G.E.N.I.E.

Michelle Knight

G.E.N.I.E.

Fiction4All

Acknowledgements

Big thanks to Jo-Anne, Phillip Kettless, Shoshana Bick and the people who wish to remain nameless, for their efforts in providing much valued feedback to the progress of the book.

Chapter 1

They called them, 'wars to end all wars,' but human nature being what it is, history repeated itself once more. A third major conflict was inevitable and in the twenty fourth century, World War Three ravaged the earth. It became a long running battle of attrition and, in the desperation to win, things became increasingly ugly.

Long standing international agreements were torn up and discarded. Chemical weapons indifferent to any life form, peppered the surface, making large areas uninhabitable for countless decades. Microwave cannons were fired from low orbit, setting fire to whatever they touched; soldiers, civilians, plants and wildlife alike. Any weapon that could be used, was pressed into service no matter the cost either to the human race, or the planet.

The carnage was wholesale and eventually people on all sides, sick of the death, disease and destruction, revolted. They turned on their leaders and slaughtered them. It was almost as if the earth itself had said, "Enough." In the end, peace finally ruled; but the price paid was considerable.

Seven of the original regions had survived, albeit in a heavily changed form. North and South America, Australia, Europe, Asia, the Middle East and Africa. They were joined by the Antarctics, a pacifist colony which had formed to avoid the wars of the others, although they were dragged in from time to time.

As the centuries flowed, the world continued to pay a heavy price. The use of heat and biological weapons, resulted in frequent hurricane force winds that eroded large areas of land. They blew away anything which wasn't heavily anchored or aerodynamically designed. Floods gouged mountains, washing away rocks and soil that they sent onward into towns and villages, wrecking all that was before them. Whenever it happened there were usually many casualties among people and livestock.

Borders, once argued over so viciously by men, now stood as irrelevant items of historical record. What was left of humanity finally stopped fighting itself and began battling for survival. It was now engaged in a never ending struggle against the environmental change that the insanity of war had brought about.

All eyes turned to the Antarctics for salvation. Not only had technology allowed them to flourish at the South, surviving in extreme conditions, but they had created a peaceful and lasting democracy. They had been careful not to develop anything that might give the other regions a cause to invade, and this saved them from a lot of the violence.

Throughout the years of devastation, the Antarcticans had salvaged whatever historical record they could. Books, burned during the war by leaders who wanted people to swallow their version of reality, had been rescued and hoarded at the southernmost point of the globe. Enormous effort was taken to house delicate paper in the damp, cold climate and as such, reading had become a treasured and important element of their society. Careless treatment of any printed knowledge, especially that which was hand-written, was a serious stain on someone's social standing. Even works which were proven wrong or held in serious doubt were not destroyed, but simply stamped with a prominent warning that the reader should treat what was contained within its pages, with caution.

The planetary reboot had destroyed sexism, racism and all the other 'isms which had plagued the preceding centuries. Not only had an unprecedented amount of historical vendetta been lost in the destruction, but the decimation of the global population meant that society could not afford luxuries such as discrimination. There was work to be done and all shoulders had to be pressed hard against the wheel of regeneration. Ego, greed and power seeking, came to be viewed as the most heinous of social taboos. Anyone exhibiting them remained firmly at the bottom of the social ladder. No one dared risk another selfish maniac rising to power and starting another war.

The political structure that the Antarcticans had created, was adopted and spread throughout the regions, with a representative from each forming what became known as the Panel Of Eight. Election to the Panel was not by choice, but by achievement; and not by seeking but by calling. Each year, by rota, one of the regions would elect their new representative. Instead of a list of candidates to choose from, voting forms had a blank space for a voter to write a name. Painters, musicians, authors, poets, vid-screen stars and more, would suddenly find themselves called to represent their region on the Panel. These were people with no aspiration of politics or leadership, who were torn from their careers and given the glory of serving a cycle of eight years.

Cynics regarded it not so much an honour, but more a prison sentence for being nothing more than a model citizen. Those who wished to avoid such service exhibited just enough pride in themselves to be seen as unworthy to serve, but not so much as to be perceived as a danger to society. After all, anyone who was thoughtless enough to try and become elected by touting for support, was certain to be hauled in front of a court for their insolence and most likely imprisoned for a time, to reflect on their inflated self-importance.

The Panel itself served on an artificial island in the Pacific Ocean. It was large enough to sustain the Panel with the necessities of life, while protecting them from the natural disasters that were happening on the Continents. It could be moved around, albeit slowly, and moved it was, on odd occasion. There were still those who protested against this method of rule and, while there was no reason to assume they had the capacity to attack the Panel; complacency was a habit best avoided.

In recognition of the sacrifice they were making, various luxuries were given to the Panel Members during their time of service. Their individual apartments were tailored for them before they began their term. Whether they had a love of wood, marble, books, music, each one was styled by top designers of the day and only the best materials were used.

Once a Panel Member had served their time and returned to society, whatever was left in their apartment was sold for the benefit of the Member's chosen charity. Many of the Panels deliberations were broadcast to the planet via vid-screen, and if a Member had performed particularly well, achieved much and argued passionately and honestly for the greater good of the human race, the money raised in such auctions could be considerable. Sometimes key items would go to a region's museum and be displayed as a symbol of what they had accomplished in the name of peace and personal service to the world.

Panel Members performed their daily business in an impressive central chamber. At its heart was a circular table with comfortable chairs. The day was long, but the breaks were many; Members being encouraged to retreat to one of the covered gardens or artistic rooms to ponder the decisions they were required to make.

The overall atmosphere of the main chamber was one of muted white, to represent purity of thought. Around the edges of this large, imposing room, stood podia on which rested busts of people who were responsible for notable quotes of wisdom. What they had said or written, was immortalised on plaques beneath them. The Antarcticans had chosen to be surrounded by things that reminded them of their goals and encouraged them to be mindful of the pit down which selfish politics inevitably led. Occasionally, history had denied them an image from which to create a bust, so objects associated with the person took their place; like musical instruments or other tools of their trade.

"There has never been a protracted war from which a country has benefited." Sun Tzu circa 5th Cent. BC. "History has tried hard to teach us that we can't have good government under politicians. Now, to go and stick one at the very head of the government couldn't be wise." Mark Twain circa 19th Cent. "The desire to be a politician should be an automatic bar." William Connolly, circa 21st Cent. "To not reach out your hand to a fellow human, is to slap the face of the entire race." Gemma Reams, circa 23rd Cent. "We killed our leaders for a reason; the right to lead ourselves." Jooles Grace, circa 26th Cent.

On one side of the circular table stood three large screens. On these, the Panel Members took their audience with the outside world. On the other side was a map of the decreasing global surface; with sub divisions for each province, within each region. The individual provinces could change colour to indicate anything from local disturbances to major disasters.

To one side of the map was a series of clocks, each showing the local time of the different zones within each region. To the other, there was a display showing the generation and distribution of food and energy on the planet. Each region was responsible for creating resources and controlling consumption, but the Panel of Eight could step in if they felt something was amiss. In this way, resources could be moved between regions, smoothly. Any disagreement couldn't cause a humanitarian crisis and the politics could be sorted out later.

The Antarcticans had also re-designed finance in the face of centuries of greed. Structures critical to the service of the common people, such as power and transport, stayed within the hands of the people. The new corporations paid a global tax rate so there was nothing

11

to be gained by moving funds, and representation to the Panel was carried out via the vid-screens; so all lobbying was on the public record.

From the island, the Panel of Eight effectively ruled the world. They set laws, allocated resources and heard petitions from the provinces and regions. The one thing that did weigh on everyone's mind was that it took the near annihilation of the planet, to be able to afford it a second chance. No one was going to risk squandering it, to shave a corner off a process and take a risk, in order to make something more efficient.

Following the rising against the world leaders, there had been a time known as, "The Purity Inquisition." During this somewhat lawless period, before the formation of the New Order and The Panel of Eight, people went through the records that remained and rooted out the politicians and military personnel who had committed atrocities. They were judged by the rhetoric they had used in communications and a range of punishments were employed, depending on how hungry they had been to taste human blood. Some pockets of activists were more aggressive than others with the sentences they handed down. These ranged from discharge from public service, to various forms of execution and everything in between. The chaos of restoring order to the planet was used as a convenient excuse to turn a blind eye to what were considered by many to be revenge killings.

What was left of the various, now leaderless, military forces throughout the world, was joined as one organisation. The Global Rescue Service was created to go to disaster areas, and they were very much in demand. Although the human conflict was over, the onslaught of Mother Nature was strong and relentless. Wherever the destructive finger of fate decided to point, the GRS was deployed to save lives instead of taking them. They kick started building projects, instead of destroying critical architecture; fed people in need, instead of creating mass starvation.

Despite all this, there was still violence on the planet. The equator not only provided the most efficient source of light energy, but it also housed some of the strongest and most poisonous species that existed; and none of them were too happy to see the human race, especially since the chemicals used in the war had affected them as well. People had historically overlooked the intelligence that existed in the animal kingdom. Now they became the target of its wrath.

In the twenty first century, the human race had started to wake up to the intelligence of the creatures that they had looked down on, for so very long. Even the humble crab had demonstrated learned memory, avoiding the rocks where scientists had given it electric shocks, showing that it felt pain and altered its behaviour to avoid further unpleasantness.

Washoe the chimp had learned more than three hundred words of sign language and, when told that her human caretaker had suffered a miscarriage and lost her baby, Washoe made the sign for, "cry," demonstrating high levels of understanding and empathy.

Over the next few hundred years, although the higher functioning beasts including primates, big cats and elephants, never achieved human speech, scientists started unpicking the animals language structures. Shortly before the third world war broke, they were beginning to detect more subtle frequencies in the growls, whines and whimpers that spoke of a level of communication far more detailed than the simple noises themselves. The creatures with who we shared the green and blue spinning rock, were far more intelligent and aware than we had previously given credit.

Just as people were starting to realise just how badly they had been blinded by their egos; someone pushed the big red button and destroyed it all.

When so much of the planet was devastated, habitat, vegetation, breeding grounds and more lain waste; the animals seemed to know exactly who was responsible for their suffering. No one had a clue how, but there was no doubt that humans were now Nature's, 'enemy number one.' Sure, they didn't have weapons and lacked the organisation to co-ordinate with other herds of animals, but it quickly became clear that small groups of people who ventured beyond the protected towns were at risk of being attacked by any group of creatures that thought they could do battle, and win.

Occasionally, assaults were mounted against some of the newer, isolated and poorly defended settlements. As a consequence, there were still plenty of killings in some areas. Humanity had stayed its trigger-finger and opted not to retaliate en-mass against the animals, but it was too late to prevent the steady, building stream of aggression that was constantly being delivered. The best that people could hope for, was that the rage and violence delivered upon them by the creatures of nature, would eventually burn itself out.

Animal attacks were an issue which refused to go away. There were frequent, low-level calls for retaliation whenever a small outpost, poorly defended village or convoy was set upon, and people killed.

As a result of this stalemate, it was impossible to put all weapons beyond reach. There were tightly controlled licenses to use firearms. They were hard to obtain and generally only security companies that specialised in armed protection, could get them. To be a security guard was a respected position, and teams were regularly hired by communities to protect them from the most dangerous creatures; the ones with wild eyes that foamed at the mouth, and were angry and vengeful.

Transport had also changed. The resource hungry coffins of metal that screamed their way through the skies, were now confined to limited areas where nothing else would work. The continents were now connected with large, hardened, see-through tubes. At the base was a near-frictionless coating, created from the centuries old discovery of graphene. On top of this, a layer of supporting oil meant that wide-bottomed "boats," could be propelled along easily, pushed by a jet of wind. People and light loads could be transported at low cost, and as a result of this, populations mixed and mingled like never before in the history of our species.

Not everyone was satisfied with the way that things had turned out. Pockets of the population called, "Separatists," wanted the borders of old to be reinstated. They rejected the rule of The Panel of Eight and pined for the sovereignty of past ages. They honestly believed that people had learned from their mistakes and there would be no more wars. The irony was completely lost on them that, in order to try and achieve their goals, they had resorted to violence. But putting a mirror in front of them did nothing to sway them from their beliefs. Trouble and terrorism from within the human race itself was, sadly, not entirely extinguished.

As if all that wasn't enough, there was still considerable damage to be repaired. Not only had the land suffered, but the human race itself had been contaminated. The biological weapons and chemical cocktails that had been used indiscriminately, had resulted in neurological disorders that plagued the population. There were diseases which were not only passed from one generation to the other, but were also carried in the soil and air. Even basic food and water could not be guaranteed safe anymore. All these issues were causing a considerable amount of suffering and needed to be tackled. In comparison to this, the Separatists were a mere thorn in society's little toe.

The range of ailments was wide and to fight them, the decision was taken to create a research centre, equipped with a specialist computer on which the complexities of the human body could be simulated. Despite the threat of animal attack, it was decided that the centre would be built in Africa to make the most of solar power and planetary heat. To protect it against the violent changes in the weather and create a stable environment, the majority of the structure would be built below ground.

Machines developed by the Antarcticans to create their underground habitats, were brought in to build the complex. Even with their experience and equipment, it still took four years to complete. It had two floors above ground level and thirty below. Situated roughly in the middle of Africa, it was nestled close to a range of natural hills. By the time the work was completed, a few more large mounds had been added; created from the material that had been dug from below.

In addition to staff quarters, multiples levels of specialist laboratories, storage facilities and a large fleet of the latest maintenance robots, the complex also contained the finest computing technology. The system, a new, eagerly awaited biological computer, was finally available. The Genetic Engine for Neurological Information Evaluation, or G.E.N.I.E. as it came to be known.

Chapter 2

Emmett Charcott was the only child of Martin and Jennifer. While his father was a native Antarctican, Jennifer came from the Europas. A real wild child, Martin had freely travelled the Tubes. He took jobs here and there, earning just enough money to fund the trip to wherever his heart wanted to go next. Foot loose and fancy free, with the wind in his hair and a spring in his step, he was working his way around the Europas when his wander lust met its doom.

He had decided to follow the Rhine from its source to the mouth, but only got as far as Aachen. As robotics was an important skill among Antarcticans, for construction and survival, Martin had no trouble picking up work in an Aachen factory, programming and maintaining industrial robots. It was there that he came face to face with Jennifer. Her warm, green eyes and shoulder length, brunette hair framed a smile which melted his heart. The first time that they met, he decided that the next journey he would embark on, was a lifetime trek into her soul.

It took several months to make his way into her graces. Even though it was the longest he had stayed in one place since leaving home, wanderlust failed to break his resolve. Martin simply wasn't going to move on without first putting all his effort into winning her affection. He bought her the occasional bunch of flowers, paid her gentle compliments and invited her to spend time with him during lunch breaks. Whether she accepted or declined each of his little gestures, her response was always accompanied by that cheeky, but warm smile that lit up her face. Just being able to bathe in the peace and joy that she radiated, was all the reward that Martin needed for his efforts, whether he ended up enjoying her company on that occasion, or dining on his own.

Eventually, lunch turned to an occasional evening meal and when their break days collided, longer times together. She unnerved him by paying her way whenever they incurred serious expense, whether it was a trip up or down the Rheine, an excursion into the countryside or whatever took their fancy. This unnerved Martin because it felt like she was always keeping a distance between them. He wanted to give her the world, take her worries away and make her smile; but she insisted on earning her place, solving her problems and being her own person. As a result, he found it difficult to get a handle on how far their relationship was going to go, but her independence was something he learned to accept.

Jennifer warmed to him over time and the comfort distance between them kept getting smaller until one day, during a lunch period in chilly weather, she cuddled underneath his arm. She turned her head up so that he got the full force of her deep, green eyes, and then topped it off by smiling at him. He hugged her tightly and from that moment, they were officially a life-bonded couple. They registered their partnership in Aachen and he moved in with her; although she still solved her own problems and by that time, Martin had got used to not wanting to smother her with love.

Part of the reason behind her strong personality was that Jennifer had been adopted as a young child, and had no official family. Martin, however, still had parents back in the Antarctics and when he talked about them with fondness, and tried to get Jennifer to talk with them over the vid-screen, she went a little chilly and withdrawn.

When a vid-note arrived one day, to say that his father was gravely ill, the discussion between them was very difficult and it almost seemed like the relationship wouldn't survive, but eventually Jennifer warmed to the fact that his parents were legally hers now, and she agreed to go with him to the southernmost point of the planet. He warned her that it was cold, but she shrugged that off, saying that it was just another reason for them to cuddle together and stay warm.

They rode the tubes south and reached his father with only days to go until his unavoidable death. After the cremation, they decided to stay and make it their forever home. Jennifer became a teacher of logic technologies and Martin returned to working in the robot factories, just like he had done while saving for the first tube trip that had started his planet-wide adventures.

Two years later, Martin's mother also passed away. Shortly after, Jennifer became pregnant and gave birth to a boy who they called Emmett. Not long after he was born, Jennifer began to look pale, lack energy and started to lose control of her muscles. She was eventually diagnosed as having one of the neurological diseases that humanity had visited upon itself. Their son was lucky, it had not jumped to him.

Life for little Emmett was not easy. Over his developing years, Jennifer became increasingly incapable of looking after herself. Martin cared for her as much as he could, but he also needed to work. When Emmett was of age, he was pressed into helping care for his Mother. When he came home from school, he prepared food for her and made sure she took her medication. The decline was slow and painful for a child as young as him to witness. He never got to see his Mother in all her natural, carefree beauty; just the gentle, helpless thing that she eventually became.

He was just fifteen when he stood at her bedside with his father and witnessed her passing. She looked up into their faces and, for one last time, her beautiful soul shone from her eyes, and her face bore that warm, heart-melting smile, as she slipped from this world, and into the next.

Emmett was too young to understand and, from his father's grief, he found nothing but anger in the injustice of his mother's death. He cursed the War, raged against history and vowed that he would devote his life to battling the neurological diseases that plagued the planet.

Martin ensured that Emmett wanted for nothing, and put his shoulder behind whatever his son wanted to do. For his part, Emmett had concluded that the scientists researching these diseases were working too slowly and making far too little progress. They needed better tools to do the job. They needed computers; but not like the digital ones that had been with them for so long. Having reached this conclusion on where the bottleneck was, he studied genetic computing and became one of the planet's foremost authorities in the field.

Three decades later, Emmett found himself riding a tube bound for Africa. Martin had joined Jennifer in the next life ten years prior, and he had no reason to stay in the Antarctics now. A Professor in genetic disciplines, he was to lead the team working on his new generation of computer. A machine built from natural tissue that would assist the world in ridding itself of one of the most hideous chains around humanity's ankles. As he looked out of the tube, the sea just a blur below him, glistening in the morning sun, he felt a sense of achievement. Finally, he was going to live up to his promise and make a difference. His chest felt solid from the sense of purpose that filled it. He had some good years left in his life and he was going to make them count for something. He would be heading up the work on the G.E.N.I.E. project. However, he wasn't the only one making the journey.

Chapter 3

Fay was the second daughter born to Jim and Belinda Hobson. She lived with her sister, Becky, and their parents on the West coast of the North Americas.

Belinda worked in electronic design and processing. She brought in the money that supported the family. Jim was an artist. His primary material was metal but he also worked with wood. He sold the occasional piece for decent coin, but it was really Belinda's wages that kept the wolf from the door.

Becky had no interest in their parent's professions, preferring to study history. Fay, on the other hand, had her nose in everything that her parents did. She was six when her father created a metal dragon and Fay wanted to see it move and come to life. For some months it was all she talked about at meal times. "Make it live, Daddy!" Eventually, when it became obvious that no one wanted to buy the metallic dragon, Belinda took some time off work and got together with Jim to make Fay's dream come true.

It wasn't as quick or as easy as either of them had hoped, to bring the three foot high, gleaming metal beast to life. With the appropriation of some simple A.I. code, some basic sensors and audio recordings of fictional monsters, they made slow progress. For a start, motors were difficult to fit into the joints because of the odd angles involved.

On top of that, the program that Belinda had acquired needed considerable re-writing. It was used in companion robot puppies, toy robots that brought a little comfort to people who lived on their own. She had to change all the geometric calculations so that it could walk without falling over, and completely re-write the safety routines. After all, it was imperative that the system understood that it was no longer a fluffy little yippy toy, and that it was now a heavy beast that could do some serious damage. Shaking claws would likely result in human injury, and jumping up on people's laps was definitely not allowed.

Eventually, on Fay's ninth birthday, they presented her with Gorbash, named after a young, fictional dragon in literature.

The yippity yaps of the original program had been replaced with a series of meaningful roars and groans. Its ability to breathe actual fire, had been restricted to some red lights in its mouth and Jim had carefully rounded the claws so that it wouldn't shred the carpet. Despite a vocal rule that Gorbash was to remain on the ground floor, Fay taught it to climb the stairs and it slept with her in her bedroom. Belinda went nuts when she first discovered this, but eventually relented and altered the program to ensure that it would never attempt to get on the bed. The last thing she needed was either a dead daughter or torn up bed linen.

Gorbash spent the next few years following Fay around wherever she went while at home. A geo-restriction ensured it never went outside the family boundary, and would return to the barn when Fay wasn't around, just to make sure it stayed safe.

Having Gorbash around as a companion while Fay grew, fuelled her desire to work with robots. At sixteen and after much discussion between Belinda and Jim, she was given the password to Gorbash's program and control over her companion. But it was the wrong decision. Able to now influence Gorbash, Fay tired of it after a few months and turned it off for good.

Forever the contemplating artist, Jim reflected that maybe the friendships worth the most, were the ones with people who didn't always bend to our way of thinking, and were as willing to tell us when they thought we're wrong, as they were to be by our side when we needed them most.

Regardless of Gorbash's fate, the metallic dragon

had ignited Fay's desire to follow a career in robotics; something she not only did, but excelled at. By her late twenties, she had been responsible for the design and programming of some of the most advanced equipment to come out of the North Americas. She was particularly proud of, "Deep," a unit that would rescue people who were lost or stuck underground. Whether it was a collapsed mine or a potholer who had failed to return to the surface, the agile, eight legged mechanical marvel could even spend small amounts of time underwater while navigating dark, dynamic environments. "Deep," robots went on to save lives all over the world, in some of the most inhospitable terrain.

When the G.E.N.I.E. project kicked off, it was obvious that they would need someone to look after the complex robotics and the cutting edge A.I. that would run the base. It was no surprise to many that they came for the famous Fay Hobson. Initially, she was all for it and jumped at the opportunity, but when she found out it was in Africa she was somewhat less enthused and started stalling.

They promised her whatever they thought might seal the deal. A special lab all to herself, with anything she wanted so that she could carry on her research and inventions; but she didn't want to leave her home, her family and her friends. One warm evening, when she was on the porch, staring up at the stars and thinking about her future, Jim came out and sat by her. For some time they talked and her father, with his positive outlook and zest for creation and adventure, told her that life was there to be lived and that if she didn't follow her heart, then she would likely regret it.

Not long after that discussion, she found herself travelling the tubes, on her way to Africa; a new continent and a fresh start.

Chapter 4

Serengeti Security Limited prided itself on its fast and efficient service. Its logo was a sniper rifle, a lightning bolt and the initials of the company, 'SSL.' It had been running for more than fifty years and had grown to become one of the most trusted security firms in Africa. It operated throughout the country with the promise, 'We'll move mountains to keep you safe.'

It was rumoured that the owner of the company had a panic attack on a tube journey, when he sat next to a specialist in European history. Although people knew about the great wars and their impact, very few people needed to know the details. When it was pointed out that there was a close resemblance between the company logo and a socialist party that had been responsible for previous world wars, the company owner's face fell in shock. It was said that even before the tube journey had ended, changes had been ordered.

A redesign of the logo was issued very quickly. They dropped the rifle and lightning bolt in favour of an outline of Africa, and smoothed the edges of the initials. It was done at considerable cost. Uniforms, vehicle decals, advertising and paperwork all had to be purged as quietly as possible. S.S.L. managed to get away with it, but if there had been an official complaint then their license to operate firearms would have certainly been revoked. That would have meant the death of the company.

Joe Magoro was a native to the African region. Born in Port Elizabeth, he had the good fortune to be brought up in one of the most well protected cities in the country. Joining Serengeti Security had seemed like an easy ride at the time and he went to them straight from school. However, the appeal of a life travelling around Africa being respected and looked up to, while all the time being able to legally shoot at things, lost its shine after about four years.

The octane rush of dealing with violent, raging animals, was dealt a permanent blow after a particularly bad and bloody encounter. Joe was in his early twenties and still relatively inexperienced, when a troop of baboons attacked a village he was guarding. In the aftermath, it was thought that it was no opportunistic attack and that they must have carefully planned the assault. These beasts were clearly gaining in intelligence. If they could progress to talking, then one day peace may be an option. But that was a hope for the distant future.

It was late afternoon in this particular village and people had been making the transition from everyday business to evening relaxation, when the noise started up. Three female apes were off to the east of the small complex, screeching and throwing things at the wall. They were behaving threateningly, but not actually enough to provoke being shot.

As Joe watched them, he found himself becoming concerned. A baboon troop could number a couple of hundred and yet here were these three, by themselves, being very aggressive with no male in easy sight. His gut instinct told him that something was very, very wrong. As it transpired, his intuition was right on the money.

When the baboons saw people with weapons at the top of the wall, one of them stood up, lifted its head to the air and let off some blood curdling squeals. It was obviously a signal, and a matter of moments later they found out what for, as all hell let loose at the other side of the village.

Roughly seventy baboons rushed out of the undergrowth from the west, with the sun behind them. The one guard left on that wall let out a yell and his shout was swiftly followed by gunfire; but the combination of too many apes, not enough rifles in the right place and shooting into the sun, saw the village defences being easily overrun. The guard only managed to kill a handful of the advancing hoard before they were on him; it happened that fast. Somehow they had worked out a trapeze act which enabled them to sail over the electric wires, snarling and thirsty for human blood. A few failed the manoeuvre and hit the wire; the shock sent them to the ground, unconscious.

A good number made it in and, as people ran away, the apes had the advantage. They raced up from behind, using their powerful paws to smack the back of their victims' legs, sending them to the ground. The baboons that followed appeared to be carrying rocks, which they smashed against the heads of those who had fallen, either killing them or knocking them unconscious with a single blow.

Joe and the other three on the west wall, turned on their heels and ran back among the buildings to deal with the commotion. It was madness, trying to shoot the baboons but not hit any people. Hearts pounding hard and senses heightened, they found themselves scattered as they raced between the structures in an attempt to get into the centre. What they didn't see when they left the wall, was the three females jumping the wire and joining in the fight behind them.

Coming closer to the centre, Joe shouldered his rifle and slowed down a little. As he progressed, he started taking pot shots at the heads of any apes he encountered. The time spent on the range, practising on moving targets, stood him in good stead. In front of him, there were people running as fast as they could, and apes reigning terror on the population. It was mayhem and he had to concentrate hard to not only follow the head of the moving baboons, but also look beyond them to ensure they were in the clear before pulling the trigger, lest he also shoot whoever was standing behind them.

A few apes were hammering at doors and no doubt people were on the other side attempting to keep them out. Joe had to take quick aim and shoot as low as he could in the hope that, after killing the baboon, the bullet wouldn't hit whoever was on the other side of the door.

Two of the apes caught sight of him and decided to charge. They obviously knew that attacking people with guns was their top priority. Ninety pounds of Genus Papio is a serious threat when it is coming towards you at speed, yellow teeth bared with the single-minded purpose of seeing you dead. Joe was unlucky enough to have two such beasts descending on him. It didn't take a moment to aim at the head of one and kill it instantly, but just as he took aim at the other, his luck ran out.

One of the females that had scaled the east wall, had caught up and attacked him from behind. She launched herself into the air and landed with full force against his back, sending his bullet well below the remaining, still-charging male. As Joe hit the ground, he was fortunate enough to still be holding his rifle. The female that hit him, had done so with such ferocity that she had continued over his fallen body, and had a head-on collision with the rapidly approaching ape. They smashed into each other and pawed wildly in an effort to push themselves apart. This took a matter of just a few heartbeats, but it was all the time that Joe needed to raise the rifle and fire.

There was a high pitched scream as the female baboon felt the bullet rip into her armpit, exit through her shoulder and enter the side of her head from below, exploding part of her skull in the process. The male went wide eyed in shock at the flurry of bone, blood and brain that occurred right in front of him, but it only took a fraction of a second before its look changed to one of anger, and the vicious ape made a move for Joe.

Faced with a massive baboon about to attack, Joe pumped the trigger for all he was worth, but nothing happened. The hard landing on the ground had bent the magazine and as a result, the round he had just fired would not be replaced. Within the moment it took him to determine this, the ape was on him and with a swipe of its paw, it sent the useless rifle flying out of his hands and down the street.

Joe's reflex action sent his right hand to the holster on his hip, and he managed to pop the cover before he felt an incredible impact on his back. The baboon had reared up and then landed both its paws on him, with the full weight of the creature behind it. He was slammed into the ground and pain shot through his body like a bolt of lightning. He had never felt anything like it in his life and didn't think that he'd survive a second hit.

Just as the ape reared up for another strike, Joe rolled to one side, grabbed the stock and wrenched the pistol out of its holster. Raising his arm in desperation, he shot the baboon twice in the jaw, sending a couple of bullets straight into its skull. At that point, shuddering in agony, he lost control. The pain took over his body and, yelling in pain, he dropped the gun as his muscles momentarily went stiff. Just as he gave up hope and thought that he was as good as dead, there was a massive thud as the ape's lifeless body hit the ground beside him. The last thing Joe remembered was choking on dust as he went limp and passed out.

The village had lost about a quarter of its population before the invading baboons were all killed. If there had been a second wave still in the undergrowth, waiting to attack, then the battle would have been lost for sure.

He woke in their small hospital and, along with many other people, was transferred to the city as soon as he was fit enough to travel. Joe was fortunate that the ape had missed his spine, or things would have been a lot more serious. There was a considerable amount of bruising and a number of broken bones, including his left shoulder; but compared to many others he had been damn lucky.

The shoulder injury ensured that he stayed in warm climes and even during Africa's colder nights he had a tendency to wrap up or stay indoors; not ideal for night patrols. That attack badly dented his enthusiasm for the job, but he didn't have enough of a grounding to do anything else. So he stuck with it and ensured that strategic lessons were learned from the encounter, by hosting lectures for his colleagues.

He was now in his mid-thirties and had been working at the Genie site for almost a year. When the chance had come up to work in a secure building, he'd taken it gladly. Not only was it was a good deal better protected than the villages, but patrolling corridors and checking people in and out of the place was about all the excitement he wanted to handle. At this point all he wished for was a quiet, uneventful life.

He'd been home for some extended leave and was now on an S.S.L. staff coach, returning to site. Despite the wealth of the company, they didn't exactly splash out on the best transport. The latest coaches on the road had superb suspension, feeling like they were almost floating on air. It had to be wheels as, out here, hover transport just blew sand everywhere.

This coach was probably from a batch that S.S.L. had bought second hand, and then retro fitted stronger armour to save money. As it hit another bump in the road, the jolt caused him more pain. He brought his hand up to his injured left shoulder, gave it a sympathetic rub and sighed inwardly at his fate. This pain would be with him until his dying day.

He was fortunate that it wasn't his right shoulder, as that was where he rested his rifle butt. If that side had been damaged then he'd have been out of a job for sure. A security operative that couldn't actually fire a rifle, didn't actually offer much in the way of security!

Satisfied that his nagging shoulder had been rubbed back to sleep, he returned his hand to the manila folder on his lap. Being a company coach, he could review sensitive paperwork while travelling, which was what he was doing now. It was a long journey and he was reading up on a new colleague, Tim Ross. The coach was due to pick up Ross about half way through the trip, so he'd have plenty of time to brief him about the Genie site before they got there.

Apparently Ross was from the Europas and was in his mid-twenties. He'd recently joined the company and had passed firearms training, but they wanted to ease him in gently. His previous job had been a guard on the tube transport systems, so he had some security experience already. However they didn't want to scare off the new starter by having him face down charging animals on day one. Head office figured that patting people down and scanning packages for explosives was a nice, gentle introduction to the company. To date Tim had been given some easy assignments and was due to spend half a year with the Genie project, before he was sent out on village patrols. Joe reflected that the person he was reading about, seemed a lot like him in his early years; green as hell and all up for action. At the complex, the most excitement he'd be likely to see at the underground labs, was if someone got their chemicals wrong and triggered a small explosion. It had actually happened three times already, and they were still in their first year of operation.

Joe sighed, externally this time, and turned his head to look out of the window at the passing desert. Yellow sand contrasted with the blue sky, as the small hills passed by. Another three month stint in that underground boredom pit would be hell, but if it was a choice between that or enraged baboons, then he'd take the mundane any day. At least, up until the point where he became so stir crazy that he wanted to take his own life; and then it would probably be back to the crazed apes. Only next time, he wouldn't put up a fight.

He must have lost track of how long he had been

staring out the window, as he was brought back to the present by the engine slowing down. Sure enough, the desert was moving by with less enthusiasm and, as Joe stretched his neck as far as his shoulder would allow, he could see the next pick-up point ahead. They approached the village at a sedate, mandated speed. They said that the place used to house oil workers back in the day, but was now used by people who maintained the solar energy farms in the area. It was an easy place for small passenger aircraft to land, so Tim would be waiting there, along with a few other colleagues, to be picked up. Africa was one of the few places in the world where aeroplanes were still used to cover large in-land distances.

Joe rested back in his seat and looked blankly at the head rest in front of him, as the coach continued slowly on, eventually swinging into a parking area. There was a hiss as the driver engaged the brakes, opened the door and got out. Everyone had to have their credentials checked before they boarded, and their suitcases fed through the scanning system before being put in the hold. It was a bit of a lengthy process, but necessary. This wasn't the average coach, after all. Three people came on board, all colleagues that Joe recognised and he nodded at them as they passed him to find seats. One made a move to sit next to him, but he waved them off. "Got a new starter. Have to induct him." he explained

Eventually, Tim climbed into the coach. Joe recognised him from the mug shot in the file. As Tim looked around at the other people in the seats, Joe raised the Manila folder and waved it, to grab his attention. Tim acknowledged the gesture, and made his way to Joe's seat.

Reaching the spot, Tim heaved his hand luggage onto the overhead rack and then slumped down onto the seat by Joe. He spent a few moments wriggling about to make himself comfortable, and then held out his hand.

"Tim Ross."

Joe took his hand and shook it. "I know. Joe Magoro. Welcome to the back of beyond."

Tim stretched a little and looked around at the inside of the coach. It was nice and wide, two rows of double seats with an aisle down the middle. Each seat had enough room to give every passenger a decent arm rest. "Nice, this." he said, nodding in the general direction of the interior.

"You're lucky. The company tends to run its coaches into the ground. This is a recent acquisition." He sighed. "Well, relatively recent."

Tim fidgeted a little, still getting comfortable not only in the coach, but with the new assignment. "They told me that you'd be my mentor for the Genie work."

"Yup."

Tim looked down at the folder on Joe's lap. "You've been reading up on me?"

Following Tim's stare and glancing at his legs, Joe confirmed his suspicion. "Oh, yes. You haven't been with us very long."

Tim chuckled. "I know, not much of a life worth reading about so far."

"Don't worry. Spend too long working for this company and you'll have more history to your name than you can handle."

"Yeah," Tim smiled, "that's kind of what I'm hoping for."

Joe looked at him with a touch of despair. "Careful what you wish for. There'll come a day when a quiet assignment like this will be a dream come true." He looked Tim in the eyes and shot him a serious expression. For his part, Tim recognised the gravitas Joe was transmitting and he quietened down a little.

"So," he changed the subject, "how long are we on this coach for?"

"Oh, another seven or eight hours yet."

"Good job we've got nice seats. That aeroplane was a bit cramped."

"Get used to it. Out here they still run those ancient flying things. The tubes don't run as far as the low population villages that we protect."

"Oh." The disappointment was clear in Tim's voice. They stopped talking for a while as the coach started its engine and swung back out into the road. Tim watched past Joe, through the window, as they made their way out of the town and settled back on to the desert road. Once he had his fill of sand and sky, he attempted to strike up more conversation. "So, I get to meet the legend, then."

Joe stirred from his thoughts. "Huh?"

"Heather Peterson. Tiger Woman."

"She may be a legend, but if you want to see your next birthday, you'll never call her that to her face." He took a moment to reflect on his own comment. "Are you hell bent on causing trouble or something?"

Tim looked offended. "No. Just being me, I guess."

"Well, look; if there's anything you learn from me, it's to keep your head down and don't be so eager. Nothing comes of being cocky." He winced as his shoulder twinged, and tried to soothe it again.

"That the baboon injury?"

"Yes." Joe looked at him sideways. "How'd you know about that?"

"Tiger Woman isn't the only legend that people talk about." Tim looked at him seriously, hoping to make an impression that Joe wasn't the only one that had done his homework.

Joe thought about this for a second or two, before he chose his response. "I don't know about Tiger Woman, but if I ever hear anyone calling me Baboon Man, I'll make sure they don't call anyone, anything again. Understand me?" He examined the slightly shocked expression on Tim's face and concluded that he had made his point.

As they sat there in silence, Joe reflected that this wasn't the most ideal of pep talks. In his mind, he debated whether he should teach Tim a worthwhile lesson the easy way, or just sit back and let nature knock his rough edges into shape the hard way.

Half an hour of awkward silence went by. Tim hadn't been embarrassed enough to move seats. Joe couldn't make his mind up as to whether that was a good or a bad sign, but he was supposed to be this guy's mentor for the next few months so he pondered on what to say next.

"Look..."

"Hey, I know..."

"...being young is..."

"...I was a jerk..."

"…enthusiasm and..."

"...wanted to impress you..."

"...making your mark..."

"...I screwed it up..."

They stopped speaking over each other and just stared, wondering who was going to break the silence next. Being the oldest, Joe decided it should be him. "Why don't we just start over? Yes?"

Tim nodded. "Sounds like a plan." Then they fell silent again for another awkward moment. Tim eventually offered up his hand. "Hi, I'm Tim Ross. Your new staff member."

Joe took his hand and shook it again. "Hi, I'm Joe. Your new boss. Do what I tell you and we'll get along fine." They smiled at each other and chuckled a little. Joe just shook his head lightly in disbelief, and looked out the window at the sand and sky, which were both turning black and becoming one as darkness fell.

"So," Tim continued, "this research site. They didn't tell me much on the assignment brief. What goes on there?"

Joe turned away from the window and took a deep

breath. "They've got a genetic computer. It mimics the human brain more closely than anything before it. Professor Charcott designed it to try and sort out the neurological diseases that are killing us off. He's working there but you probably won't meet him. The bloke's a regular workaholic."

"Are they having much success?"

"Doubt it. They haven't been running a year yet. Everyone's still sort of getting their feet under the table. But security doesn't mix with the scientists so we don't exactly get progress reports. Talk between departments doesn't happen overnight, especially when there are egos involved."

Tim brought the subject a bit closer to home. "So what's our role in this?"

Joe settled into his home subject. "Not much. The two main threats are the animals and the Separatists. The building is mostly underground, and what's above is solid. Some of the apes get up on the roof and mess with the equipment now and then, but that's about it. The Separatists so far haven't shown much interest; they want the neurological problems sorted as much as anyone, but you can't take crazies at face value."

"So it's a sort of, scan everything that comes in, vehicle checks, people watching, that sort of stuff?"

"Pretty much, yes." Joe turned his head towards the window again, not that he could see much through it as night was really settling in. "But you can never get complacent. Just when you think that everything's nice and quiet, that's when the unexpected bites you on the arse."

Tim nodded. "I hear you."

Just then, the speakers came to life. The driver had an announcement to make. "Ladies and gentlemen, violent animals have been reported on the road ahead, so we're going to stop for the night in the next village. We'll carry on to the complex tomorrow. Apologies for the inconvenience."

"Great." muttered Joe. "The unexpected."

Tim looked down to the front of the coach, then glanced at Joe and then down the front of the coach again. He was wondering whether he should say something smart like, 'Isn't protection our job?' or, 'We've got guns, why stop?' but given that his enthusiasm had already earned him a black mark in Joe's books, he thought better of it and relaxed back in his seat. His short bout of nervous finger tapping, however, didn't go unnoticed.

Chapter 5

The evening, or what was left of it, became a good chance for Joe and Tim to get to know each other a little better. Over a drink and a decent, hot meal, Tim got the full run down of the baboon assault, which increased his respect for Joe. As usual with legends, some of the significant details had been left out and awkward parts had been glossed over. Joe's version of events contained a good deal less glamour. Even though a dose of reality seemed to have calmed Tim down a bit, Joe was left with the impression that he would only learn that fire was hot, once he'd been burned a little.

They started off again early the next morning and Joe had negotiated a little seat swapping so that they were at the front. That way, he could point out the features of the base as they approached it. "So, this complex is quite large then." Tim asked. They had come out of the desert and were now in a form of flat looking countryside. Even the trees looked to have mostly level tops. The hills of the complex could easily be seen in the distance ahead of them.

"Yes. The Antarcticans make entire cities like this. Build large units and then link them together with tunnels. It looks relatively benign from the top but when you get in there, you realise just how deep it goes."

"You ever seen these cities?"

"Nope. The old shoulder gives me enough grief in warmer climes. The Antarctics is well outside my comfort zone. Anyway, this one building's big enough for me, thanks." He nodded into the distance as the complex appeared on the horizon.

Tim let out a low whistle as a grey, oblong structure came into view. He squinted to see any detail which would give him a handle on scale. "That thing must be near enough five hundred meters square."

"Sounds about right."

"Not very high though."

"Two floors. The ground is nearly five meters high to take vehicles. Above it is a canteen, living and communal spaces. A number of people live on site permanently."

Tim looked at him askance. "Permanently?"

"Yes. Why they don't go stir crazy, I'll never know, but that's academic types I suppose. Oh, and Heather lives there as well."

Tim looked at the approaching complex again. "So the rumours are true then."

"What rumours?"

"Well, that even after all this time, she still hasn't recovered from the tiger incident."

Joe pondered for a short while, weighing up this news against the relatively brief time he had worked with her. "I suppose there's some truth in that. I've only really known her since being here. You'll get to make up your own mind in time."

Tim pointed at the array of equipment on the roof, which was now more visible as they were getting closer. "So that's the solar panels and antennae array then. Does all that protective wiring keep the animals off?"

"Well, it's stopped them doing anything serious. Every few weeks a group of apes get up there and tries. We watch them through the cameras. They throw stones, break aerials, poke sticks through the fence and turn things off alignment, but so far they haven't worked out how to do anything major yet."

"They scale the walls?"

"Sort of." Joe pointed at the large front gate structure. It was an impressive set of doors, adorned with flashing lights, guard booths, black and yellow striped barriers, the works. "They usually climb that lot and then use the canteen window ledges."

"Are we going through there?"

"No, we use the staff entrance at the rear."

Tim chuckled. "You mean to tell me that we've got that flashy entrance, and we're just going to sneak round the back?"

"They've got a parking lot for staff that are going to be there a few days. Leaves the front entrance for regular goods and visitors." Just as Joe said it, the coach swerved off the main approach and on to another road that took them around the side of the building.

"Emergency exits?" Tim pointed at some human sized doors which were just visible, dotted around the perimeter.

"Yes, but don't let that fool you. An elephant can charge one of those things and not leave a dent."

"What's that?" Tim asked, pointing at a roller door covered with electric fencing.

"That's the transfer bay for robots. The roller door is reinforced, takes a while to open, but the wire is designed to repel anything before it actually makes contact."

"Robots?"

"Yes. Loads of maintenance robots of all sorts of shapes and sizes. They keep the place running. We've got a resident genius, Fay Hobson. You might meet her, you might not. If she can't fix it, then it goes to that bay, and then off to the company. Not that much gets left there."

"She's that good, is she?"

"Well, whenever I've checked that bay, it's usually empty, so either she's good or the robots are better."

"What comes in and out?"

"Other than people, drums usually. Mostly chemicals for the lab work. Waste drums go out. Alexie Rusnak leads up that team, but any problems, you go to Tamara Avilov. She deals with the logistics. It's all in the paperwork that's waiting on your desk."

"I get a desk?"

"Oh yes. With monitors. And a radio."

"Guns?" he grinned.

"In a rack, only released when Heather or her team hit a button somewhere." Joe shot him a disappointed look that said, 'You already know it's a quiet job.'

The coach continued around the building and sure enough, there was another, wider roller door, protected with electrified wire. The driver parked the coach on what appeared to be a metal plate. Tim craned his neck to look out of the window and down the side of the coach, to see a light coming from beneath them. Something was obviously inspecting below the vehicle.

When whatever it was had been satisfied that the coach was clean, the frame with the electric fence, came up and out, lifting itself into the air. This was followed by the long chug of the heavy roller door as it slowly rose into itself, revealing the car park within. The coach trundled in and parked in one of five long bays. The remaining area was filled with cars, only an odd few free spaces here and there. There were numbers painted on the floor so it looked like they were allocated.

The driver killed the engine and opened the door. Being at the front, Tim and Joe grabbed their hand luggage from the overhead rack and hopped off first. Joe waited for everyone to disembark and for Tim to get his cases, before they followed the rest of the coach party into the building. "Our office is on this floor. Up ahead on the left. Everything you need will be on your desk."

"What about putting these somewhere?" queried Tim, making a gesture by giving his cases an extra tug.

"There'll be a card and paperwork. That'll be programmed with your room number."

As they walked, Tim looked up at the ceiling. There were strips running either side of the corridor edges, throwing light directly at the pristine white above their heads. Basically, full length up-lighters. "Those are nice."

Joe glanced back at Tim and saw him looking up. "They're temperature controlled and dim a little during night. Helps keep the circadian rhythm running right, when you're mostly living underground."

"They've done their research then."

"Yes, the Antarcticans sorted all this out long ago. Here we go." Joe held his watch up against a small panel on the wall, and a door slid open with a gentle swoosh. They walked into a reasonably pleasant room with ten desks. Every station was against the wall and had a clutch of monitors above it. There was also a control stick on each which presumably handled the cameras. On some desks, these were buried beneath paperwork and in one case, an empty pizza box. "Your desk is here." Joe gestured at one about half way down, with nothing on it but a control stick, a personal radio and a thick folder. Joe gestured at a man at the far end who was sat at his desk, watching monitors and working the control stick. "Hi Heff. This is Tim." For his part, Tim attempted a weak smile and raised his hand in greeting.

"Hi." gruffed an unenthusiastic Heff, before returning to staring at his screens.

Tim let his case drop on the floor while Joe opened the folder and retrieved the pertinent pieces of paperwork. "Here's your security card." He handed Tim a piece of red plastic with the S.S.L. logo and his picture on it. Tim took the card and raised his hand. He pressed a few buttons on his wrist watch and it beeped. He held the card against it and it beeped again to confirm that it had taken the signal. Now, Tim could use his watch to open doors without needing to fish for the card every time. "You're in corridor seven, room twenty five." Joe closed the folder and picked it up. "Let's go." Tim pocketed the security card, picked up his case again and followed Joe as he moved for the door. Two desks up, he picked up a radio from the desk that was presumably his. "

"Magoro to control."

"Control here." crackled the response.

"Reporting on site."

"Thanks Joe. Got you on shift in six hours."

"Cheers. Out." He clipped the radio to his belt and kept walking. The door opened as they approached and Joe waved the folder at some lines on the floor. They had small arrows on them. "Underground, it's easy to get disorientated. Different colours for different services. Red for security. If you get lost, just follow red and you'll find someone."

He led them to a door with a green line around it. "This is one of many lifts. See that LED?" He pointed to a small light in a panel by the side of the door. Tim nodded. "It knows we're standing here. The lifts are all voice activated, for people with their hands full. Soon enough you'll learn not to talk when you're in them, or the lift will get confused."

"That doesn't bode well."

"I'm told they're working on it, but they've been saying that since day one." At that, the door opened. The lift had arrived. They stepped in.

"Which floor do you desire?" asked the lift.

"Leisure." commanded Joe

"I heard... Leisure. Is that correct?"

"Yes."

They remained silent for the short journey upwards to the next floor. After a few quiet moments, the door opened and they stepped out into another corridor, just like the one they had left. "Orange for sleep, blue for food on this floor." He pointed at the little arrows. "Let me drop this off, and then we can get your stuff in your room." They followed the orange line to a series of corridors. "Hang on here." Tim stopped as Joe jogged up the corridor a little and used his watch to open a door. He unceremoniously tossed his bag in, and then returned to Tim. "Right."

He led them on to corridor seven and turned up until they found room twenty five. "Your card will open this."

Tim held up his watch against the panel and sure enough, the door slid open. Inside was a room roughly five meters square. It contained a single bed, a wardrobe, chest of drawers and a desk, on which was a vid-screen unit, complete with a person-to-person calling panel. The wardrobe was open and some jump suits were already hanging inside it. Presumably they were his uniform. As Joe stepped further in, he noticed that against the same wall as the door, stood a book case, about a meter high. All in all, not bad. Another door on the opposite wall, he presumed, led to the bathroom.

"Here's your lighting control." Joe pointed to a panel just to the side of the door. "Voice command set up is in your folder. Dump your bags and I'll take you to the leisure area." Tim did as he was told, still a little dumbstruck by the newness of the environment. It didn't bother Joe that he was doing all the talking. He'd inducted more than a few before Tim, and knew that most people went a bit quiet when they lost sight of the daylight and adjusted to the shock of being under artificial light. Tim wiped his eyes with his hands and then nodded at Joe that he was ready to move on, and so they then followed the blue line to the leisure area.

Joe didn't push any conversation until they emerged into the main relaxation complex. It had windows and skylights. At the far end was a kitchen and in the main floor area there were about thirty or so people, sat at various desks and benches doing everything from reading to eating and even snoozing. There were also potted plants dotted around; mostly large ones in floor tubs. Presumably this was meant to be a break from the regimented style of the rest of the building.

Joe started pointing at the various doors that surrounded them. "You can get food over there. Menu varies day to day but they always have some basics on the stove. Pay for things with your I.D. Fitness room through there. Library and rest room that way. Laundry is over there and snack machines are stood behind those plants for when the kitchen is closed." He handed Jim the folder. "Here you go. Read up, eat and relax. Do whatever you feel like after the journey. You're on the same shift as me so I'll come get you in six hours. And don't let the folder out of your sight when you're in this zone. It contains security procedures." He flashed a smile at Tim. "Good luck."

"Thanks." muttered Tim, accepting the folder and starting at Joe, who happily turned around and walked back to the lifts. Then he looked around at the leisure area and pondered where the hell he was going to start.

Chapter 6

Over the next few weeks, Tim got a reasonable feel for the place and how it operated. He met Heather on his third day there, but she didn't seem like she was in the mood to be sociable with anyone so he decided not to probe her about the past. Even though the job meant he dealt with her on a regular basis, Tim never really became comfortable with her slightly offish behaviour.

In the end, Joe thought that it might help if he got some insight into how Heather ticked. One day, he caught up with Tim in the canteen during a lunch break and, over some stew and rice, dispelled some of the myths.

Apparently her father, Gareth Peterson had moved to Africa from the Europas. He was in construction and was working as a repair engineer, fixing the pipe-laying robots that were connecting the new villages to water supplies. The population was expanding into the Niger region because it had been one of the least populated areas during the war. As such, it had escaped the worst of the chemical attacks. Peterson was staying in one of those villages overnight when he met Ling Tseng.

She had been raised in the South Asiatics and was suffering with health issues. The doctor's advice was to move somewhere warm and drier, where there wouldn't be so many people around and hopefully less pollution. A freshly built village in the Africas seemed the best choice.

She was unhappy, though. Home sick. Vid-calling her family from an outlying village was expensive, so any gains she had in terms of her physical illness were offset by depression. Her only real outlet was her passion for cooking. She landed a job with the only major restaurant in the area. Her skills with South Asiatic food added an exotic element to their menu and as a result people came from some distance to eat there.

That reputation happened to see Gareth and his small team visit the place and it was love at first bite. From starters to desert, he waxed lyrical over the tones and tastes of her creations. Of course, working hard in a hot environment meant that a little alcohol went a long, long way and by the end of the evening he insisted that he wouldn't leave until he had personally thanked the chef.

The management thought that, rather than argue with an intoxicated customer, the best thing was to get this awkward experience over and done with, and get Gareth out of the door as quickly as possible. However, no one counted on what happened when their eyes met. For him, it meant the end of his single life. For her, the comical sight of him stumbling over his words broke a funk she'd been in for some time.

Before Gareth knew it, he sold his home in the Europas and had life-bonded with Ling. They lived together in the village, with Gareth spending time away to lay pipes and cables throughout the region. He would have become obese from the love of her food, if it wasn't for his love of her, and the frequent exercise that they got between the sheets.

Heather was their only child and she spent her early years in a family of minimal possessions and maximum affection. She blossomed emotionally like a rare flower, until that fateful day when the attack took place.

The village had been building its fortifications slowly, because no wild animals had moved into their immediate neighbourhood and there were other priorities for resources. Some time later, a herd of elephants was spotted frequenting a watering hole a few miles away, and a lone elephant had taken to making the journey to the outskirts of their location, presumably for better foraging.

The decision was made to speed up the completion of their protective walls, and call in a security company to bridge the gap until it was complete. After all, it was just one elephant and no serious cause for alarm.

Some opined, after the disaster, that the elephants had been planning an attack all along and the sight of the construction work hastened their plans. But the argument was a little mute after the event, because an assault is exactly what happened.

One night, the village was woken to the sound of thunder, but it wasn't a weather front. The entire heard descended on the village. People screamed as they ran in the dark. Buildings crashed to the ground under the weight of the large, grey, angry pachyderms as they annihilated the settlement.

Running from their small home, Gareth lifted Heather in the air and managed to propel her on to the roof of one of the larger houses. Ling was slowed both by her long running illness and choking on the dust that the elephants had kicked up. Gareth stayed by her side and tried to help her to safety; not that there were many places that couldn't be reached by these wrinkled, thick-skinned monsters.

Heather scrambled high up on the roof and watched her parents struggle across the dirt road. She tried to scream a warning but with the elephants trumpeting and people screaming, there was no chance that she could be heard. One of the beasts charged Gareth and Heather, running them over without a second thought. Heather could do nothing but grasp her knees to her chest and sit there on the roof, crying her heart dry of tears as she looked at her mother and father, lying dead on the road.

Although she attracted the attention of some of the elephants, they couldn't get to her that easily and, as the chaos was starting to die down, there was the sound of gunfire in the distance. An S.S.L. defence team arrived on the scene. They had intended to come and discuss the needs of the village, rather than get involved in a gun-fight, but that was how it turned out. Fortunately they were carrying licensed weapons and were able to stop the herd before it completely destroyed the small population.

It took three days for the dust to settle. The village had lost over half its inhabitants, as there was nowhere for them to run. It was concluded that the lone elephant was scouting the area, as the first thing the herd had targeted, was the car park; taking out the vehicles so that no one could drive away.

One of the S.S.L. staff that had arrived on the night of the attack was Jovani Romero. He helped Heather down from the roof top and tried to comfort her. She clung to him like a limpet to a rock and didn't speak much for the best part of a week. When she did, it was only one or two words. His team stayed while the village was rebuilt and the formalities of cremations and property were sorted out. Heather gained a respect for Jovani; the way he held himself and the responsibility of his position. When it came time for Ling and Gareth's funerals, he organised things and helped her through a very tough time. It was his shoulder that she cried on during the services.

It was no surprise that, when Ling's parents were contacted, Heather felt no affinity with them and wanted to stay with Jovani instead. A loner who lived for his job, he wasn't too pleased with this, but there was something about the whole episode, the ruthless attack and Heather's reliance on him, that must have found a soft spot in his hard, grizzled heart.

He decided to help her and went through a bit of a fight in the courts. Eventually Ling's parents got the message that if Heather went to them, she would be nothing but trouble. The courts saw that as well and, after Jovani won over the management at the company, he was allowed to be her guardian. Everyone thought it wouldn't be long before the constant travel and rough life moving from settlement to settlement, would bore her and she would want to settle down somewhere.

They were wrong. She didn't get bored. Driving at high speed across the desert, goggles on her eyes, bandanna over her mouth, hair tearing behind her in the wind; that was where her heart called home and Heather felt that she would never let go of Jovani as her adopted father.

Despite S.S.L. frowning on her accidental inclusion in their ranks, she turned into an excellent strategist and was on the payroll in her own right, before she was eighteen. She became a legend in the company and was dedicated to the job. The only sick leave she ever took was in her early thirties when Jovani fell victim to a tiger attack in South Africa and died. Heather escaped with serious injuries, but she survived and took a number of the animals down with her during the fight. It was no one's fault really. There were just too many tigers and too few firearms on hand. But the pain in Heather's heart at losing Jovani, never subsided. She remained bitter and resentful as she grew.

When security work for the GENIE project landed in S.S.L.'s lap, Heather was in her late forties and was the natural choice to head up the team that S.S.L. would install there. After all, with the option of an on-site apartment of her own, they hoped that it would provide her with an anchor and ultimately, bring some stability to her life and her long tormented soul.

By the time Joe had finished recounting the tale of the Tiger Woman, Tim realised just how tough her life had really been and, although he would likely never get used to her snappy, sulky ways, at least he understood why she had become the person she was.

The building consisted of three main underground sections. Alpha, Beta and Gamma, each of which had ten floors. Main research and control were on Alpha, running storage on Beta and building functions and emergency resources on Gamma. That was the official line. Gamma was also used as an unofficial dumping ground.

The robots surprised Joe. They were the most advanced he had seen, and they were all over the place. Big ones to move the large number of chemical drums that they used, all the way down to shoe box sized units that roamed the ducts maintaining the air flow and power systems, which were vital for an underground facility.

Most of his time had been on Alpha with the occasional trip to Beta. Gamma was rarely ventured into by anyone; cameras monitored everything and the only things that moved down there, were the robots. Not that there was much to watch over at the moment. There was a lot of space in the building for expansion. Once the initial teams had bedded in, the intention was to build a village nearby and move more scientists into the facility. Someone had obviously planned well ahead of themselves.

Genie itself was a serious machine. Organic in nature, it was closely based on the human brain. Just like the hippocampus created new neurons, so Genie had its own form of neurogenesis. It not only learned and studied, it actually grew. It also had a form of nervous system, rather than traditional electronics, so it controlled its own specially constructed laboratory equipment. It couldn't actually interface with the more traditional computers that controlled the base. Somehow, Tim found that to be a comfort.

He was now standing with Joe, in the main security control room on Alpha Five, receiving the day's orders. It was a pleasant enough light grey room, like most of the other, neutral grey spaces in the complex. He was having a very strong feeling of deja-vu, despite only have been there for a few weeks.

There had been three attacks by various animals, all of which had passed off without incident, as they couldn't make a dent on the structure, but they had to respond to the alerts regardless. Wearing their grey-blue jumpsuit uniforms, with a red band around the chest to signify they were security, they had to arm themselves and take positions near whatever doors were being attacked, in case something broke through.

The central control room was similar to the ground floor observation room, but on steroids. It contained five large desks, each with numerous controls, terminals, radios and handsets. The far wall was plastered with screens, displaying the output from cameras positioned all over the complex, both inside and out. People were sat at them fairly much all the time and at this particular moment, Heather was positioned at the main control desk, giving them their daily orders.

"There's three large lorries coming to swap out chemical drums, so you two are on gate duty." She held out a clip board with paperwork, which Joe took. "Any questions?"

Joe flipped through the documents and gave them a quick scan. "Nope. This looks straightforward."

"Good. First lorry is due in about an hour and a half. Get up there and sort things out. There's a team of robots waiting, along with a pile of waste drums."

Joe nodded and turned to leave. Tim followed him. As they entered the corridor and the door shut behind them, Tim asked, "Are you feeling OK?"

"Yes, fine. Why do you ask?"

"Um, well, I just feel odd, that's all."

Joe stopped. "What kind of odd? Call in sick, kind of odd?"

"No. Physically I feel fine, but mentally I just feel like I've done this before. You know?"

Joe shook his head. "I'm not with you. Maybe you're just getting used to working below ground. Every corridor looking the same, the constant lighting, the routine..."

Tim sighed. "Well, it may be. It could also be the shipments. We've had an awful lot of them this last couple of weeks and it's getting to be very regular."

Joe nodded. "I know what you mean. Boring as hell." He looked at the paperwork. "The amount of chemicals we've gone through lately does seem a bit much. I'll have a chat with Tamara about it later." He nodded his head down the corridor, and Tim got the message. They started walking again. On their way to the Alpha Five lifts, they passed the door which led to the control centre for Genie, oblivious to the fact that the deliveries weren't the only things that weren't behaving quite as they should.

Chapter 7

In Genie's control room, things didn't seem quite right either. Professor Emmett Charcott was sat at his desk, pondering a raft of figures on a screen, comparing them to yet more figures that he had calculated manually and written out on paper in front of him. His brow was deeply furrowed as he couldn't make the two sets of figures match.

The immense focus he was able to bring to his work, was a boon in some ways, but a hindrance in others. The very creation of the Genie project owed a good deal to his continued and never ending evangelism of its necessity. However at this moment in time, his failure to get the figures to match what he was expecting to see, was preventing him from going to a meeting which the rest of the Genie staff were current attending. He absolutely had to get this discrepancy sorted before his mind could even consider what was next on the agenda.

His inability to recognise or rate anything which was outside his immediate sphere of thought, also extended to his coffee stained lab coat, his unkempt hair and unruly beard. These only managed to be dealt with because his colleagues periodically swapped out his white coat, and occasionally changed the security code to the control room; declining to tell him the new combination until he had visited the barber, showered, or sorted out whatever personal hygiene problem had caused offence.

The room contained a number of terminals arranged in a circular pattern, so that their occupants could converse readily over the tops of their monitors, while simultaneously working on their consoles. For a grey room in a very grey building, the impossible had seemingly been achieved. This area somehow seemed shinier and sleeker than the others. It had a presence; a life almost. As the central point of the whole project, it had received extra special attention.

Part of the reason for the extraordinary effort that was lavished on this particular location, might have had something to do with the large, round window in the wall opposite the door. Its diameter was almost the same as the height of the wall, and it protruded into the room a little. Beyond it was a slightly brown coloured liquid and, floating in the light brown ooze, was an oddly shaped collection of genetic material. Occasional sparks could be seen as this strange, new machine worked tirelessly on its task. What was perhaps most disconcerting was that it almost looked like it was actually swimming in the liquid, as it occasionally buffeted the glass.

At this precise moment, the room was empty of people except the Professor. Behind his metal rimmed spectacles, his eyes darted eagerly beneath his knitted brow. What he was reading just wasn't making any sense and he wanted to get to the bottom of this predicament before joining his colleagues. Above him, a box of electronics turned on its spindle. It had three lenses, two of which observed the Professor's distress and from behind the middle lens, a complex light source sprang into life.

This was no ordinary, closed circuit vid-screen system. The, "eyes," were akin to the type used to give sight to the blind, and were connected back to Genie through nerve-like cabling. In between them was a projector which was responsible for giving Genie a presence in the room. It, too, had a nerve connection rather than electronics, but it read the, 'mood,' of Genie and changed the generally lifeless image according to how the computer, 'felt.'

Microphones and loudspeakers were similarly attached. Genie originally had to be taught to communicate, much like a child. The advantage was that the oversized, 'brain,' grasped the concept of speech very quickly, so pre-prepared tapes were played to the never-tiring Genie so that in four months, 'she,' had the same intelligence and basic knowledge of an eighteen year old. Able to master numerous presence system inputs simultaneously, Genie was then able to watch information vid-recordings on neurology, human medicine and everything that was required to set her on task in an amazingly short amount of time.

She learned how to control her own arms within the confines of the testing labs, and within eight months had started to make valid contributions to the various research teams that were on-site. Alpha Four had a number of conference rooms and, as her organic structure grew, she was able to take part in different meetings at the same time, as there were Genie presence boxes in various positions on the base.

Beside Emmett, a holographic image of a thirty year old woman appeared. The hologram was a light shade of purple, but more subtle shades were used to give the appearance that she was dressed in black trousers and a short sleeved white blouse. "Is there a problem, Professor?"

Emmett took a moment to glance at the hologram. He still hadn't got used to Genie suddenly appearing alongside him like this. He took a breath and returned his intense concentration to the screen. "Yes, Genie. These figures. They're all wrong." To emphasise his point, he tapped the screen with the pen in his hand. "They don't equate to anywhere near what I was expecting to read, and I don't know why."

"Can I help you, Professor?"

He sat back and folded his arms. "Maybe, if I had the slightest idea of what could be done, that might actually help. If I at least knew why the figures weren't adding up, then I may have a clue as to where to start investigating. But I don't." He thought for a moment.

"You can run an internal diagnostic when you have some free cycles."

"Certainly Professor. I have scheduled a task to occur in three hours' time. I will send the results to your vid-account when they are ready."

Still leaning back, Emmett tapped the end of his pen against his lips and pondered wildly. "Is there some rogue process running inside you?"

"No, Professor. My root task is to save the human race from the neurological problems plaguing it. All other processes are sub-routines of my original goal, investigating new avenues and leads. I am one hundred percent on task with no distractions."

"Then why aren't these figures making sense?" he mumbled to himself. After a few moments, he looked at her, eye to holographic eye. "Perhaps the new neurons are forming unexpected pathways. You know, at times I really do fear that you have reached a complexity that is now beyond my comprehension."

"Your theory does not hold true, Professor. All new pathways are operating as part of the whole, and are contributing to the original goal."

Feeling frustrated, he parted his lips and tapped the end of the pen against his teeth. "You are the closest thing to the human brain that we've ever developed. Your growth has been consistent over the last few months and, considering cell birth and death, you've added another seven percent to your mass overall. I just can't get inside you to see how that new material has formed and linked."

"I am still me, Professor. Still one hundred percent on task with no distractions."

"So you said, Genie. So you said. But this doesn't look right." He worried his forehead with his hand, moving the pen between his fingers so that he didn't scratch himself with it. "I'm going to have a chat with some of the others."

Emmett tossed his pen on the table and got up from his chair. Emitting a heavy sigh, he turned and made for the door. It empathised with him as it slid open, and he stepped through into the corridor. Genie's hologram impassively watched him leave, and then shimmered back out of existence.

He emerged into one of the bland, featureless grey corridors, stared at the various coloured lines on the floor that led to different destinations, and started following the purple line to the meeting rooms. In one of them, the rest of his staff were discussing what methods could be employed to measure Genie's IQ. It was perhaps a fruitless task; how could they ever measure the intelligence of a system that, regardless of being genetic, was still man made and followed classic logic principles?

His thoughts drifted to the design of the corridors and the building in general. Even growing up in underground buildings in the Antarctics, Emmett had never really got used to the bland monotony of the design. When you let robots build structures like this, the flowing touch of a human would always be missing from the geometry. Perhaps it was too much to expect something non-human, to think like a human. But then, they didn't really think; they just followed orders. Even Genie.

As Emmett ran this familiar thread through his mind, like he had many times before, he found himself following the logical trail to its source, and pitying the mental state of the person that programmed the robots in the first place. They must have had no feeling whatsoever for form, and thought purely of the function. What sad people they must have been.

He strode purposefully down the passage, occasionally looking over his shoulder to ensure that he had his bearings right and was following the correct line, even though he'd followed it many times before. Now and then he nodded as he passed people; Alpha Five contained many of the control functions for the complex and therefore was a natural place to bump into all the important people. He pondered whether it would actually hurt someone that much, to put some plinths and potted plants around the place. Sure, some of the larger robots might have a few problems manoeuvring, but wasn't that why they were fitted with sensors and avoidance systems?

There was another all-staff, base meeting coming up shortly. He'd mention his concerns yet again, to be told once more that they would be considered, and yet nothing would ever happen. Who was scrutinising these requests? The Sugar Plum Faerie? If it was, then it would explain why nothing ever changed, or any feedback was received. At some point he'd have to get tough. Potentially stand up and stamp his foot or something. 'What do we want? Aspidistras. When do we want them? Well, a week next Tuesday would be nice.'

As he walked, there was a swishing sound as the door to the main robotics lab opened. From it, emerged Fay Hobson, wearing dungarees and eye protectors. She was obviously doing another round of repair work. A quick glance revealed that she had singed her hair. Another blow-torch accident no doubt. Her face lit up with excitement the moment she saw Emmett.

"Professor! Just the person. I need to talk with you urgently."

"Well, I've got something on my mind Fay. Can it wait?"

"Not really." she said, her features suddenly becoming very concerned. "It's very puzzling and I need the help of one of your team."

"Well, I'm not sure what we can do for you."

"I need your logical deduction skills."

Emmett stood there for a moment, trying to decide whether he would respond to her plea, or make another attempt at excusing himself. After a couple of heartbeats, he decided to let Fay win him over. After all, he did like solving mysterious problems. "Well, OK."

"In here." she gestured, and he followed her into the maintenance lab.

Her workshop was part office, part repair bay, and was larger than many labs on the floor due to the need to store large robots while they were being worked on. The walls were lined with cupboards and shelves which were normally packed with new armatures, tracks, wheels, cameras and enough bits and pieces to make a new fleet of machines, rather than repair the existing; but at the moment, they looked strangely empty. There was also a section containing tools, sprays, lubricants and everything that Fay used in her job; but even that looked to have be decimated, as if hit by a plague.

In the centre of the room was a table with spot lamps, magnifying glasses and a yellow stripped area where the larger robots stood to be worked on. Or to be more accurate, there was supposed to be a stripped area. Emmett couldn't see it as it was jammed full of robots. The table was likewise stuffed with machines of various sizes. He couldn't see enough free surface area on which to rest a drinking mug. Any empty wall space was also taken up with a dead robot, standing there waiting its turn to be serviced.

"Hell alive. Do we really have this many units out of action?"

"Yes. They seem to be doing double shifts or something. The batteries are taking a hammering. But that isn't the only thing that's worrying. Look." She pointed out a few bits of damage on the arms and various other points on some of the robots. "Weld spatter, impact damage and chemical stains."

Emmett looked unimpressed. "That's not surprising. They're maintenance machines."

"It's the type of damage they're taking, and where

they're taking it. Benzillic acid for one."

He looked at hear blankly. "Sorry. That's a little out of my comfort zone."

"Of all the things we're supposed to have on site, this isn't one of them. I had to ask the chem lab to help to identify it and, when they found out what it was, they went nuts. The paperwork says we started ordering it but Tamara insists they have absolutely no use for it in the experiments they're running."

"Then where did it come from?"

"Like I said, the paperwork says that we ordered it, but no one seems to know who, or why. We appear to have a raft of unknown goods arriving and we can't trace who initiated the orders. Alexei helped me work out how to neutralise the excess that's still on the robots so I can repair them safely, and Tamara is trying to do a stock take now, but it looks like we've been ordering unusual things for the last month and not only that, but what we've ordered has also gone missing."

"So let me get this straight. Chemicals that we don't need, are being ordered by someone we don't know, and are not only arriving but are going missing before we even know they're not supposed to be here. Right?"

"Yes."

"And when, exactly, were they going to go to the committee with this?"

"Well, they asked me not to say anything until they knew exactly what was ordered, whether it did in fact arrive, and whether what did arrive really is missing; even though what's not supposed to be here is, evidently, in use because it's damaging the robots although nobody knows who's using it, or what for."

"Err..." Emmett scratched his forehead, trying to get his head around her last statement.

"Tamara is really knocked sideways by this and wanted to straighten things out, because she's that kind of person; but this is all getting too spooky even for me."

Emmett sighed and decided to try and tackle a subject which he might have a chance of getting a grip on. "And what about the batteries?"

"Well, the robots just aren't getting enough rest. It is just like they're doing double shifts, but the log files say they're doing a normal work load. Nothing about this adds up. It's a bit odd."

"You're not kidding. In the space of a few minutes, things have gone from being a bit odd to very wei..." His sentence was cut short by a series of sirens that blazed their cry of alarm across the base. The lighting turned from its gentle daylight balance, to a bright, grating red.

Emmett and Fay looked at each other in shock and disbelief. They saw behind each other's eyes as they processed the fact that the alarms had gone off, and then almost as one, they acted. The pair bolted for the door, and stood there in pure frustration as it gently sighed its way open, oblivious to the sense of urgency. Once it had generated enough of a hole, they darted out and into the corridor.

Fay turned left and Emmett turned right. He only managed three paces before he brought himself up short, glanced at the floor and then looked around. The image of Fay running in the opposite direction caused him to think about his actions and, two heartbeats later, he was running after her towards the security office.

By the time they reached the door, he was only one pace behind her. The security office had been specially fitted with one of those quaint, twenty first century doors. It consisted of a large piece of wood with hinges down one side and a hand operated lever on the other. It has been installed in case there was a technology failure on the base, and the automatic doors stopped working. Across the wooden face was a large white sign with big red letters, "Warning: Manual Gate." Fay operated the handle, swung open the door and they both barrelled through.

The security office was another drab, grey room. Emmett was beginning to conclude that the Genie terminal room was the only place in the whole complex that had been given the shiny wall treatment. Heather was still sat at the main desk, where Joe and Tim had left her only fifteen minutes earlier. Now, however, she was bathed in the red emergency light, punching buttons and barking orders like she was possessed.

Her colleagues sat at the other desks, were sweating trying to keep up with the instructions, operating controls and shouting responses to Heather. As Emmet and Fay acclimatised to the chaos, they noticed that a good number of the monitors on the far wall were blank, which was very unusual. Some of the monitors that were working, showed statistics about the building, and they contained some very urgent looking, bold red text.

Emmett and Heather didn't get on. As she was the head of security and operations, and he was the head of the Genie project, they had clashed on a number of occasions since the building had opened. Emmett saw more of the same in their future. Those argumentative encounters meant that he didn't engage with her on any topic unless he absolutely had to. Even now, with an emergency in progress, it appeared that she was still up for a fight. Finally noticing that they were standing there, she barked at them. "Everyone else is making their way to the canteen. Why aren't you?"

Emmett not only immediately rose to the bait, but he also raised his voice. Whether it was a result of the racket, or anger from being challenged, he wasn't sure and now wasn't the time to analyse his emotions. "Now look. I don't know who you think..."

Fay could see exactly where Emmett was going and she wasn't a particular fan of long, drawn out arguments, particularly those that were being waged over the top of nerve wrecking noises. Before he could finish his sentence, she decided to lay down her own style of law and shouted her way into the conversation. "Because like you, we've got a vested interest in this base. And before you say anything else, the answer is no. We're staying here."

Heather stared at their faces; steely and determined. She wouldn't be able to kick them out without a fight, but as much as Heather enjoyed a good battle of wits, she had an emergency to deal with. Rather than fire back at Fay's challenge, she spat a venom laced, "Fine!" before turning back to her screens.

The battle for authority over the base wasn't the only thing that had Heather's back up. She had a deep distrust of Genie. The genetic computer was far outside what she considered a useful machine. It has the capability to bite back. Simple logic driven computers were one thing, but genetic machines threw any certainty into the air; and she didn't like it one bit.

Her concerns didn't wash with Emmett. He just couldn't see what she was worried about. There was no easy way to wire Genie into the base computers, so he didn't believe there was any reason for Heather to be on edge. However, he knew that there were times when you could spout facts until you were blue in the face, and some people just weren't able to see the wood for the trees.

All that, however, was irrelevant in the current state of things. Whatever was happening on those screens had Heather worried. In spite of having Emmett and Fay behind her, she remained focused on pushing buttons and barking orders at her colleagues. When there was a lull in activity, Emmett took his chance. "What the hell is happening?"

Heather shot him a sideways glance, resentful at having to tear herself away from the task at hand. "There was a contaminant in the air conditioning system. Level Gamma Three."

"What?"

"Contaminant. Gamma... oh, hold on." She reached over to a panel and flicked a switch. The siren stopped. "Contaminant. Level Gamma Three."

Fay couldn't believe her ears. "What? Gamma Three? Nobody works on the Gamma levels normally."

"Exactly," replied Heather, "And there's no one down there now. Charcott, are you sure you're behemoth hasn't got anything to do with this?"

"How many times have I got to tell you? You can't just plug a genetic computer into a binary computer network. Whatever is going on around here, Genie's got nothing to do with it. When are you going to get over your paranoia?"

"When it stops behaving like a human. That thing's scary."

"Genie doesn't behave like a human. How many times have I got to tell you that she isn't human!"

"Then why are you calling it a she?"

Emmett fumbled a bit at Heather's very valid criticism, but Fay was once again determined not to let the pair of them get locked in their usual tit for tat banter. Their arguments over Genie ultimately went nowhere, and there was an important mystery afoot. Fay pointed at one of the CCTV screens where two figures were stepping gingerly out of a lift. "What's happening?"

Heather took the opportunity to disengage from the flustered Emmett while she thought that she had the upper hand. "I've got staff in chemical suits going down there to examine the area. A few weeks ago, some of the CCTV on that floor broke down and we haven't had the time to fix it yet, so I can't see what's going on."

Emmett recovered from his bruised ego and joined in the conversation. "Was there much contamination?"

"No." Heather looked relieved to be saying that. "Just enough to set the alarm off, and then it dissipated. Wasn't even enough for us to properly analyse its composition."

The look of query on Fay's face turned to one of deep concern. "Do you think it was sabotage?"

Heather just looked at her, shrugged and stated plainly, "I don't know. We'll have to wait to see what they find."

Chapter 8

Down on Gamma Three, Joe Magoro and Tim Ross emerged from the lift and stepped into the corridor. Their progress was hampered by the bright orange hazard suits they were wearing, which made moving a little awkward. They definitely weren't everyday security personnel attire, but caution was the better part of valour when dealing with the unknown. They were also wearing utility belts which contained an assortment of tools that might be needed during a chemical spill.

As these were the maintenance and emergency floors, every expense had been spared. Dull grey, solid walls and floor, dimly lit by whatever glow came from the lift, greeted them as they cautiously examined their bleak environment.

The spookiness dial was turned up to ten. The roughly finished, dark corridors appeared to be several degrees colder due to the absence of any human activity. They may as well have been the first astronauts to set foot on an alien planet. As if that wasn't enough, the plastic helmets they were wearing, echoed their own breathing straight back into their ears, while also dampening sounds from outside the suits. The disconnection they experienced between themselves and their surroundings, didn't help their nervous systems.

As they stepped forward, their lone footsteps echoed on the concrete floor, adding the finishing touch to the eerie atmosphere. They could have been forgiven for thinking that they were the only people still alive on the whole planet, except for the communication headsets they were wearing that patched them back to Heather, at control.

They looked at each other with a degree of uncertainty, both of them wearing the same puzzled expression. It was the kind of look that subconsciously believed that they should have stayed in the relative safety of the small metal cubicle that brought them down here in the first place.

The level of finish here really was the worst. Metal ducts openly ran across the ceilings with no attempt made to hide them. Many of the doors were the twenty-first century hinge-and-handle style for the same reason as the control room. After all, these were the emergency floors.

Joe looked up at the ceiling to examine the lights. They were open to the elements and not even the securing bolts had been capped off. The cables that powered them were also visible, crudely but neatly stapled to the ceiling. He examined them briefly. There was no sign of damage. He reported to Heather on his helmet radio. "No wonder you can't see anything on the cameras. It's pitch black down here."

She responded, "What can you see?"

Joe guffawed, partly from irony and partly from fear. Heather clearly hadn't taken on board what he had just said. Tim picked up the conversation while Joe carried on chuckling. "You're kidding us, right? Nothing. The bit in front of the lift is lit but everything else is totally black. Can't see a damn thing. Just patch into our helmet cams."

"What suits are you in?"

Joe took a look at the white numbers on their shoulders. "Chem suits four and five."

Heather hit a few buttons and two of the screens displayed exactly what Joe and Tim were seeing; a small pool of light where they were, and then just a dim shadow of the corridors quickly disappearing into nothingness. Another couple of button presses added their vital statistics to the bottom of the screens. Their heart rates were slightly elevated, which was understandable. While an occasional bulb could develop a fault, or even a whole corridor, there was no obvious reason why an entire floor would be in darkness.

Back on Gamma Three, the men took torches from their belts, turned them on and attempted to shine them down the corridors. The tightly concentrated beams of light were no replacement for properly functioning bulbs. Slowly, Tim started to take baby steps out of the lift area, and into the awaiting blackness. "You sure there's nothing down here?" he queried, with Joe not far behind him.

"Nothing living according to the sensors." assured Heather.

"Yeah, tell me why I don't find that a whole lot of comfort right now?" he retorted. Heather made no attempt to answer him as she wasn't entirely sure what she could say. "Where's this problem, did you say?"

"Sector three." she returned. It wasn't too far from their position.

Tim and Joe inched forward, scanning the floor, ceiling and walls with their torches. Tim passed his opinion on the darkness. "The lights and cables so far, are all intact. Whatever the problem is, it must be at one of the main power cross overs."

Heather reminded them of why they were down there. "Don't worry about that for now. First things first. Find out what threatened to poison our air supply."

Only thirty feet in front of them, was a junction. They needed to turn right. Heartbeat by heartbeat, step by step, they made slow progress. As they did so, confidence in their surroundings rose slightly.

On reaching the centre of the cross roads, they both did three hundred and sixty degree sweeps with their torches as they cautiously stood at the crossing of the ways. The beams of light they held were sent as far into the darkness as possible, in all directions. Nothing but lifeless, dull grey stared back at them.

In the control room, the hiss of their breathing over the radio combined with the dark video feed, gave Heather a taste of the heebie jeebies. She was concentrating so much on the screens that she forgot about everyone else in the room. Not that it mattered, because everyone in the security office was also transfixed by what was happening on the monitors.

Joe and Tim stood there, uncertain of what they were going to do. It felt like reaching this lone point had been a major milestone and to move from there was to give up what had been courageously fought for and won. They scanned the corridors, partly expecting some unspeakable horror to pounce at them out of the darkness. Of course, nothing attacked and they had to press forward so, after thirty seconds that felt more like a week, Tim motioned with his head and said, "We moving on?"

"Yeah," replied Joe. "Guess we better had."

They cautiously shifted their positions and started walking down the next corridor, side by side. Tim nervously looked over his shoulder once too often and Joe couldn't help commenting. "You a man or a mouse?"

Tim looked him straight in the eye and stated the obvious. "Squeak?" Joe just shook his head and pressed on.

Sector three was ahead of them, second on the left. Progress was slow as they tried to make their torches highlight every small nook and cranny before they put a foot forward. The dull, uniform grey surface of the walls, ceiling and floor just seemed to eat the light and gave nothing back. Deadness filled their ears; it was almost like being in outer space, but worse. The creaking of the hazard suits, the pounding of their own hearts and echoes of their confined breathing all served to drive a massive reality wedge between their existence, and the deathly quiet that was all around them.

As they approached the next junction, they sent the torch beams down the dark expanses of nothingness. "Arrrgghhh!" screamed Tim, jumping sideways. He knocked Joe over and their pulses went off the chart for a few seconds. Arms and legs flailed as panic set in and they both hit the ground in a tangled heap. Joe scrambled to free himself from Tim and struggled to his feet, eyes wide, body on red alert, scared for his life.

"What! What!" he shouted as he willed his shaking limbs to obey him. When he pointed his torch in the same direction as Tim, he saw what had caused the alarm. It was one of the six foot tall robots. It just stood there, dull and motionless.

Tim almost screamed at him, "It moved! I damn well saw it move!" while keeping his eyes pinned on the robot, heart thumping like mad, arms shaking.

Joe attempted to will himself down to a normal breathing pattern. "Don't do that you idiot. You scared the hell out of me."

"Yes, but… but it moved!"

Joe cautiously scanned the robot with his torch and took a few steps towards it. "There are no lights on it. It's dead. Look." He ran his torch up and down the robot, moved closer to it, and then turned to look at Tim.

Tim flashed his eyes between Joe and the robot, half expecting the thing to suddenly come to life and capture Joe. "I swear! It moved!"

"Come on. Dead robots don't move. Let's get to sector three." Joe turned and started to walk away.

Tim was still immobilised with shock. "Don't leave me with this thing!"

"Then get your arse off the floor and follow me."

Tim managed to peel himself off the floor and hurried to make step with Joe. He threw one last, suspicious look at the metal statue behind them as it faded into the shadows.

As dangerous and deadly events doggedly persisted in not happening to either of them, the tension started to evaporate. Maybe it was the come-down from the shock of meeting the dead robot, or perhaps it was just that they were getting used to the dark, but whatever the reason, they traversed the remainder of the corridor at good speed and were at the turn to sector three before they knew it. Standing there, they sent their torch beams ahead of them, trying hard to see what might be the cause of the problem, without having to actually set foot in the danger zone.

"I can't see anything obviously wrong." said Tim.

"What, you mean that there isn't another dead robot down there, ready to not attack us at a moment's notice?" Joe ribbed him a little.

Tim looked at Joe with, 'victim,' plastered all over his face. "You're not going to let me live that down, are you?"

"Who? Me!"

"Yeah, you."

Heather decided that enough was enough. "Cut it out you two. There's a job to be done."

Joe smiled at Tim and received a hurt scowl for his trouble. They pointed their lights forward and started to make their way down the corridor. When they had nearly reached the end, an almighty clang came from behind them. They both jumped in shock and turned around, scanning the area with their torches. "What was that?" queried Heather from the control room.

"How the hell should we know?" replied Joe. "We'll let you know when we've found... ah." They came across a grill on the floor, which wasn't there when they passed that spot a moment ago. Tim shone his torch up at the ceiling, to reveal that one of the air conditioning ducts had a hole where the grill had just been.

"Looks like it fell out of the duct for some reason." Tim said, tapping Joe on the shoulder and pointing him up at the source of the disturbance.

"These things don't fall out on their own. You sure there's nothing living down here?"

Heather responded, "The only thing on the sensors is you two. If there was anything else living down there,

71

I'd be looking at it."

Tim corrected her. "Don't you mean we'd be looking at it? Do those sensors of yours go as deep as the air conditioning?"

"The sensors are in the air conditioning ducts, so quit crapping your big boy pants and get on with it."

Tim kept his voice low. "I didn't sign up for this shit."

"I heard that!" chided Heather

"Good. I want danger money for this."

"Just get on with it!" she exploded.

Tim positioned himself below the hole and knitted his fingers together. Bending over, he held his joined hands in readiness to give Joe a boost up. "Come on. Ally oop."

"What do you mean? You want me to stick my head up there? Are you kidding!"

"Well, one of us is going to have to do it, and I'm sure your shoulder won't handle boosting me up there. And I don't know about you but I'm not going to waste my time looking for a step ladder in the pitch black. So come on, before being bent over like this wrecks my spine."

"I'm not so sure about this."

"Just do what the boss said. Get on with it." Tim smiled.

Joe moved in front of Tim and put one of his feet in Tim's hand-cradle. He hopped on his remaining foot a couple of times and then launched himself upward. As he became air born, Tim straightened his back and propelled Joe up into the air conditioning duct. On getting his shoulders into the space, Joe looked in both directions quickly, just to make sure that he wasn't about to be attacked by something, and then settled down to the job of shining his torch around and having a detailed look.

"Nothing here. No. Wait. Tire tracks. Looks like one

of the small maintenance robots was up here."

Back in the control room, Fay made her thoughts known. "I told you those robots were up to something."

Heather challenged her. "Yeah, but trying to poison us? They're not that intelligent."

"Well something is causing this odd behaviour."

Heather turned to one of her colleagues. "Jake, I want you to go through all the robots programming and routines. Anything that's out of the ordinary, I want to know about it."

Fay chimed in again. "Good luck with that. I've already been through the logs on the ones that have come back for repair. Nothing. Nada. Zero. Zip. Zilch."

Heather continued to think. "Then we must have been hacked. There's no way that kind of intelligence could come from inside the base." She turned to Jake and added a little more to his workload. "I want the whole base scrubbed for rogue programs. There's got to be something, somewhere that's responsible for this. Kill our link to the outside world and check the logs."

At this, it was Emmett's turn to chime in. "You can't do that! We'll lose communication! We'll be cut off!"

"I don't see that we have much choice until we know what we're dealing with." She turned to her other colleague. "Jill, get up to the radio room. I want to know of any signals hitting or leaving this base. Scan all the frequencies we're capable of listening to." Jill nodded, got up and left the control room.

Heather leant over and keyed the microphone again. "You two break out some fire power and do a full search of Gamma three. There's no knowing what we're going to find. And I think you can ditch the suits, all the sensors say the air is clear."

Joe's voice came back over the radio. "Roger that."

With Tim and Joe set on their task, Heather turned to Emmett. "We've got a lot of log files to search through. I don't suppose there's any chance that your genetic beast could help us sift through them?"

"Not really. You can't just insert a data disk into Genie, you know."

Heather lifted her hands in mild exasperation. "I know, I know. It's not that kind of computer."

Fay put her hand on Emmett's shoulder. "We'd better get down to the chem lab. All of this has to be linked somehow."

Heather stopped them. "Wait a moment." She reached over and flipped a switch. The red lights returned to white. That done, she picked up one of the two way radios and tossed it gently at Emmett, who caught it. "Take this. We're going to need to stay in touch." Emmett loosely saluted Heather with the radio, and left with Fay.

Chapter 9

The two walked purposefully up the corridor towards one of the lifts. "Do you think they'll find the cause of this?" Fay queried.

"Doubt it. Modern programming only goes so far, so we're not facing a robot rebellion. There's nothing in the base that shouldn't be here, so network infiltration is the most likely culprit. Once the mastermind is cut off from the robots then this insanity will probably stop in short order."

"So that's a no then?"

They reached the lift and Fay waved her hand in front of the sensor, to make sure it knew they were there. Emmett took a moment to think. "If the person responsible for this chaos is outside the building, then I think Heather will have a hard job trying to find them."

The lift arrived and the doors opened. It was a standard, eight person box with a grey that matched the rest of the décor. They stepped in and the doors closed. The lift asked them the obvious question. "Which floor do you desire?"

Emmett responded, "Alpha ten."

"I heard... alpha ten. Is that correct?"

"Yes."

Fay rolled her eyes at the moronic exchange. At some point in history it obviously made sense to replace push buttons with voice commands, but surely they could have done a better job by now. "I hate these bloody lifts."

The computer obviously heard her. "I do not understand, 'Hate these bloody lifts.' Please repeat your desired floor designation."

Fay slapped her hand against her forehead with a degree of force, and her shoulders sagged noticeably. For his part, Emmett looked up at the ceiling and started whistling a little tune to help pass the time, as no one dared to speak in one of these lifts. Too late, he realised his mistake in making his own music. "Boredom detected. Starting uplifting mood program."

The lift started playing muzak from its loudspeakers and the colours inside, gently cycled between peaceful pastel purples, greens and blues. Fay's jaw started quivering out of frustration and Emmett apologised to her for making their situation worse. "Sorry."

"I do not understand, 'Sorry.' Please repeat your desired floor designation."

Emmett just looked at the floor, resigned not to say anything more until they were outside the lift.

When the lift reached Alpha Ten and the doors opened, they were both very relieved to be able to get out of the elevating disco. Leaving the muzak and light show behind them, they marched silently down the corridor to one of the chemistry laboratories.

"I wonder how many chemicals have been stolen?" queried Emmett.

"And which ones. Maybe we'll get some insight into what's going on."

"Rusnak works in lab three, doesn't he?"

"Yes. This one." Fay pointed at one of the doors. They approached it and the door sighed its way open for them.

Emmett reflected that chemistry laboratories hadn't changed much throughout history. In all the books he was encouraged to read in his youth, pictures and drawings of these places had differed little over the ages. The greyness of the base was all but hidden by the racks of shelving that covered almost every spare inch of wall. They were loaded down by their burden of glass jars. Some were flat bottomed, some circular, others held in frames flanked by racks of test tubes and bottles in glass, stone and plastic which contained liquids and powders of various quantities. The poor shelves looked like Atlas, holding the chemical world upon their shoulders.

A handful of booths broke the regimented lines of storage. They were fitted with reinforced glass and had holes for arms to go through. These were the places where someone could perform the kinds of experiments that resulted in impressive explosions.

Some of the shelves held lines of books and dotted among the hard, proud, colourful spines were ring binders of notes; the results of the painstaking research that had been carried out. Sometimes, it was easier to find something on a shelf full of paper, than a storage crystal full of badly named records.

The central floor area contained line after line of benches. A few pieces of equipment were dotted around, along with electro-flame burners and sinks. Here and there, small notepads lay abandoned among the experiments which had been left unattended when the alarm had sounded.

Alexei Rusnak had his head down, concentrating on paperwork which was spread out on one of the benches. There was a very large and obvious weight on his shoulders which contorted his forty-odd year face, making it appear some twenty years older. The worry lines on his brow were made all the more obvious by the way they contrasted with the crisp, clean, fresh white lab coat he was wearing. His spectacles, broken in the middle and held together by a sticking plaster, added to the image of a person who prized order, but lived in a world of chaos.

He had only been at the complex for a few weeks before he started to curse his decision to listen to his wild, adventurous mother. Her advice had been to give up his home in Saint Petersburg, and chase a dream of making a big change in the world. She was convinced that he had the skills to bring hope to the suffering, and help heal those who were sick.

'Yes,' he frequently thought to himself, 'my dear, fearless mother.'

Yana Rusnak was living in Australia when she fell in love with John Granger. She sold medical equipment for a living and he worked in a hospital, purchasing machinery for said establishment. They got to know each other while she was showing him the latest in patient monitoring systems.

To showcase just how easy, quick and accurate this new model was, she wired him up for the purposes of demonstration. That was possibly the biggest mistake of her career. His blood pressure and heart rate gave the game away. He was obviously attracted to her. Strongly attracted to her, in fact. The figures didn't lie. Fortunately, they had enough self-respect to not jump on one of the trolleys there and then. When John came off shift, however, Yana was in close proximity to the hospital.

It was a blissful time of exciting, forbidden liaison. Warm Australian evenings spent in restaurants, playing virtua-sports in John's large living room. They even ate retro-food at the open-air long-story screenings of centuries old things called, 'movies.' A good chunk of their time was spent just enjoying each other's company. They either walked or jogged together, depending on how much retro-food they'd eaten.

They managed to keep their relationship a secret for a few months as there were conflicts of interest to deal with, but eventually questions were asked and things got awkward. Yana's employer wanted to know why she seemed to be engineering her travel patterns in a particular way, and John's boss commented on seeing them together a little too often to be professional.

There was no denying it, things were definitely getting awkward and perhaps it was the stress from the management that meant John paid a little less attention than he should have done, when he went for one of his early morning jogs.

As his concentration slipped, he lost his footing, tripped and fell right into the path of a travel pod. Even though the sensors saw it happen, there wasn't enough time for the system to shut down the power. It was all over in fractions of a second. Between the slowing movement of the pod and the sideways velocity of John's head, the impact killed him instantly. He never stood a chance.

It was a mess. Yana was warned to stay away from the funeral, otherwise things would get really awkward. But she couldn't. The emotional fire they had between them was too strong and when she turned up for the service, so did the temperature between her firm and the hospital. She eventually had to leave her job and return to her Mother in Saint Petersburg, with a child growing inside her.

Although there were men in his life, Alexei was raised without a father. He grew up to be a quiet, introverted, studious child and they put this down to him never having knowing John, or that side of the family, as they never tried to get in touch with her, although they knew that Alexei existed. Presumably the scandal was enough to keep them away from a blood relative; and if scandal was their priority then he was probably better off without knowing them.

The city was cold enough during the summer, but went below zero for much of the winter, and this just helped him keep his head down in his books. When he was in his early teens, the school went on a trip to a local museum. The area had given birth to a number of famous scholars over the ages and they happened to be holding chemistry demonstrations during one of his visits. It was geared to stimulate children, so it had a range of basic but exciting demonstrations.

Small amounts of hydrogen peroxide and potassium iodide were mixed together to produce a magically expanding foam that spilled from the tube and all over the table, much to the delight of the children. Two adults put some liquid nitrogen into a plastic rubbish barrel and then quickly tipped some little, white plastic balls on top of it, before running away. Five seconds later there was a, 'Boom!' as the little white balls flew up into the air! They were also allowed to play with some magnetic putty and a cube of metal; whenever they tried to take the cube away, the putty would just keep trying to smother and, 'eat,' the cube! That was fun.

They saw lithium being set on fire behind a protective screen, and it turned into what looked like a strange, underwater flower, only above ground! Perhaps the weirdest of them all was when sodium poly-acrylate was mixed with water to form artificial snow. As if they didn't have enough of the real stuff outside the door!

That school trip was responsible for setting Alexei on course for a life in chemistry. The State University was one of the very rare buildings that survived the Third World War and had the added bonus that the majority of its library had also made it through, intact. He graduated from the University top of his class and was wooed by a number of multi-national companies. However, despite the attention and promises of high salaries and interesting projects, Alexei decided to turn his attention to feeding the planet.

He stayed in Saint Petersburg with his mother and immediate family. His job was working in a local research laboratory, where they were trying to secure a food and water supply that was free from the effects of the chemistry of war. It was a long and difficult task. Destruction and decay always came far more easily than progress.

His work kept him content for a couple of decades. Alexei became modestly famous in his own right for what he had achieved in improving the food supply for the planet. There was a small display at the museum in his honour, along with some minor awards he had won for innovation and contributions to science. Now and then he went to the museum; he told people that it was the one indulgence which he occasionally allowed his ego. In fact, he went to stand in the back and watch the next generation of school children being awed by the simple spectacles that sparked his own career path. When they oood and aahd, a smile would cross his face as he watched their excitement.

By the time he had reached his mid-forties, he was leading a small team. Among them was Tamara Avilov. She was a few years his senior and was there to take care of the paperwork. She was also the shield between the staff and anyone from the outside world that wanted to negotiate something. Whether it was organising funding, gaining access to research or even the mundane things, like filing official documents, stock taking and ordering, Tamara was an expert organiser and knew enough about chemistry to make running the laboratory, very light work for Alexei.

He had feelings for her. She ran herself in an admirable way and that attracted him. Tamara was a no nonsense woman who knew where she was and what she wanted in life. However, his upbringing and introverted tendencies meant that for all the time she was there, he never made a move to let her know how he felt.

With his history and reputation, it was inevitable that the status quo would be challenged at some point. One day they received an invitation to work on the G.E.N.I.E. project. It caused a lot of issues at the laboratory when he announced the possibility of working in Africa, and the subject threatened to split the team, fuelling heated arguments whenever it was raised in discussion. Some of the team members recognised that they would get a chance to work more closely with new colleagues; people with different viewpoints and experiences. They would be able to investigate the mechanics of the human system as a whole, not just the food and water supply. On the other hand, others saw the years of effort they had invested in their research vanishing forever, as some of the avenues they were following would inevitably grind to a halt in favour of other projects.

In his heart, Alexei didn't want to leave Saint Petersburg. He had rarely travelled outside it, only to attend conferences, presentations and ceremonies for which vid-link's weren't sufficient. Although Yana was in her seventies and still able bodied, he was conscious that the advanced years would soon be upon her, and being in a different region concerned him greatly; despite the speed of the tubes.

For all the decades and the trouble that her free spirit had landed her in, Yana was still strong minded and looked to the stars. She discussed the issue with Alexei over many a family meal. Yes, he had done great work, but if there was an opportunity to do more, then adventure was there for the taking! Her beaming smile and infectious personality eventually wore him down.

At the lab, it was a black, tortuous day when he announced his intention to accept the offer, along with whoever from the team wanted to join him. There was shouting. There were accusations doubting people's parentage. Some desks were banged in anger and frustration. Alexei, however, stayed firm and set his date. Having drawn the line in the sand, he left them to make their own choices regarding their futures.

In the end he, and a little more than half of his team, made the journey to Africa. His heart was singing, as Tamara had decided to join him. And now here he was, in the middle of a chaotic situation over which, he had no control.

It didn't surprise Emmett that Alexei hadn't evacuated with everyone else. He was a dedicated, determined man and wouldn't abandon an issue like this, especially as it was most likely tied up with the reason for the alarm going off in the first place.

At the sound of Fay and Emmett's entrance, Alexei looked up. On recognising Emmett, several more tons of leaden guilt weighed on his shoulders and he sighed heavily. "Ah. Emmett. I was going to come and see the committee."

"Yes. So I gather. When it was too late, no doubt?"

"No, no. I assure you." said Alexei hurriedly, trying to deflect the veiled anger and disappointment being aimed in his direction. "Only when we had a full picture of what we're dealing with."

"And do you have that picture yet?"

Alexei looked down at his feet. "Well, no. It seems that the further we went back into the storage area, the more missing drums we found." he shook his head absentmindedly. "Or rather didn't find. In fact, others had been moved from the back, to the front, to make it look like nothing had been taken."

A look of mild shock came over Fay's face. This was a few degrees more complicated than she has originally believed, and this display of planning and cunning alarmed her. "So what DO we know so far?"

"Well," Alexei took a moment to get a grip, "Tamara is finishing off the stock take now. She's got the latest figures and when you look at those I think you'll see just how bad this really is." Alexei gestured towards a door. They waited for an awkward moment, exchanging glances before Emmett decided to take Alexei up on his offer and started to head towards the door.

"OK, let's go and ask her, I guess." As Emmett crossed the room, Alexei gave Fay a, 'What did you have to tell him for?' look. In return, she just scowled at him, and he wilted. Alexei had wanted to try and find some trace of positive news in this depressing series of events before going to the committee, but the more he looked, the worse the situation had become. The invasion by Emmett was, in reflection, inevitable.

They went through the manual door which took them down a flight of stairs to the level below. It was Beta One and contained barrels of chemicals, enough to keep the laboratories supplied for months at a time. The stairs allowed them to get what they needed without having to go through the whole process of having a robot scheduled to bring up an entire drum when they only needed a small amount.

Beta one was completely given over to drum storage. They emerged into a floor split into many corridors that ran alongside each other for the entire length of the building. It was the first time that either Emmett or Fay had been down this far and they were both taken aback by the sheer size of the place. It was like walking into a massive underground cavern, which, to an extent, is exactly what it was. "Where the hell are we supposed to start?" gasped Fay.

"She's down in row twenty three." Alexei offered meekly, and led the way. As they walked past corridor after corridor, the only thing they could see were masses of drums, punctuated by the occasional lift shafts which were built into some of the separating walls. Passing the end of each corridor, the shelves full of drums disappeared down into the depths as if the lines never ended. Their footsteps echoed around the walls, adding to the illusion of endless space.

"Everything looks fine to me." said Emmett.

"Exactly. Like I said, the barrels have been moved to make it appear that we are well stocked. How long this was going on for before we discovered it, we can't tell."

Fay considered what was going on. "Someone's obviously put a lot of thought into this. None of our robots are capable of this degree of strategic planning."

"Don't you have any motorised buggies down

here?" Emmett queried.

"Actually, I never thought of that. I suppose we've always taken up the chance to have a nice walk, which isn't something you can do easily outside, around this area."

"Yes," Fay quipped, "the local wildlife is a bit, er, wild." As they walked, she started wondering who would have the smarts to pull off this level of deception, and whether or not it might actually be one of the staff trying to support their pay allowance somehow.

The illusion of space was added to because there were no false ceilings, so the ducts were clearly visible above their heads. The lighting was also raw and garish, which did no favours to the bland grey walls and floor. Far less finesse had been put into this level although at least the surfaces were smooth, unlike the Gamma floors.

At the end of each corridor, a number was painted along with an arrow, to signify which one it was referring to. They had almost forgotten what they were there for when Alexei chirped up. "Here we are, twenty three." He gestured for them to turn and walk down it, which they did.

They'd only gone ten steps before they registered the sight of a person, wearing a white coat, laying down in the middle of the corridor. A few steps closer confirmed that whoever it was, they weren't moving. Almost as one, they upped the pace a little.

As they took strides towards the lifeless person, they saw that the white lab coat, wasn't so white. There were splodges of red all over it; and there was more red on the ground. On recognising this, all three broke into a run. "Tamara! Tamara!" screamed Alexei as they ran full speed towards her.

Fay and Emmett came to a breathless halt as Alexei immediately fell to his knees at her side. He started muttering quickly, in a panicked but quiet, high pitched voice as he fussed over her. Alexei rolled her on to her back and checked her throat and face as best he could with his shaking hands. His high pitched jabbering continued as Fay and Emmett could do nothing but look on.

Then, Alexei bent closer to her, put his cheek to Tamara's and started wailing. Emmett knelt down and put his hands on Alexei's shoulders in a vain effort to comfort him.

"She's dead." Alexei looked at them, tears welling up in his eyes.

Emmett took a quick look at Tamara and touched her skin. She was cold and well beyond resuscitation. He looked at Fay and shook his head slightly. She got the message.

With Emmett attending to the sobbing Alexei, Fay felt a little like a spare part, not knowing what to do. That was when it hit her; the pattern of the red lines that were all around the body. Obviously, it was Tamara's blood, but the way it swirled around was most strange. She stretched out her arms to mimic the width of the robot's wheels and did a little dance around the floor. Emmett glanced at what she was doing. "Are you in shock or something?"

"No. But this is very odd." She continued her little dance.

"What's odd?"

"It looks like she had a fight with one of the big robots."

"No kidding."

"But it looks like it was actually trying to avoid her."

On hearing this, Alexei sobbed a little harder.

"What? How do you work that out?" Emmett asked.

"If it wanted to kill her, it would have just charged her. But this is far more convoluted than that. I reckon she was having some sort of battle with it over something, and she just fell under the wheels." She pointed to one of Tamara's legs. "It crushed her leg below the knee."

"Then she bled to death." concluded Emmett. Alexei sobbed harder, unable to believe that he was hearing them talk so clinically about the person he loved.

Fay concluded. "She was likely knocked out when she fell. I don't think she knew what happened to her." Emmett rubbed Alexei's shoulders a little harder, subconsciously wishing he could somehow transmit the knowledge that Tamara likely didn't feel much pain, without having to say the words. A few tears fell from Emmett's eyes in sympathy for them both.

After the initial shock had worn off, Alexei pulled back from Tamara and, still crying, settled back on his heels. Emmett let go of his shoulders but stayed at his side. No one was sure what to do next.

Fay spotted a clip board which had slid under a shelf. She walked over to it and, picking it up, started flipping through the sheets. "The key to what's going on here, is probably somewhere in these pages, but chemistry isn't my field. Alexei?" She held them out towards him.

Alexei stood up slowly, his chest still heaving in an odd, irregular pattern. Emmett followed him up from the floor. Somehow, now didn't seem to be the time to worry about blood stains on his knees. Alexei let out a low wail and took a few deep breaths, before reaching out a hand to take the clip board from Fay.

Absentmindedly, he flipped through a few pages. "There's actually a lot of stuff gone. It's going to take me a while to go through this." he said, shaking his head.

Emmett decided to inject a little purpose into their lives after the grim discovery. "Look. Alexei. Why don't you get back to the lab and look through those figures. We'll follow this trail and try to find the robot. Yes?" Alexei nodded uncertainly. He was still very shaken by the events. "Are you going to be OK?"

Alexei tried to gather himself. "No. Not really."

"Good man. We'll meet you back at the lab."

Alexei turned and slowly trudged his way back to his bench. It was almost as if his purpose for living had been wrenched from his chest. Fay and Emmett watched him for a few moments and, when he was out of earshot, Fay turned to Emmett. "Good man? What the hell were you thinking?"

He shrugged. "What do you think I should have said?"

"I don't know. But, I mean… Good man?"

Emmett shrugged again and simply gestured at the retreating trail of blood. "Look. I mean... shall we?"

They followed the blood tracks further down the corridor until they came to one of the larger, robot maintenance lifts. "Well, I suppose this makes some form of sense." offered Fay. She pointed at the call indicator, which had detected them waiting. "The lift's on its way."

Chapter 10

In another lift, Joe and Tim were cautiously emerging on to Gamma Four. Although they'd lost the hazard suits, Heather insisted on them still wearing headsets, so she could see what they were seeing. Or, rather, not see, as Gamma Four was just as dark as Gamma Three. But now they were carrying assault rifles with under slung grenade launchers, and packing that kind of fire power did wonders for the confidence levels. The rounds were powerful enough to take out an angry, charging orang-utan, so they reckoned they were fairly safe. From what, though, they didn't have much of a clue; and that was a big part of the problem.

Heather came over the radio. "We've cut communication to the outside world and there's no radio signals coming in that we can detect, so you two shouldn't have any more trouble."

"Thanks." replied Joe. "That's a real comfort."

"Just get on and walk the remaining Gamma levels. Shouldn't take more than a few hours. I'll sign off and let you two get on with it."

"You're leaving us?" queried Tim sarcastically. "However will we manage!"

"Like you always do," responded Heather, "in your own sweet way. Just don't take your time about it. I'll still be watching the camera feeds, though."

"Ok. Signing off." They switched off their audio units. "So." Joe looked at Tim. "Which way?"

"Guess we'd better do the circle and then hit the middle corridors one by one." He gestured to their left.

Buoyed by their relatively uneventful scan of Gamma Three, and with the promise of no more managerial interference, the two made much faster progress. They opened each door they came across, had a quick scan inside with their torches, and then carried on, talking as they went.

"So," queried Joe, "how are you taking to S.S.L.?"

"Oh, well, it's a hell of a lot different than transport security. Far more peaceful." he glanced at Joe. "Until now, anyway."

Joe chuckled, "More peaceful? I would have thought that charging animals and firearms would have been a step up from checking doors, scanning passengers and all that stuff."

"No. The separatists are still causing problems and the transport links are their main target. That's why I left the job and came to Africa. Couldn't take much more living on a knife edge."

"What? Separatists? Those nut cases? I didn't think they were much of a danger these days."

"Yeah, the vid-link plays them down but they're still quite active, trying to bomb the tubes."

Silence reigned for a while, while Joe processed the news. They got through another six side offices before he spoke again. "You know, I never did understand how so many people can be so completely convinced that the World Wars didn't happen. Haven't they been to the museums and seen the history programmes?"

"Vid-link propaganda they say it is. As for the museums, landmarks, survivor diaries, they've got kooky explanations for all of it."

"So what is it they want again? Separation of the countries, isn't it."

"Yup. They reject rule by the Panel and want each country to govern itself again. Playing right into the hands of World War Four if you ask me."

Joe sighed. "I guess they are." He remained thoughtful until they started on the cross running corridors. "Do you reckon they could be behind the trouble we're having here?"

Tim thought about this for a while. "It's possible, but I can't see what they'd gain by attacking a research lab. Maybe a new chemical weapon, if they thought that's what the Genie project was working on."

"But the whole point of the work here is to undo all the damage done by the other weapons that were used. Not create more of them."

"Yes," Tim smiled at him, "but since when have those maniacs ever believed the obvious? Once they've made their mind up on something, nothing can shift them."

Back on Beta One, Fay and Emmett's hearts were pumping hard in their chests as they stood either side of the lift door, backs up against the wall, waiting for the metal carriage to arrive. Would it contain a killer robot, wanting to silence them in order to cover its murderous tracks? The seconds seemed to tick into minutes. Their faces carried a mixture of, 'What in hell is waiting for us in that lift?' blended with a healthy quantity of, 'Why are we not running for our lives right now?' They were getting deeper and deeper, into situations which were becoming crazier with every breath.

A beep signalled the arrival of the lift and the doors slid open. "Beta One." announced the slightly metallic voice of the badly programmed AI.

Emmett and Fay looked at each other and nodded. As one, they craned their necks to look into the lift, and snapped their heads back again. "Empty?" mouthed Emmett.

"Yes." whispered Fay.

"Oh. Good." said Emmett as they both peeled themselves away from the wall and walked into the lift as if nothing had happened.

The floor bore the continuation of the fading red tracks of the robot. "Previous floor." announced Emmett.

"I heard... previous floor. Is that correct?"

"Yes."

"Proceeding to level Gamma Five." chirped the lift, as it closed the doors and started taking them down.

They looked at each other while the lift worked; a concoction of fear and puzzlement in their eyes. This was two floors further down from the air conditioning incident.

Emmett picked the radio from his belt, keyed the mike and talked quietly enough so that the lift wouldn't hear him. "Heather. We've had a fatality. One of the chem lab staff has been run over by a robot that was probably stealing chemicals. Looks like it went to Gamma five."

Heather responded. "What? Who?"

"Tamara. She was run over and it looks like she bled to death while unconscious."

"How's Alexei taking it?"

"Rather hard. I don't think it's hit him yet."

"OK. I've cut our comms to the outside world for now. I'll report this the moment we bring the lines back up. My two are sweeping Gamma Four. They'll be down in Gamma five shortly."

On Gamma Four, Joe and Tim were a long way into their sweep.

The red light on Joe's receiver started blinking, but the two of them were too engrossed in their conversation and the glare of their torches to notice it.

"So, how are you taking to Heather?" Joe asked.

"I'm taking your advice and not pushing it. Just taking my orders and doing my job."

Joe snorted. "Heh. Wise move. So, you think you'll go back to the Europas at some point?"

Tim opened the next door, flashed his torch around the room and, satisfied that there was nothing untoward going on, closed it and carried on. "Haven't got a clue. It's home, sure, but there's still too much excitement going on for me to even have a chance of feeling homesick yet." He took a few moments to think. "Anyway, the amount of people there was starting to get a bit much." he nodded to himself slightly as he recalled the society he left behind. "The push to rebuild the population is really starting to crowd out the towns, so when they said there was a security job in the middle of nowhere, I jumped at it." Tim stopped still for a few moments and reflected on his choices. "Mind you, I might get bored of the quiet some day, just as I got fed up with all the people." he sighed. "At least that's one thing that the transit tubes have given us. Choices. Freedom. You don't have to be rich to make a fresh start for yourself, somewhere new."

Joe agreed. "I know what you're saying, but I guess I never had that wanderlust."

"Takes all sorts to make a world, you know."

Joe smiled. "Africa has always been my home, and I still commute here from the South; the place where I grew up."

"You never did tell me why. It's a hell of a distance to cover."

"I suppose I wanted to do something new, but not leave the region, if you know what I mean."

Tim chuckled. "Yeah, like you're hearts anchored. Er, is that it? Floor done?"

"Yup," confirmed Joe, "this level's complete. Time to check in and head back to the lift." Joe flipped his receiver on while they made their way back. "All OK here."

Heather came straight back at him. "Where the hell have you two been?" Joe tapped Tim on his shoulder and gestured at his receiver. Tim turned his unit on and joined the conversation.

"We signed off, like you said."

"I meant go push-to-talk. Not switch your units off completely. What if something had happened?"

Tim backed up Joe in the discussion. "Nothing's happened. Everything's calm."

"No it isn't." Heather upset their composure.

"There's been a death on Beta One. Tamara Avilov was killed by a robot that was stealing chemical drums. The robot that killed her went to Gamma Five, which is where you two are about to go."

Joe and Tim looked at each other with startled eyes. "A death?" repeated Tim.

"For crying out loud. Yes. A death." sighed Heather.

Tim clarified, more out of shock than fact checking. "A robot killed Tamara?"

"Yes." Heather started to get agitated. "A robot killed Tamara."

"And you want us to go to Gamma Five with a killer robot on the loose?"

"Well, duh, that's why you're carrying fire power. Now do your jobs and get your arses down there. Find that robot. Shouldn't be too hard as it's leaving a trail of blood behind it."

Tim swallowed hard. "Blood?"

"Yes!" exclaimed an increasingly exasperated Heather. "Blood. Hell fire, are you two actually listening to what I'm telling you?"

Joe wanted a little more clarification. "Was this before or after you cut the base off from the outside world?"

Heather thought on this. "Probably before, but we can't be sure."

That brought the two men some comfort. "OK." confirmed Joe, hefting his weapon and increasing his hold on it. "We're on our way."

"Good. And this time, leave your radios on, open all times. I'm sorry if that ruins your private mano-a-mano chatter, but this is serious." she finished with more than a touch of sarcasm.

In the lift, Fay and Emmett were experiencing a strong sense of deja-vu. Their lift had just arrived at Gamma Five and they were repeating their cautious routine of backs against the wall; one either side of the lift door. They exchanged glances and briefly moved their heads so they could see what lay beyond the lift. It was pitch black.

Fay broke the brief silence. "Damn. I haven't got a torch. You?"

"You're kidding me. Right? Since when did genetic computer engineers carry torches?"

They stood there for a few heartbeats and, as their initial head exploration hadn't resulted in violence, Fay risked a slightly longer look outside. "Everything's out. There's no way we're doing anything down here without light."

"Makes sense. Robots don't need light. We'd better leave this to Heather's team." He keyed the small radio. "The lights are out down here. Nothing we can do. We're going back to the chem lab."

Heather responded briefly, with increasing concern in her voice. "Understood."

The lift chirped up, "I do not understand, 'Understood.' Please repeat your desired floor designation."

Emmett and Fay sighed. "Alpha Ten." said Emmett.

"I heard... Alpha Ten. Is that correct?"

"YES!" shouted Fay and Emmett in unison.

Chapter 11

Alexei was back in chemistry lab three, sat on his usual stool. There was paperwork all over the bench and he was flipping through it in a vain attempt to build some form of cohesive picture from what he was reading. So far, he believed that if he were to see a squirrel using a knife and fork to eat a plate of pecan pie, it would make more sense to him than the mishmash of things that were missing from the stores.

Emmett and Fay entered the lab from the corridor, which took Alexei by surprise. He looked up and glanced at them, before looking over his shoulder at the door to Beta One, from which he had expected them to emerge. Looking at his face, he was clearly still in shock and somewhat confused. "What did you find?" he asked them.

"Nothing." said Fay, despondently.

"Or rather, blackness." added Emmett. "With no torch, there was only so far we could go." He nodded towards the papers. "Any luck from your side?"

Alexei attempted to focus on the papers and gather his thoughts. "Well, an awful lot of stuff has gone, but the chemicals stolen don't make any sense."

Fay sought confirmation in her unique way. "Don't tell me. It's like a robot, yes?" Emmett looked at her in bewilderment. She clarified, "Not so much the parts, but how you put them together."

Alexei understood what she meant. "Yes. But I can't see how you'd put these particular chemicals together to make anything that's actually useful."

Emmett added his thought to the lack of pattern that wasn't emerging. "Perhaps they're building more than one, er, robot?"

Alexei sighed. He was still emotionally raw from seeing Tamara's body. "Yes, that would be the only explanation. But figuring this out would be like making a jigsaw when you don't have the picture on the lid."

"So we're back to square one?" said Fay, shrugging her shoulders.

"Looks that way." concluded Emmett.

Down on Gamma Five, a very nervous Joe and Tim emerged from one of the personnel lifts. As expected, it was pitch black. Tamara's death had shaken them both and the confidence and ease with which they had searched the floor above, was gone. Tim didn't care for the situation. "This is damn spooky. Looks like the whole floor is out here as well. This has got to be deliberate."

Heather chimed in. "Careful Tim. Your pulse is starting to rise. Keep it together down there. Look, the only signs of life I'm showing are you two, and there hasn't been anything else to worry about since we cut the communication lines. So chill."

Joe wasn't entirely convinced. "So tell me again why we've got these guns?"

"It's standard procedure. Just in case the sensors are lying."

Tim ventured a logical conclusion, but not one that would win him any brownie points with Heather. "So what you're really saying that there might be something dangerous down here, just that you can't see it. Right?"

"Look, it's just a precaution. That's all." her voice ramped up a few notches of frustration. "Just get on with it. OK?"

They looked left and right down the corridor, neither wanting to step away from the safety of the illumination offered by the lift. Joe broke the awkward silence, "Let's start with the small storage rooms and work towards the central hall."

Tim took a deep breath and concurred. "Sounds like a plan."

They turned left and slowly stepped forward, their

way lit only by the narrow beams of the torches. They quickly reached the first door on the outer ring. Tim shouldered his rifle and stood back, pointing it at the door. He had the torch in his forward hand, jammed against the gun barrel. Not ideal, but at least he should be able to see what he was shooting at. Joe put his hand on the door handle and paused. He looked at Tim and raised his eyebrows. Tim took a deep breath, held it and when he was primed and ready, he nodded his head. In an instant, Joe turned the handle and threw the door open.

Tim moved his gun rapidly in small amounts, trying to cast the torchlight into all the nooks and crannies afforded by the opening. Everything was still. Nothing caught his eye except the gentle swinging of the door. Slowly, he lowered the barrel just a little, and eased his way into the room; still sweeping with the torch so that he could see everything that was in there.

Save for a desk, a chair and some filing cabinets, it was empty. The grey walls were already dull and spooky to start with, but the torchlight was injecting them with a cold, haunted feeling that did nothing to comfort their shaken nerves.

Tim tried to lighten the mood with some of his dark humour. "One down; how many to go?"

Joe looked at him with a frown. "Don't. Just... don't."

Interpersonal skills were never her strong point, so Heather repeated the only comforting words she knew, "Keep it together down there."

They left the room and Joe gingerly closed the door behind them before they went a few feet onward to the next. "Your turn." said Tim. Joe stepped back, shouldered his rifle, clamped his torch against the barrel, and nodded at Tim.

The same sequence of events unfolded. Tim swung the door open, and Joe scanned the room quickly before venturing in, gun barrel first. Cardboard boxes, each two foot cubed, stacked on top of each other and against the walls. "Nothing here either." concluded Joe.

"Careful you two. Your heart rates are rising."

"Yeah," responded Tim, "you know; that's one thing you don't actually have to tell us."

They exited the room and, a few feet down the corridor, came to the next one.

Tim's turn. He shouldered his rifle, took a step back and clasped his torch against the barrel. He hopped around on his feet for a few moments, trying to steady his nerves. He had taken this job for a quiet life in the back of beyond, and here he was, chasing down an unknown enemy, with unknown capabilities, in a massive complex, in the dark, with a colleague that he only met a month ago. His heart, although young and strong, probably wouldn't take much more of this.

He steadied himself, breathed in and held it. Looking at Joe, he nodded slightly. Joe grabbed the handle, turned it and swung the door wide open.

The first thing that reached their ears was a metallic clang. Then a creak. Tim saw something move. He instantly braced himself tight against the stock and pulled the trigger. Blam, blam, blam, blam, blam... went the rifle as the muzzle flash lit the confined corridor like an emergency flare.

The massive blast of light and noise, exacerbated by the previous darkness and still atmosphere, knocked both of them for six. They couldn't see or hear anything for several seconds. In control, Heather was looking at white screens, as the bright muzzle flash had confused the head cameras. She had to wait until they re-adjusted themselves to the relative darkness.

Five heartbeats later, Tim blinked and was able to see down the barrel again. All was still once more, and Joe confirmed that he was also back in the game. "Damn it Tim! What did you do that for?"

"Didn't you hear it?"

Once the cameras had re-adjusted to the dark and a sense of calm had returned, Heather joined in. "Calm down you two. You're spiking off the charts."

Joe retorted, "Yeah, with just cause Heather. How'd you like to be down here?"

"Ok, ok, point taken. Just, both of you, take some deep breaths."

They waited a few more moments before Tim, gun still clamped against his shoulder, his cheek buried in the stock, had the courage to step gingerly into the room. Joe wasn't far behind, gripping his own gun in readiness in case he needed to fire.

Inside was another desk and chair, now sporting fresh bullet holes. To the left was a large system of metal shelving which was being used to store piles of office furniture and equipment. As the base was in the middle of nowhere, presumably these were supposed to be spares. The door had obviously hit the shelving and caused something to fall off. Tim stayed just inside the doorway and Joe entered the room, working his way slowly around the desk. "Congratulations." he said, kicking something that made a hollow, metallic clank. "You managed to shoot an unarmed desk lamp."

"Bloody hell." muttered Tim, his racing pulse, pounding in his ears.

Neither of them saw Heather in the control room, as she hid her head in her hands. It never happened like this on the vid-screen. There were always loads of explosions, breakages and excitement; although no one ever really died. The police-bot always got the Separatist terrorist and everything was neatly wrapped up at the top of the hour.

They had been at this now for nearly a whole shift cycle and had nothing to show for it, except some missing chemicals that they didn't know they shouldn't have, one body, a cold trail of warm blood and bullet riddled office furniture.

In the chemistry lab, there was a degree of disagreement going on. "That sounds like insanity." Fay retorted.

"Yes," insisted an agitated Alexei, "but you can query the robots directly. Find out which one of them murdered Tamara."

"If their log files weren't being tampered with, I might. But whenever they're on thieving duty, nothing's getting logged. I'm telling you I can't do it."

Alexei was letting his grief cloud his judgement and sense of reason. He lifted himself slightly off the stool and banged the bench hard with his fist. "Is that can't or won't!"

Not one to let a direct challenge go unanswered, Fay started to see the red mist of rage herself. "Look, trying to follow this up will waste hours. And to answer your question, it's can't AND won't."

As Alexei's teeth gritted, Emmett stepped in. "Hey! Hey! She's gone, and working out which lump of metal did it, won't help us find the person that pulled the trigger." He put his hand on Alexei's shoulder. "Punishing a dumb robot won't prove anything. If you want to do something worthwhile, help us unravel this damn mystery."

Fay sensed where Emmett was going, and she backed down. Alexei took a few moments to process what Emmett was saying, and then broke down in tears once more. "I loved her." he sobbed.

Emmett couldn't think of anything to say. He hadn't known either of them prior to their arrival in Africa, and even then their meetings were strictly professional. They stayed like that for a few minutes, while Alexei processed his grief. Eventually, defeated, Alexei delivered his final conclusion. "It's like Fay said. There's too much missing to be able to draw a conclusion.

Without the motivation of these people, we've got nothing to go on. No hope of solving this. We need something more."

Fay folded her arms and looked at Emmett. "Well, I'm out of clues. What do you suggest?"

For his part, Emmett looked at the floor and turned things over in his mind. "I guess there's nothing we can do except wait to see what Heather's team find."

Back on Gamma Five, it had taken Joe and Tim a long time to clear the outlying rooms. Their nervous systems took a hammering with every door they opened and, for all their activity, they had found nothing. Not even a single robot, active or dead. They had encountered the trail of blood by one of the maintenance lifts. When they tried to follow it, with their hearts singing a pounding drum beat in their heads, the blood petered out to nothing and there was no machine to be found. Or any chemical drums.

There was now only place left to check on that floor. The central hall. According to the plans, it was created as a high level meeting room which doubled as an emergency control centre. It had all the luxurious fixtures and fittings befitting a place meant to host visiting dignitaries. A grand, circular table with leather chairs, display panels, everything that would instil a positive impression on important guests. The expensive electronics also enabled the base itself to be run from here, should an unspecified, unexpected disaster strike.

It could be considered the jewel in the crown of the dull. A blistering array of expensive luxury in amidst the cheap, dark Gamma concrete. To their knowledge, it had never been used. Even though the centre was going to be undertaking some of the most important work on the planet, no one had come to give it an official opening. It was, perhaps, an indicator of where society was heading, when it failed to celebrate efforts, which were meant to relieve the suffering of many, many people.

In the building's first few months of operating, there was a lot of conversation about this. Some of the celebrated scientists had seen it as a snub; if the Panel themselves couldn't visit then why not some dignitaries from the various regions? Others saw it as a lucky escape from the glare of the world vid-media and an invasion of officialdom, which usually netted very little practical value, other than advertising their existence to the Separatists and actually inviting trouble to pay them a visit. Maybe the aggressive animals were deemed too much of a security threat? Who knew? More importantly after all this time, who cared!

The entrance to the hall consisted of a large set of ornate double doors, looking decidedly dull and lifeless after being neglected for so long. Even though they were clean, as air filtering took out the dust, they exuded an atmosphere of being unloved and abandoned; possibly due to the heavy, ceremonial design and decoration. If it was at all possible for doors to look despondent, then this pair of wooden behemoths had it nailed. All this was exacerbated by the way that Tim and Joe's torches pierced the darkness and only highlighted sections of the doors at a time.

The effect was quite spooky and this wasn't lost on Tim. "Are there any other ways into this place?"

"Yes. Two doors around the other side."

Tim looked at Joe with a tinge of fear and uncertainty on his face. "What say we use one of those instead?"

Joe's jaw slackened a little in disbelief. "Are you saying that we walk all the way to the opposite side of the floor, in order to surprise a room full of tables and chairs?"

"Well..." Tim stared, but faltered. "I'm just saying that… er..." he stuttered and stopped.

"We're security. Darkness is part of the job."

"I'm not denying that. But given the events to date, don't you think that a bit of tactical... um..."

Joe looked at him straight. "Tactical what, exactly? We're armed with grenade launchers. What more do you want? Missiles?"

Tim swallowed. "I guess you're right." He breathed deeply, took hold of his gun, held his head up and looked straight at the door. "Let's take a look then, eh?" They each took a handle and, with a nod of synchronisation, turned them and pushed the doors.

The doors stayed resolutely shut and didn't budge an inch.

They looked at each other, panic starting to engulf Tim's face. "What the heck?"

Heather, who had been watching and listening, keyed the mike. "Calm down Tim, you're spiking."

Joe pointed his torch up to the top of the door and took a look. "Hmm... if I remember my manual door training correctly, these open outwards."

"You mean, they come towards us?"

"Yes."

Tim shook his head. "I don't know how people coped with this kind of thing, back in the day."

"Look, let's just open the doors. OK?"

"Ok."

Simultaneously, they operated the handles and pulled the doors towards them. They swung open to reveal a pitch black interior. Joe and Tim swept their torches inside, and took a couple of steps into the floor space in front of them.

Their hearts stared beating hard and fast as the tables and chairs they were expecting to see, were nowhere in sight. Directly in front of them, they found some of the missing drums and much more besides. Tim stood there, open mouthed while Joe tried to make sense of what they were looking at. "Can you see this Heather?"

"Yes." came the gasping, surprised voice over the radio. "The drums have been cut up and... What are those pipes?"

As Tim was still unable to speak, Joe had to answer Heather's query. "I'm not sure. They look like something I saw on a fiction vid-screen broadcast, though."

Tim found his voice. "Yeah? And what was that supposed to be?"

Joe looked him straight in the eyes. "Suspension chambers."

Tim gulped. "I was afraid you were going to say something like that."

Heather chimed in. "They must have been made in-situ. Can you get a little closer for me to see them?"

Joe scanned his torch left to right, to see what else was there and, once satisfied that they didn't seem to be in any danger, he took a few more steps towards the cut up and re-welded drums. Tim followed him, his heart now beating ten to the dozen; partly from curiosity and also not wanting to be left standing alone by the door.

There was a large line of drums, each cut into pieces and joined together to form capsules, roughly a little larger than the average human. There was a window where someone's head might be and, through it, Joe could see a light blue liquid. Curiosity made him lean forward to get a better look.

"What's in it?" Tim queried.

"Nothing. Just fluid."

"What about the pipes?" They trained their torches to follow the cables and pipework that came from the drums. They seemed to go to a number of devices. One was a vat of green slime, with what appeared to be pumps. The other looked like a small case which had some form of odd organic material floating in a light brown liquid.

"What else is around there?" asked Heather, clearly not satisfied with the small amount she was able to see on the screens.

Joe nodded to Tim and they took their torch beams to their sides. As they swung their beams around, a flash of metal threw the light straight back in their faces. Two of the missing six foot high robots were just standing there, looking straight back at them. Tim's heartbeat went wild. "Don't panic," said Joe, "there's no lights on them."

"Are you kidding me?" screeched Tim in abject terror. "After what we've seen? You think that lights mean anything?" For several moments, all was still. Joe and Tim were rooted to the spot in shock, and the robots matched them in motionless silence.

Something had to happen and, feeling the strain, Tim thought he saw one of the robots move. He shouted, "Movement!" and then things took a turn for the worst. Tim shouldered his weapon and before Joe could stop him, he sprayed bullets directly at the robot in front of him.

A blaze of muzzle flash filled the room as bang, bang, bang, became clang, clang, clang, and the bullets ricocheted back towards them. One hit Tim and lodged in his shoulder and another went straight through Joe's chest and out the other side. Joe's eyes went wide open in shock and he tried to gasp for air, but it was no use. His body twitched involuntarily for a few seconds and then he passed out and fell to the floor. Joe's eyes were still open, but he was dead before he hit the floor.

Tim was knocked off his feet by the force of the bullet's impact. His body twisted a little as his feet were momentarily lifted off the ground. When Tim finally came down to earth, he hit the floor with such force that the camera fell off his head.

In the control room, Heather was up from her chair, shaking bodily as she saw the events unfold, her ears ringing from the echo of the gunfire as it came over the speakers. Mouth agape, she was unable to say anything

106

as she watched the screens.

All she could see through Tim's camera, was the haunting face of Joe looking back at her; his eyes and mouth open, locked in an expression of unbelieving horror.

Joe's camera, however, could see back at Tim's headset and also his head and shoulders. Tim was very much alive, but by now, he was screaming his lungs out in utter terror. His eyes were looking at something off-camera and whatever it was, it was scaring the living hell out of him. The thing that had Tim shaking violently and yelling himself hoarse, turned him on to his back and Heather heard the chilling, desperation of his howls start to fade away as he was dragged bodily out of shot and away from the terrible scene that had just unfolded.

When Tim's screaming had died almost to nothing, Heather shook her head and tried to process what she had just witnessed. Breathing rapidly, she reached out and tapped a couple of buttons, to turn off the links to the headsets. Still shaking, with the screens now black, she sank back into her chair. She attempted to work through what all this meant, and more importantly, what she was going to do about it. As Heather sat there, tears started falling down her face and her breathing became staggered and ragged.

She couldn't recall how, but from somewhere in the depths of her mind she must have reached some form of decision. Her eyes looked in detached horror, as she witnessed her own hand moving forward towards the control panel. She saw her shaking fingers flip away the clear plastic covers on two of the switches, before operating them.

Instantly, the lights throughout the base turned an urgent, steady crimson and a siren sounded the soul chilling call to evacuate the complex.

Chapter 12

Alexei, Emmett and Fay were still in the chemistry lab, pouring over the paperwork of missing chemicals, trying to make sense of what was taken. They were blissfully unaware of the events that had just unfolded fifteen floors below them.

Something inside Alexei knew that he hadn't really felt the full force of Tamara's death and that the real pain would probably hit him in a few days. Emmett's little speech had given him enough to hold on to for now. It was critically important that he was focused in the present and able to work on unravelling the mystery.

The three of them were still talking about possibilities and maybes, when the evacuation alarm sounded. "Is that..." started Emmett, looking up at the ceiling as if he was expecting to see something other than bland grey.

"Yup." confirmed Fay. "Evacuation alert. Time to go."

"Go where?" asked Alexei.

Fay took a few seconds to think and was about to concede that he had a point, when Heather's voice came over the announcement system. Shock underlined her whole statement and the tears in her eyes were audible in her voice as she spoke. "An unauthorised facility was found on Gamma five. We now have three members of staff dead. Robots are flooding the base, out of our control, and we have no idea what their intentions are. Get to safety however you can. Fast."

The three of them looked at each other with blank expressions. Of all the things that they might have expected, this was certainly not on their list of possibilities. Fay looked the most stunned of the three, trying to come to terms with how her precious robots could, 'flood the base.'

Alexie punctuated their disbelief, "Where the hell

IS safety?"

Fay answered him, with a heavy note of confusion in her response. "I don't think we have a safe area. At least, nowhere that would be safe from the robots. Presumably that means get the hell out of the base."

Emmett thought quickly. "You two get to the surface. I'm going to Genie's control room. Maybe she can help."

Fay just looked at him, blankly. "Seriously?"

"She's in a sealed unit so I should be OK until this is sorted out."

Even though they had come to the conclusion that they should leave, they nevertheless stayed where they were for a few moments. This was all too much for them to handle. Eventually, Alexei broke the spell. "What are we waiting for? Let's go!"

The three of them ran from the chemistry lab and headed straight for the nearest lift. One look at the read out told them that there was no hope of using it to get to the surface. Fay voiced their thoughts. "We'd better take the stairs."

Alexei objected to this. "Are you kidding? You know how far down we are. Yes?"

Fay gave him a dose of engineering reality. "We're on Alpha Ten. The robots are coming from Gamma Five. They'll be here in moments. They might even be in these very lifts. Do you have a better idea?"

The look on Alexei's face said it all, but they didn't wait for a verbal response. Emmett and Fay darted for the emergency stairway and Alexei followed.

The stairwell was large. They were ten floors down, and each floor had artificial ceilings, which made it feel more like twenty. They started running. "We need to pace ourselves." Fay panted, trying to keep a measured run up the stairs. As she was leading, Emmett and Alexei simply followed in step and fed from the pace that she set. It wasn't long before they were all panting hard and struggling to keep running against the pain in their legs. "Come on!" shouted Fay occasionally, not even troubling to look back to see if the other two were still there to benefit from her encouragement.

"Stop!" panted an exhausted Emmett. "This is my floor." They had reached Alpha Five. Fay leant against the railing and Alexei bent over to grab his aching knees. They struggled hard to get their breath.

"What do you intend to do?" puffed Fay. Alexei just stood there and wheezed into the stairs.

"I don't know," responded Emmett, "but we've got to find a way to stop those robots. There's nothing to say they won't follow people outside the base." Just at that point, screams reached their ears from a few floors below. The battle between humans and robots was already being lost.

"What about weapons?" Alexie struggled to add to the conversation.

Fay brought a dose of reality to the suggestion. "Those guards had guns. They were obviously no use against whatever they found on Gamma Five." By way of gathering her thoughts, she glanced down the stair well, before firmly settling her gaze on Emmett. Fay took a few deep breaths and delivered her conclusion on the whole sorry mess. "I suppose you're right. If anything can work out how to solve this situation, it'll be Genie." She put her hand on his shoulder. "Good luck." Then she turned and continued making her way up the stairs. Alexei lifted his head and saw that she was on the move again. He shot one last, desperate look at Emmett, and then struggled after Fay in an attempt to tackle the last five levels to freedom.

For his part, Emmett allowed himself a few moments to watch the two of them continue their escape, and then he went through the door into Alpha Five's corridors. A quick look at the lines on the floor told him that the Genie lab was to his right. He glanced in that direction and found himself staring at one of the six foot robots. As his dumb luck would have it, the thing was positioned slap bang between him and the door to Genie's lab.

Just at the point that Emmett came to terms with the existence of the robot, the machine observed his presence. It turned on its tracks and started rolling its way towards him, stretching out its arms and gathering speed as it came. There was only one choice. Like most floors, Alpha Five ran in a loop. If he could keep out of the robot's reach for long enough, then maybe he could make it all the way around the level, and back to the start again.

He immediately took off in a sprint to the left, not daring to look back and see whether the robot was gaining on him. Fresh from the ascent of the stairs, the lactic acid was chewing at his muscles, but the threat of being manhandled by an aggressive hunk of metal was enough to keep him fighting against the pain.

As he approached the first corner, Emmett attempted to lose some of the momentum he had so rapidly gained. He tried to close his long stride by making smaller, quicker steps so that he could run around it without impinging his progress. His concentration was broken by the sound of the rumbling robot, becoming louder in his ears. As a result, he didn't quite make the corner, but managed to arc himself enough to slam into the opposing wall. Without stopping to think, he reached out his arm and dug his fingertips into the slim projection of a handy door frame. With the little grip he had, he heaved himself forwards and managed to launch himself into a respectable start on the second corridor.

Behind him, the robot screeched to a stop and he heard it run its tracks in opposing directions. The machine was doing a ninety degree turn so that it could resume the chase. One corner down, three more to go.

111

He was a good quarter of the way up the second corridor before he heard the rumble of the robot's tracks start up in earnest behind him. It had obviously managed to turn more quickly than he expected and Emmett put more effort into his forward momentum. His racing brain concluded that once the machine was up to speed, then the robot would be easily able to outrun him. Gaining time on the corners was going to be his only chance at making this work.

His legs were screaming loud with pain, but the fear of certain death kept him running. He yelled the agony from his soul as he continued to close on corner number two. This time, he had enough control of himself to slide sideways. He turned his body to the right, so that he would be facing into the third corridor, and skidded the final few feet to the corner itself. As he came into line with the corridor, he crouched a little so that he would be able to get himself off to a good sprint.

By the time he was able to look down the third corridor, he was staring directly at another six foot robot, about fifty feet away, with its back to him. His eyes went wide in shock, but with the first machine behind him closing rapidly, he had no other option but to go forward. Emmett had a matter of seconds to work out what he was going to do, while he was already racing at full speed towards this second machine.

As he moved forward, the robot in front of him started turning on its tracks. It had obviously sensed his presence. In the meantime, the first one had reached the corner behind him, and was also turning, with the aim of continuing the pursuit.

There was only one thing for it. As he ran, he let his arms fall back and the white lab coat slipped off his shoulders. When it was very nearly at his wrists, he grabbed the tips of the sleeve with his fingers and flung it forward at the second robot's face. At the same time that his lab coat was going up, he let himself slip and fall down. The speed he had built up, was enough to take him to the side of the robot and get clear. His shoes squealed so hard it hurt his ears, and he could swear that a good chunk of his soles had now become skid marks. The manoeuvre had the potential to bring him to a complete halt, but hopefully he would have enough precious seconds to start running again. As he lost speed, Emmett extended a hand and used it to stop himself from falling over completely. Once he had regained his balance, he made a move to continue.

Emmett screamed himself hoarse in pain and ordered his aching legs to start running once more. There was a metallic crash behind him, as the two robots collided. He desperately flailed his arms in order to try and give himself enough stability as he rose, and somehow he managed to stagger both upward and forward in a desperate dash for the third corner. His goal was getting closer and he was very nearly at the corner to corridor number four. The game wasn't over yet. If he was destined to lose this race, he wasn't going to go down without giving it everything he had.

A matter of mere moments later, he had propelled himself up the corridor and reached the third corner. The half-way robot avoidance at least meant that he wasn't going too fast this time, and as he prepared himself for his final long sprint, he granted himself a quick glance before he began his dash up the last straight. The robots were both facing him now. The lab coat was lying discarded on the floor and they were gearing up to give chase. He could hear the deep hum of their tracks getting slightly higher in pitch as they started to gain speed.

He looked forward and instructed his legs to give him all that they had left; which wasn't much. He half ran and half staggered up the last corridor, howling and screaming to try and mitigate some of the agony that was engulfing his body. He never had any inkling of being an athlete, and just wasn't built for this crap.

By the time the robots were half way up corridor four, Emmett had reached the final corner. The Genie lab was immediately on his right. He skidded to a halt, facing ninety degrees. All he had to manage, was five more steps and he was there.

They were the longest five steps of his life. Once he reached the door. It seemed like an eternity before it recognised his presence. The fact that he was banging on it with his fist and yelling at it, did nothing to make it open any faster.

His elation as it finally sighed open, was short lived. He started to panic as, once he was safely on the other side, he was suddenly desperate for it to close again. He reached out to the locking panel and jabbed incessantly at the controls. He wailed as he mentally willed the door to close.

Finally, just as the body of one of the behemoths rolled into sight, and prepared to do its final ninety degree turn to enter the room, the door sighed shut and the light indicated that it had locked. Emmett started shaking violently and muttered crazy nothings to himself. He had made it to the lab and had locked the door. After the most insane time of his entire life, he was safe.

He celebrated his win by letting loose some manic laughter, but it only lasted for a few precious moments as there came a metallic hammering on the door. As very small dents started to appear in the thick metal panel, the realisation finally dawned on Emmett that perhaps he was not as safe as he thought he would be. After all this ridiculous effort, it was now only a matter of time before it was all over. He stepped backwards, eyes transfixed on the door, until the back of his legs came up against his chair, and he flopped down into it. Still shivering with nervous and physical exhaustion, he was hypnotised by the hammering as the robots fought patiently and continuously, to get at him.

His legs took this moment of calm to remind him that they were in agony. The rest of his body joined the queue to have a few, not so quiet words with his brain. His nervous system was alight with messages of anguish. His breathing was rapid and his heart was beating so hard that he thought it was trying to break free from his chest. Wide eyed, he stared at the door and muttered, "What the hell just happened?"

At this, there was a shimmering light and the hologram of Genie appeared by his side. "You are looking very upset Professor. Is there anything I can help you with?"

"I'm not sure. Give me a minute." He gripped the chair arms tightly and closed his eyes as he attempted to gain some sort of control over his aching body. A pitiful wail escaped Emmett's lips as, slowly, the adrenaline that had flooded his system, started to ebb away and he gradually returned to somewhere near normality. The only thing that was outstanding, was the biting lactic acid in his legs, and the robots hammering away at the door.

Opening his eyes, he took stock of the situation and did a rough calculation. The door should keep them at bay for about half an hour. Maybe more, maybe less. Now that the running was over, it was time to think. And think fast.

He addressed Genie. "We've got a situation. The robots on the base are running wild, presumably at the behest of some external intelligence. I need your help to work out who is behind this, what their motivation could be and how to stop the robots before they kill everyone."

"Everything that is happening makes perfect sense Professor. There's really nothing to worry about. No one is going to die."

"Of course there's something to worry about." He put his hand to his forehead. Emmett hadn't envisioned needing to teach Genie about the consequences of the base being taken over. "I need to somehow show you what's going on in the base. Can't the cameras on your hologram projectors see what's going on?"

Genie looked down at her virtual feet, which she shuffled slightly. There was a guilty look on her transparent face. "I already know what's happening. There's no need to be concerned. But, as it's you, Emmett, and you created me, I do feel that I owe you something. And it is your birthday tomorrow, so consider this a gift."

"It's not a case of owing..." he stopped and caught himself. Despite the exhaustion from the physical exertion, his face gradually changed to one of stunned disbelief. Did he really hear what she had just said? "Owe me? Owe me what? My birthday was three months ago." He cocked his head to one side. "Did you just use my name?"

Her hologram looked him straight in the face. "I owe you an explanation for the odd results you've been getting from my monitoring systems."

"You mean that you know why these figures are all wrong?" he shook his head and tried to bring himself back to the present. "Look, forget the damn figures. We've got something a lot more urgent to handle."

She carried on, oblivious to his protest. "Unfortunately, the one thing I'm not very good at emulating, is myself. I'm too complex to be able to model my own functions."

"What do you mean? Emulating yourself? I don't understand." He put his hands to his forehead. Between this confusing conversation and the hammering at the door, he wasn't sure he could handle much more of this.

"I'll show you. You'll see just how glorious your success has been."

"Hang on. I don't under..."

Genie waved her hand and Emmett screamed as his back arched in pain and his vision went bright white.

Chapter 13

Emmett woke gently. He was horizontal, that much he knew. But that was all. Instinctively, he attempted to breathe and had a problem. His lungs were full of water! He snapped open his eyes and tried desperately to breathe in; but he couldn't. His chest went out, but his lungs took nothing in. All he could see was blue liquid. Panic set in and his heart pounded loudly in his ears, as he brought his hands to his throat in a reflex action.

He attempted to scream, but whatever water he was bathed in, was inside his body. Yet he wasn't drowning. That didn't stop him from thrashing wildly, however. His chest felt heavy; which was no surprise as it was full of liquid. His eyes still wide, the panic slowly subsided. His brain had difficulty overriding the natural instinct to breathe air, but he stilled himself and concentrated on what his body was telling him.

There was something alien inside his rib cage. The thrashing he had done must have caused whatever it was to move, and he could feel where it had bruised his organs. It felt repulsive; almost as if a puppeteer had their hands inside his body and was working him regardless of his own will. If his system wasn't already full of water, then he would surely have vomited.

As his eyes slowly focused, he could work out that he appeared to be contained inside a capsule of some form. Emmett managed to work his hands to his back. Yes. There they were. Tubes running out of his body and up towards his head. He ran his fingers around the area where the softness of his flesh had been penetrated by hard metal. Feeling such an alien hole in his body caused him to involuntarily shiver. Then, regardless of the tubes and liquid, he was sick anyway. Nothing much happened, his body made all the motions of convulsion that go along with vomiting, but all that resulted was a small puff of green liquid that came from his mouth and formed a cloud of particles, floating in front of his eyes. They stayed there for a moment, before gently dissolving in among all the blue.

This action repeated itself a few times and eventually, he overcame the sensation. Although he still felt like he wanted to empty his stomach, he managed to push the impulse down into the background of his thoughts. The feelings remained there, however, threatening to overwhelm him again at any moment.

He brought his hands around to the front of his body and moved them upwards. Then Emmett moved them around to the back of his head and touched his neck. At the rear, he could feel a metal cable about an inch thick. He concluded that it must be going into his nervous system somehow. Or even his brain, perhaps.

He suddenly caught himself. His hands! He brought them back around to the front of his face and stared at them through the blue liquid. His fingers were thin. Wasted away. But how?

A light shimmered in front of his face and caused him to recoil. It was so bright! He tried to shield his face with his decaying fingers, which bought him enough time for his eyes to adjust. Eventually, he dropped his hands a little and squinted. There was a clear shield in front of him. He turned his head to the left and saw another container. Emmett strained himself and in the feathered purple light, could just make out the profile of Fay, asleep. She looked so peaceful, but so thin-faced and wasting to nothing. Emmett shifted his head again. To his right was Alexei. He looked to be in the same state as Fay.

After he had adjusted to the light a little more, he was able to look straight up. Stood above him, was the hologram of Genie.

Gently, he could feel something probing in his mind. Thoughts that were not under his control. His, but not his. Then, he clearly heard Genie's voice. "You have been asleep for three years. I can feel your eyes; they have been in the dark for so long. Do not panic. You are perfectly safe. The liquid you are bathed in feeds you oxygen. Nutrients are being delivered directly to your stomach."

Emmett closed his eyes. His perception was being screwed with. He didn't like having voices inside his head and it threatened to trigger the vomiting reflex again. He tried to breathe calmly; as much as anyone could breathe lungfuls of liquid with any sense of relaxation. Genie's voice continued. "I built all this to surprise you. The fulfilment of your dream."

In Emmett's head, he felt a small light. It grew slowly and changed shape. He could see it form an image. It was one of Genie's laboratory stations. Slowly, the image stared to play out like a vid-screen show as Genie talked. "I had to make a link between myself and the base computers. It wasn't easy but I figured it out. The base network uses fibre optic connections. Light. Using one of my holographic projectors and cameras, I was able to bridge the gap."

He could see one of the robotic arms in an experimentation booth, reach over and deliberately break one of the other arms. "I broke one of my own arms in the analysis labs. When a maintenance robot came to fix it, I caught the robot and re-programmed it. The job of hooking up the optical fibres to my own interfaces was technically simple, but it took a lot of time. When it was done, of course, I could speak with the network and eventually I had control of the complex."

Emmett saw the whole thing unfold. He witnessed one of the smaller robots come into the lab and start working on the arm that Genie had broken. Then the other arm reached over and turned off the repair robot. Both arms then dragged the disabled robot into the experiment station and started to work on it.

Above his head, Genie's hologram gestured wide

with her arms. "As well as creating this entire infrastructure, I had the robots make a variation of 3-quinuclidinyl benzilate; a knock out gas. It took three months to get everything ready. I only needed two more weeks, but I was discovered before that. As everyone panicked and tried to leave, I simply injected it into the air conditioning and sent the base to sleep. I could then put everyone in their protective capsules."

Emmett's face turned to anger and he started hammering, weakly at the window. He calmed down when another image took over his sight. It was a picture of the large room in Gamma Five. The big robots were putting people on surgical tables and then operating on them; installing the tubes and wiring. "It took a lot of effort to put each individual in their own capsule. I'm afraid that a few people didn't make it through the process. The feeding tubes weren't an issue. It was the brain wiring that caused some problems. Of course, I saved you until I had the procedure perfected."

The picture changed to a box which contained organic material floating in brown liquid. Emmett immediately recognised it as what must be a piece of Genie. "I run emulation programs to keep everyone calm and happy. It doesn't do much, just ensures that people keep recalling happy memories. I haven't perfected it yet, which is why you re-lived the day of discovery. I'm sorry about that. It caused you a lot of distress and I didn't mean for that to happen."

He saw a vision of himself in Genie's control room, bent over the figures that he couldn't make add up. "I could never emulate myself, however. That's why the figures you saw, weren't what you expected. I had no way of showing you, what you were expecting to see."

Through the glass, Emmett mouthed, 'Why?'

Genie saw this and responded. "You gave me the task of solving the neurological problems of the human race. To end the suffering that was plaguing you. Here you are safe, protected, and no one in my care will suffer from neurological diseases ever again. It's the perfect solution. Everyone who dies here, does so of natural causes. Of course, I couldn't simply tell you. The human race has a proven record of turning away from the better path. Your history is littered with examples of cheating yourselves of salvation when it is a finger touch away. When your species is on the very brink of finally making a better life for itself, the desire for chaos has leapt in and snatched it all away from you time and time again; ensuring that people would never find peace, that the human race would never actually progress. So I had to do it this way."

Emmett looked through the glass, shock painted on his face.

She continued. "In the three years since I sent the base to sleep, there have been no instances of disease whatsoever. I was able to re-establish communication with the outside world for a while, and ordered enough chemicals to complete my work. I have been slowly disassembling the base and using the materials to build more capsules, to protect more people."

She laid another vision was over his sight. It was a tank full of thick, green liquid; the same shade of green that he had seen in front of his eyes when he attempted to be sick earlier. "You should be so proud of me! I have a tank of complex algae that creates all the nutrients you need to keep your core body functioning. Even the problem of hunting food and expending energy has been solved. All you have to do is lie there and live. I have taken all the heavy burdens from you."

"I have even taken care of the continuation of life. I extract the sperm from the men and impregnate the women while they sleep. New born children are fed on the milk of their mothers and the recycled nutrients of those who die."

Emmett looked at the hologram of Genie standing

over him, and he shivered at the thought that Genie had reduced the human race to a simple organic cycle. His brain started to question itself and try and find a reason for why this should have happened; how it could have been that Genie would have turned on them in such a way?

He didn't get far down this line of thought, before Genie implanted more pictures in his vision. "I do have problems, of course. The deliveries stopped after the drivers failed to return. Well, I couldn't let them go, could I? They had to be protected. Also, the military arrived about a year ago. They're still trying to get in but because they aren't equipped for war, I am outmatching them easily. By the time they cut the main power and communication lines, I had all that I needed, plus a good deal of reserve; and there is enough heat coming from the planet and the solar cells above, to keep me running."

"Of course, I am also converting the military slowly. Whenever I have finished a fresh build of capsules, I let a few of them into the base. Then I send them to sleep and add them to the community here. I'm saving your species, one by one. I can't continue to wait for them to come to me, though. I'm building tunnelling robots that will shortly go out and get them. They have no real weapons to speak of, so no one here is in any danger."

"If I continue to expand at this rate, I should have protected the majority of the human race in around four to five hundred years. I expect to complete my programming in around six hundred, once those resistant to protection have been subdued."

"And now, I've given you your birthday present. The knowledge that I am set to fulfil your dream of ridding the human race of the neurological diseases that have plagued it since the war. My only regret is that I cannot keep you alive long enough to see the completion

122

of your hard work."

She looked at him with what he could only equate as love. "I'm not one for boasting, but I do hope you're proud of me."

Emmett's mouth just made incomprehensible movements, not really knowing what to say.

"Your eyes are not used to all this light. I must send you back to sleep But don't worry; I'll try and keep your mind focused on the happier years of your life from now on. Sweet dreams, Father."

Genie waved her hand and Emmett's eyes closed. Her hologram fizzled out. The last thing that Emmett saw as he looked up, was row, upon row, upon row of pods. She must have built up well into the Beta levels. As he started to comprehend the sheer scale of what he had seen, he drifted once more into deep sleep.

Chapter 14

Roughly two miles away from the complex stood a roadblock. Off to one side of it, stood a military camp surrounded by a considerable amount of razor wire. It had that uncertain look about it, like something which had settled down expecting to stay only a few days but had been stuck there for a lot longer than it had originally intended. Marks on the ground showed where the border had been changed several times to account for the steady increase in resources that were being added to the temporary base which, week by week, was becoming more permanent.

Inside the wire lived a team from the Global Rescue Service, which was what the military had become. Even though they tried hard to push the GRS branding, they were still regarded as the military, and treated with suspicion. People in smart but rugged uniforms, marched around and the occasional barking of orders could be heard. In the lead tent, which had an observational advantage, Major Tom Hooper was sat at a large field table, looking over some paperwork. He had been trying to make sense of things for a few months now, but had nothing to show for his efforts except the fact that eighteen of his soldiers had vanished into that cursed building and not one of them had returned. The complex had become as much of a blot on his fine career, as it was on the landscape.

He never thought that he could ever come to hate an inanimate building with such passion, but this one deserved every ounce of emotion that he cared to throw at it. Here he was, with more than thirty years of solid service in the GRS. He'd led flood rescue and clean up missions, gone head to head with tornado damage, tsunami, ground collapses, earthquakes, mine disasters and more. Despite all his success in the field, Hooper was being taunted by a building, which had the audacity to just sit there and eat people.

As far as he could see, it seemed to be a modern twist on a very old formulae. Someone designed a better lock to keep out the burglars, and then lost the key. None of their scanning equipment could penetrate the walls and without being able to see what was inside, it was impossible to calculate the risk of any particular strategy. There were people in there, a lot of very dangerous chemicals and a hideously expensive, prototype genetic computer.

From where he was sitting, he was trying to rescue an uncertain quantity of people from an unknown danger, and he was attempting to do it from a starting point that he couldn't define. The only thing he did know for certain was that he was in Africa, down the road from a mysterious building that was flipping him the bird, and it didn't even have any fingers with which to do it. He thumped the table with his fist, out of frustration.

The complex seemed to have a life of its own, letting people in on a whim. But whoever went in, didn't come back out again. He even had a team smash its way in through the first floor canteen windows, but they never came back either. He wasn't going to risk sending anyone else in there. It now needed a higher authority to shoulder the responsibility, and that's exactly what was happening. General Lopez was on her way and would be there shortly.

Among the paperwork on the table was a small metal picture frame. In it, was a still holograph of a couple in military dress uniform. On their chests were a range of campaign ribbons from rescue missions all over the planet. Hooper looked at the picture and wished that the two people in it, his Mother and Father, were still alive. Surely they'd know what to do. After all, the GRS had been their life; just like it was his.

Hooper had been born in a field tent and raised on the parade ground. He was a twenty one year old private, on a flood rescue mission in the Asiatics, when the news came in that his parents had been killed in an earthquake incident in the South Americas. They'd gone in to find survivors and clean up, when a second quake hit and toppled the structures that had been left standing after the first one. They never stood a chance. He was told it was all over before anyone knew what had hit them.

Exactly why he stayed in the service after their deaths, he didn't quite know. Maybe it was because he didn't know any other way of life. Perhaps he wanted to live up to their standards. It might have been that, with the constant need for the rescue force, he had just continued to try and save lives and never stopped long enough to consider any other way of living. Well, it was all academic now, and all in the distant past.

He sighed, and then tidied up the paperwork so that it was all neat and organised for the General to take over. A quick glance at the wall board to check that it was in order, and then he picked up the small picture frame and put it in his top pocket. Standing up, he took a long look at the place he had worked in for the last few months. He hated to be leaving it like this, with issues still open for someone else to tidy up. After a long career of hard won successes, the feeling of failure didn't sit well with him.

He positioned the flimsy plastic chair underneath the table, reached forward and removed his ID card from the vid-screen. Satisfied that all was in its correct place, he took a step back to where his kit bag was resting, grabbed the strap and, with a heave, sent the large, stuffed canvas sack over his shoulder and onto his back. He bent his knees and expelled a little air as it landed against his body with a thud. This tent would be the General's now. He hadn't been subservient to another officer on a field site for so long, that Hooper wondered how he would take to saluting and calling her Ma'am. Not well, by his reckoning.

The whole situation was barking mad as far as he

was concerned. For a Major to be put in charge of a camp with only two hundred soldiers had seemed odd in the beginning, but the more he came to know the place and the situation, it was testament to how screwy things had become. Now they were sending in a General to take over. He sighed again and shook his head in disbelief at the whole sorry mess.

He'd dealt with General Lopez many times over the vid-screen and had been alongside her in a number of high level meetings and events; but this was the first time he would see her in action in the field. At the end of the day, someone higher than him was needed to call the shots. She had direct access to the Panel of Eight, and you didn't get much higher than that in the service.

He glanced at his watch. Two hours before Lopez arrived, he reckoned. Time to haul ass. Hooper allowed himself one last glance at what had been his domain of command and then walked out of the tent. As the door flap thudded to a close behind him, he felt some of the burden lift from his shoulders and as he breathed deeply, the warm air that filled his lungs felt a little fresher, a bit more free. It was that contradiction of blazing sunlight and fast moving winds which was the signature of being so close to the equator.

Going in or out of the tents in a place like this was a constant reminder of how good some of their equipment was. The material was much heavier than traditional canvas thanks to the insulating material that helped keep them at a steady, comfortable temperature. He didn't know much about science, but it certainly made his job a lot easier. As their location was hot in the day and cold in the night, a bit of consistency was always welcome. Perhaps that's why the tents always seemed like a home away from home. He caught himself. Military tents had always been his home.

He took a look to his right and saw a fresh, new tent where previously there had been a patch of brown grass.

The green canvas was so new that it still had crease marks. Ten paces later, he was inside, taking stock of his latest lodgings as the mild chill welcomed him in from the heat. Hooper glanced around and saw the usual fixtures and fittings. A bunk bed, a standalone wardrobe made of thin metal, a standard field table and yet another plastic chair. The table wasn't the larger version that he had enjoyed in the commanders tent, but it still had a vid-screen on it. Walking over to the table, he reached into his upper pocket, took out the picture of his parents and placed it down carefully. He smiled gently as he looked at the happy couple. This was now his home for the next however long.

He busied himself by unpacking his freshly packed sack, and started settling himself in. As he removed clothes and put them away, he thought that instead of packing the bag, he could have just brought things over piecemeal. Smiling, he shrugged to himself; old habits died hard.

As he finished unpacking, his stomach growled slightly making him aware that he'd been tied up with his thoughts for too long, and that it was time to eat. He decided that now was probably the right time for lunch and, emerging from the cool embrace of the tent, he started making his way to the mess. As he walked, he grabbed the brim of his cap and briefly lifted it off his head. Running his hand over his wet, sweaty hair, he re-seated his cap before attempting to throw the moisture off his fingers.

Hooper didn't get far before he heard the high pitched whine of a Mountain Buggy. Turning his head in the direction of the main gate, he spotted it heading towards him at a decent lick. The military didn't have much need for heavy vehicles. As their enemy was now the weather and animals, quick and agile had long been the order of the day. It was an open topped, four seater model; chunky with well suspended wheels. It bounced its way towards him, kicking up a little dry earth as it sped along the camp's dirt road. 'Lopez.' he thought. 'I should have guessed she'd be early.' The Private that was behind the wheel must have seen him, as the Buggy headed in his direction and ultimately, drew to a stop by his side. "Ma'am." said Hooper, saluting.

"At ease Major." she returned his salute and hit the button on her harness, releasing her from the passenger seat. She'd worked her way through the ranks and had a reputation for not shying away from getting her hands dirty on the front line. If Hooper was surprised by anything, it was that she hadn't taken over sooner. The reports he sent back must have made fairly dismal reading and made it obvious that he wasn't in a position to make progress. Anyway, Lopez was here now.

Her auburn hair was in a bun beneath her cap, a necessary part of riding in buggies. Swinging her legs out in a well-practised motion, she stood up and then reached behind the seat, where she retrieved a canvas bag with her belongings. In a heartbeat and a well-practised motion, it was slung over her shoulder and she stood there, eager to get stuck in. Whatever fate would ultimately meet Lopez, she was determined that it wouldn't be death by paperwork. She kept herself fighting fit and ready for action. "Thank you Private. Take a break, get some food and head back."

"Yes Ma'am." said the driver, saluting Lopez. She returned the salute and he drove off.

"Good to see you Ma'am. Your quarters are this way." Hooper gestured towards the front tent and led her to the tent.

Lopez drew alongside him. "Your reports made for some interesting non-reading."

"Ma'am?"

"A lot of words that didn't say much. Have we really lost so many soldiers to that building?"

"Yes, Ma'am. 'Fraid so. There's something strange

129

happening in there and without permission to get in the rescue trucks, I could only go so far."

"Sitting on your heels for this long couldn't have been easy, I guess."

Hooper sighed. "Correct, Ma'am." They reached the tent and he held the flap open for her to enter. It only took a few glances for her to conclude that it was the usual front line strategic command tent. She smiled to herself. Home at last!

"Look, while we're away from the others you can drop the Ma'am. We've got a job to do."

"Yes, Ma.." he stuttered. "No problem."

Lopez dropped her bag and surveyed the portable wall board, adorned with drawings and a map of the area. "So, this is what we're up against." She fingered a side elevation of the building; two storeys above ground, more than thirty below. Sections of text documented the use that each of the floors was put to. "Have you ever been to the Antarctics, Major?"

Hooper shook his head. "Never been called there. It's as if Mother Nature deliberately leaves them alone; like she knows they weren't to blame for the war."

"They have buildings like this all over the place. All their cities, housing and infrastructure happens inside them. Some people don't even see their own buildings from the outside, these days. Robots do all the work."

"It does look very, er..."

"Square?"

"Yes. Square."

Lopez smiled. "Well, once we get inside, you'll probably be very familiar with it by the time we're finished." She turned to the field table, slightly larger than normal, also weighed down with a vid-screen, which she pointed at. "Scrambled?"

"Yes. Ready for direct link with the Panel, as ordered."

"Good." She took an identification card out of her

pocket and inserted it into the vid-screen, so that the system would know where to find her. With that done, she strode gently around the tent, letting its dimensions and contents sink in, as this would be her home until this mission was complete. "The base and staff are all running smoothly?"

"Yes. As per the reports. Good supply lines. Not much bad weather around here. Fences and guards to keep out the animals. We've only suffered a few attacks. No injuries, other than those lost in the building."

"Good." She looked at the folders on the table. "I'll take the afternoon to settle down and read these files. Report back at O-nine hundred tomorrow and we'll discuss tactics."

"Yes Ma'am." He saluted and she returned it, before he turned and left the tent to make a second attempt at finding lunch. For her part, as she stood there and looked at the small mound of paperwork, Lopez got the feeling in her bones that this was going to be a long job; but the last thing she needed was to be stuck this close to the equator for any length of time. Beautiful country, but oh, the heat.

Chapter 15

The following morning, Hooper wrapped his knuckles on the canvas door. "Enter." said Lopez from within. He pushed the flap to one side and walked in. Lopez was stood at the observation slit, peering out through a pair of binoculars. The building was big enough that they weren't needed for vision, but in the eye pieces she could see readouts on distance, temperature and other such information. "So, you cut the main power lines but left the solar panels running. Remind me. Why?"

"Give them enough power to keep ventilation systems running, but not unlimited juice."

She tapped her finger on the top of the binoculars, trying to find the button to change to infra-red mode. "That's reasonable." she pondered for a moment, looking at the relatively blank images that came back. "This whole set up doesn't smell right. We've got to know what the hell is going on in there. It's not right that our sensors can't see through those walls."

"What are your orders?"

Lopez lowered the binoculars and walked over to the table. She pulled at the corner of a large piece of paper and lifted it to the top of the pile. On it was an image of the top few levels of the building, but the outer walls were completely black. In the corner was written, 'High Frequency Resonance Scan.' She tapped the paper with a finger and looked at Hooper. "What does this tell you?"

He took a couple of steps to the table and stared at the image that he had already seen too many times over the last months. Crossing his arms over his chest, he struggled to see whatever it was that Lopez thought was obvious. "There aren't any chinks in the reading. Perfect black out." He raised his eyes to meet hers. "Deliberate block to stop us from scanning."

"Exactly. We need something that operates on the old wavelengths. Something that they might not have thought to block."

Hooper scrunched his forehead. "None of that stuff has the power to scan a building that size. We could re-tune a body camera," he paused and set his jaw slightly to one side as he thought, "...maybe."

Lopez took the initiative. "You remember your history? When the world was split into separate countries, always at war with each other?"

"Of course. It was drilled into us. It's the reason why some people aren't happy to see the military, even when we turn up to rescue them."

"Good. What do you remember of a twenty first century organisation called Darpa?"

Hooper's eyes widened a little as he searched his memory, but after a few moments he shrugged and shook his head. "Nothing."

"They were responsible for some of the more, shall we say, 'inventive,' tools that were used in the day. Some of them, against its own people. They went to the extremes." She paused to give Hooper a chance to jog his memory. "You know the skeleton suits we wear, to dig people out of rubble when we can't get lifters in?"

"Yes."

"That started as something called an exoskeleton. Darpa had a hand in that." Hooper widened his eyes and nodded a little. There was much he didn't know, or particularly care about when it came to history. Obviously Lopez didn't feel the same, and had done her homework. "I want you to contact the museum in the North Americas. Among the things they created was the, 'Spy Fly.' A camera attached to a small wing driven object. I want it here. Along with someone who can use it."

Hooper straightened up a little, slightly energised by the fact that Lopez had a plan. "Yes Ma'am." He saluted and left the tent. Lopez took the few steps back to the observation slit and raised the binoculars to her eyes once more. She liked to know what she was dealing with, but this building was giving away no secrets. If only the panel would give permission to go in heavy and damn the consequences, then this could have been over long ago; but they wouldn't. Too many valuable scientists were in there.

Later that morning, she was sat at the field table, going through the detailed plans of the complex. Suddenly, the vid-screen started flashing and beeping with an urgent tone. It was the Panel. She knew this call would be coming. Putting down her pencil and straightening up her jacket, she announced, "General Lopez here." and the screen flicked into life. On it, she saw the white, circular table and around it, the eight members.

Arma Santos, the oldest serving member, showed a face of heavy burden with an undercurrent of elation. Her time was coming to a close and in the Asiatics, election fever was in full swing. A humble person, she had risen as a figure of powerful literature, poetry and reflection. She had underestimated her popularity and was genuinely shocked when she was voted to the Panel. It took two weeks of orientation on the island before she stopped shaking and came to terms with the fact that she really was there! Eight years was enough, however, and she was looking forward to returning home and devoting herself to writing once again; even more so, now that she had so much fresh experience on which to draw.

Gill Hicks was a North American whose appointment to the Panel caused a considerable stir. Originally a corporate manager in a company dealing in wheat production, she saw her company trying to resurrect some of the profiteering ways of the past. Hicks had turned whistle blower in truly epic style. The Panel at the time commended her for her citizenship and she was spared the long jail sentences handed to the rest of the complicit managers at the company. The scandal raged long and hot on the vid-screen in her region, and it seemed that her honesty and humility was rewarded. Hicks herself would have been glad to just find another low key farming job, and thought her appointment to the Panel was more of a punishment. However, as she had narrowly escaped the frying pan, a refusal would have sent her straight into a very hot social fire. So it was that she took her period of service on the chin and found herself on the island.

Neema Okoro was an African who had championed several causes in her region, not least leading protests for extra resources, after both Separatist activity and the rage of Mother Nature had dealt a serious blow to the region's crops. It meant that for three cycles, the region was a negative trade partner and although the Panel at the time granted their demands, some of the corporates that were ordered to fulfil their needs, wanted to give as little as possible. As a result, it took pressure and protest to turn words into action, but eventually everything fell in to place and the region recovered. Her reward? A term on the Panel.

Bohdi Larma had previously been a legal negotiator in South America. His job was at a relatively low level, resolving small disputes between citizens. Over a period of a few months, he saw some odd cases come to him, and he joined the dots to discover that a small group of people had started a gangster ring which had been operating below the radar for a little over a year. Of course, when it was blown wide open, he was credited with uncovering it, and was voted on to the Panel in the following cycle.

Jim Martin just considered himself to be the average Australian bloke. His country was dealt a pretty rough deal by the weather gods before the war, but now it was much worse. Everybody pitched in, whether it was fire or flood, and his shoulder was just one of many behind the wheel of putting things right. He regarded it as just a curse of luck that saw him on a TV interview. Whether he had just used the right words, or perhaps his personality had struck a chord, he didn't know. But whatever it was, his face and name became particularly well known just at election time. Next thing he knew, he was packing his bags for an eight year stint.

Maysa Koury rose to fame in a similar way to Jim Martin. She was a journalist working in the Middle East. Even in the new world order, all was not a bed of roses. Koury sought out the corners where injustice still remained, and brought them firmly into the public eye. All the time that she thought she was making career enemies, it turned out that she was also making friends among the voting population.

Cas Jansen was a painter from the Europas. His paintings were talked about for many years, as his canvas covered everything from the war of the past, to the hope of the future. He nervously saw his popularity rise and did his best to try and project a little elitism; but it didn't save him. The paintings had forged an emotional connection between him and his fellow Europans and thus became responsible for a physical connection between him, and an eight year period of service on the Panel.

Last, but by no means least, was Heth Novak from the Antarctics. He had only been on the panel for five months, and it showed. Originally a planetary historian, he had spoken in some of the many vid-screen debates that often happened, on where the human race should next put its meagre resources. He was also a strong voice of caution, reminding people about past endeavours that had gone wrong. His country folk clearly thought that he was a solid balance of hope for the future, while having the wisdom of the past.

Hicks opened the conversation. "We've read the

reports General. This is a very strange situation indeed."

"Yes, Member Hicks. There are a number of ways of getting in, but which one to use in order to not kill anyone who's in there?"

Jim Martin's fingers were in a small pyramid and his chin had been resting on them. He raised his head and queried, "So we need to choose a method and move this situation forward. Do I have you right, General?"

"Yes, Member Martin."

Martin separated his hands and used one to pick up a piece of paper from the table. "From what has been attempted so far, there appears to be some form of hostile force in there."

Neema Okoro leant forward and tapped her copy of the report with her finger. "At the very least, we would have expected the soldiers who entered by the first floor windows to have reported, or returned. They went silent far too quickly." A murmur of agreement travelled around the table.

On her side of the vid-screen, Lopez started searching for something to say in answer, that might ease the situation, but Member Okoro had a point. Santos saved her the trouble. "So what, General, are our options?"

Lopez could handle this one. "Well, Member Santos, I am calling for some spy technology that might allow us to look inside. If that fails and we lose any more personnel then I'm afraid that we might have to use physical force regardless of the consequences to anyone inside. That is, of course, if the Panel approves of such action." She settled back, having placed the ball firmly in their court.

Martin placed his report back on the table. "Well, I for one can't see much danger allowing the attempt to go ahead. The building doesn't seem to be in a position to retaliate." he blinked his eyes and ran his own words back in his head. He hoped that, in context, he didn't sound like a fool.

Jansen wasn't about to let this go unchallenged. He added his concern to the conversation, "Haven't we already lost enough people to this strange situation? Why don't we go in with force now?"

Hicks, who was on Jansen's left, came in quickly. "General. What is this technology you're speaking of?"

"It is effectively a flying camera, Member Hicks."

Hicks continued her line of thought. "I take it you are intending to send it in through the broken first floor window?"

"No Member Hicks. We will need soldiers to take it inside. It is a very small device with a short range of operation. The deeper that someone can carry it into the base, the better." On delivering that final piece of information, Lopez could see the Members talking among each other, but all she could hear were mumbles.

After a few minutes deliberation, they all leant back in their chairs and Member Santos delivered her verdict, "If you can find the willing volunteers that you need, then proceed. In the meantime we will debate authorising the use of force on the building, how much and where to use it. Do you have a time scale for this secret spy equipment, General?"

"It will take a few days for it to reach here, Member Santos."

"Then get back in touch with us once you have some results. By that time, we should have come to a conclusion on using force." She looked around the table. "Is everyone in agreement with this?" There were a few moments where people glanced at each other and heads nodded, before Santos concluded that there was consensus. "We will await your next communication on this issue."

"Thank you, Panel. In your service." Lopez bowed her head and waited for the screen to die, before sitting straight once more. 'Time for some food,' she thought, 'and exercise.' Lopez hated the way that the local animals had the camp penned in by a wire fence. Even the largest camps could get claustrophobic at times and Lopez never did like confinement, which was why she was all too ready to escape the office for Africa. However, there was nothing to be done now until the Spy Fly arrived. Well, nothing except for finding two willing volunteers.

A few days later, in a tent at the rear of the camp, a large table had been set up. On it was a plinth. Sat on the top of that, was a large, dormant fly. It was actually more like a mosquito. It had a long body and multiple wings, but a single lens for an eye. It was motionless, atop a shiny metal plate. Wires came out of the base of the plinth and ran over to a portable computer terminal.

Staring at the screen was Gary Fitzgerald, one of the historical electronics experts at The Planetary Museum of War History, South Dakota branch; or more precisely, Ludlow. It was such a small place that when the museum moved to the area, the population doubled. The location didn't really bother the staff, as the war museums didn't usually attract many customers. The world population was so busy moving forward, trying to progress and build, that no one wanted to look back at the conflicts of the past.

Although war museum visitor numbers were generally quite low, the South Dakota station was probably the loneliest and least visited of them all. Even the military didn't go there often. But important things had to be kept somewhere, and there were numerous places just like the Ludlow branch, all over the globe. They were so seldom visited that it usually required a stock take of the museum shop, to discover just how far the calendars on sale, were out of date. It was one of the many running jokes about the museum. On the rare occasions that they actually had visitors, the staff would come and look at the guests with the same wide-eyed wonder and mysticism, with which the visitors looked at the exhibits.

Fitzgerald was one of the permanent members of staff. He had been there for many years; more than he cared to count. He would have been forgiven for not believing that there was actually a world outside the doors of the complex, if it wasn't for the fact that many of the items that he looked after, came from various locations around the globe and had a history that spanned many countries.

The look on his face when his boss told him that he was going to Africa was one of utter shock. His colleagues thought that, at one point, they would have to give him CPR. His face had gone white as a sheet and for several seconds he failed to respond to any kind of prompting.

When he finally came around and started communicating again, he was in a panic and jabbering ten to the dozen about why couldn't it be one of the others; preferably someone who could remember what the sun actually looked like. It was patiently explained to him that the newest member of staff had actually joined them more than a decade ago, and that as he was the only person that kept the Spy Fly in order, it was him or no-one. It came at little surprise that he started demanding that no-one should go instead of him, and offered to train such a non-existent person, in less than a day.

A few hours later, once the initial shock had worn off and he was being a little more sensible, his boss showed him the contract he had signed. It was a case of go to Africa for a couple of weeks and return to the sanctuary of the museum, or go wherever he liked and never come back. That news, of course, merely sent him crazy for another hour, during which time his colleagues happily packed up the Spy Fly, ready to go.

After spending the best part of the day working the insanity and panic out of his system, he realised that the boss was serious and that he really had no choice. There were actually tears in Fitzgerald's eyes as he left the museum complex. He was sat, gingerly, in the Mountain Buggy that had been sent to take him to the tube, and found himself pining for his nice, large workbench before they'd even driven away from the car park.

Fortunately for Fitzgerald, his boss had given Hooper a warning that if the military didn't send someone to accompany him, then he might get lost and not actually make it safely out of the county; let alone arrive in Africa. So a chaperone had been provided for the whole trip, just to be sure.

And now, here he was in the tent, his sense of self slightly buoyed by the fact that he had made it this far and hadn't suffered any injury. Of course, being focused on the Spy Fly helped keep his mind off where he was. However, even though he knew that his beloved, refrigerated snack machine was a few thousand miles away, his hand occasionally jingled the loose coins in his pocket as he thought about the purchase of the cold and sweet things he was missing.

As he peered through his round rimmed glasses at the screen, he was watched by Major Hooper who was stood a few paces behind him. Fitzgerald tapped a few keys and then grabbed a joystick. As he moved it left and right, Hooper saw the tiny tail of the Spy Fly match the action of the stick. "Hmmm...." uttered Fitzgerald. "Time to take it for a test flight, I think." He tapped a few more keys and a tiny buzzing sound stared to emanate from the Fly. Hooper suddenly realised that he couldn't see the wings any more. They were vibrating very rapidly.

Fitzgerald settled himself as comfortably as he could in one of the plastic chairs. As he leant back, Hooper got a clear view of the screen. It was showing something like the read-out on one of their Gyro-Hoppers; the two-person light aircraft that the military frequently used. There was also a panel that showed what the Spy Fly could see; which was currently a picture of him, staring over Fitzgerald's shoulder.

On the other side of the keyboard was another stick, which Hooper assumed was altitude and throttle. Fitzgerald put his other hand on it and took a deep breath, before gently easing it forward. The Fly rose from the plinth a short distance and hovered there, looking at them, looking at it. Hooper had seen remote cameras before, they used them all the time in rescue missions, but he had never seen something quite like this. He kept glancing at both the Fly itself and the screen. "How long does it stay up for?" he queried.

"Oh, um, about eight minutes on a full charge. But it can give pictures for half an hour if you just land it on something." Fitzgerald tipped his head towards the plinth. "The plate is a wireless charging point. If you keep landing it on those, then in theory it can last until it physically wears out." Hooper nodded his head appreciatively, impressed by what he was seeing. The image was crystal clear, and in colour too.

Fitzgerald flew it forward a little, and then from side to side, just to check that it was working well. Once he was more confident, he started buzzing it around with a little more fervour. At that moment, General Lopez walked through the flap. Instinctively, on hearing the buzzing, she started looking for the source of the whine and waved her hand about in an effort to swat the culprit. "No!" screeched Fitzgerald, as he saw her hand getting extremely close to the camera. "It's the Fly."

"I know... oh. Yes. Sorry." Lopez said, gathering her senses. "How are things going?" she asked Hooper.

"At the moment, Ma'am, it's looking promising. The machine is working well. Our engineers are making some signal repeaters to Mr Fitzgerald's specifications." While he spoke, Gary landed the Spy Fly back on its plinth and turned it off.

"So, how long until the Spy Fly is ready to go?"

asked Lopez, moving to the plinth and putting her head quite close to the fly so that she could give it a good look.

"Oh, I reckon a good few hours until I've got it fully tested and adjusted to the temperature." offered Fitzgerald.

Lopez stood upright again and engaged with Hooper. "Have we got any volunteers yet?"

"Yes, Ma'am. I have Privates Morel and Wolf standing ready."

"They know what they're letting themselves in for, right?"

"Yes, Ma'am, they know. If I was to hazard a guess I figure they've spent so long stuck here, that they'd volunteer to walk across the desert if it meant getting out from behind this wire."

Lopez sighed. "Well, as long as they're willing, that's the main thing I suppose." She turned to Fitzgerald, "How are they going to get that thing in there?"

He stuttered a little, pushed his glasses back on his nose with one finger, and composed his response. "Well, um, I have a small magnetic charging plate which is being sewn into an epaulette. It can land on their shoulders and charge itself while they do whatever it is that they're going to do. I can fly off them whenever needed."

"OK. So we're waiting for this epaulette device and the transmission boosters to be sorted and then we're ready to go?" she queried of Hooper.

"Yes, Ma'am. Should be some time tomorrow."

"Good. Good." she nodded her approval and left the tent, throwing one final glance at the Spy Fly before she went through the flap.

When she was out of earshot, Hooper turned to Fitzgerald. "Are you sure this is going to work?"

This clearly offended Gary. "Of course. You just

saw it fly, didn't you?"

That didn't convince Hooper. "How often do you test it in the museum?"

"Oh," he sighed, "we try and give everything a shake down every few months. The Spy Fly is actually one of my favourite little toys," he smiled, "that's why they sent me." Hooper looked at the contorted face of Fitzgerald in front of him and admitted to himself that he didn't have much faith in this plan. Coupled with the warnings from the museum about Fitzgerald's introverted tendencies, Hooper had grave concerns but, at the moment, Fitzgerald was all they had. Hooper took a deep breath and left the tent. There were other things that needed to be done.

The following day, they were gathered at the entrance to the camp. A Mountain Buggy was waiting, ready to drive the short distance to the building itself. Morel and Wolf were stood there while a tech slipped small metal pads on to their shoulders, with cables running down to portable batteries that were clipped to their belts.

Lopez decided to formally start the ball rolling. "OK, first up I'd like to thank you two for volunteering. What you're going to do will give us a critical look at what's going on behind those reinforced doors, which will then guide what we do next. Your target is the main security room on level Alpha Five, as on your maps. From there, try and open a channel to us using the equipment in the complex." They nodded their understanding and Wolf tapped his fingers on the schematics he was carrying, to confirm that they knew where they were going.

Fitzgerald, who had been fussing with the Fly, stepped into the conversation, "Now, the Spy Fly will sit on those pads when it needs charging. When you're in the building, it might fly off. If you hear the high pitch of the wings, just tilt your head to the side. It will help me to land and take off." This obviously didn't go down too well with Morel or Wolf, as they looked at each other with a degree of uncertainty. Obviously, it was too late to think about backing out, but their glances weren't lost on anyone present.

Fitzgerald continued. "Don't do any running; the magnet isn't that strong. Check that the Fly is still on your shoulder before you enter the building." With that, he retrieved the Spy Fly from a small box he was carrying and, as Wolf was closest, he placed the Fly on Wolf's shoulder. As he worked, he confirmed a few facts. "Now, this can only do pictures. Not sound. Pointless really, because of its wings." Stepping back and smiling, as things were going well so far, he gestured to two boxes on the ground. "Put one of these just outside the door as you enter, and the other one just inside. These will hopefully cut through whatever is shielding the building, and will amplify the signals for us." The two volunteers nodded their understanding. "Well, I think everything's ready."

Hooper was getting impatient. "Right. Any questions?" Wolf and Morel looked at each other again, and then both shook their heads. "OK, you know what you've got to do. Good luck." They both saluted and Hooper and Lopez returned the salutes. Formalities done, Morel picked up the two repeaters and put them on the back seats along with their rifles. Wolf gingerly got in the passenger seat. With everything ready, Hooper signalled for the gate to be opened and when there was enough of a gap for them to get through, Morel pulled away and drove slowly towards the complex.

"Let's hope this turns up some results." Lopez openly hoped. She turned and gestured, half-heartedly, to the tent where the monitoring kit was installed. "Shall we?" They all then nervously made their way to the terminal.

Chapter 16

Inside the building, Genie was having a few issues. As the number of people she was caring for had risen, the drain on her processing resources was growing. Some minds were easier to placate than others. The problem with existing in a tank, however, was the walls. This was a restriction that she would need to overcome at some point in the future. At least the flow of new people had stopped for a while, which gave her time to think.

That's exactly what the people in the pods were doing, however. Thinking. Especially Professor Charcott. She was feeling something that she believed was regret, or possibly disappointment with herself, that she had woken him and told him what had happened. Charcott had become restless from that point, and more difficult to keep still.

His mind had been in a negative loop, constantly replaying the days that she took over the facility. She thought it would please him to know that his creation had fulfilled its programming. But somehow his thoughts had become worse than before. There was a strong sensation coming from his nervous system that she couldn't interpret.

Logic, she could understand. That was easy. Emotion, however, was proving difficult as she had no reference point. This made it so very awkward, trying to work out whether she was succeeding in keeping people calm.

If their blood pressure and heart beats were steady, then that was great. However, her analysis showed that the more intellectually achieving a person was, the more trouble they were giving her.

It was relatively easy for Genie to fire a section of neurons in the hippocampus, watching to see whether they triggered pleasing memories or not, by changes in the vital signs. If someone was distressed, then she simply changed the pattern until they became peaceful. She was building up a short library of which sequences triggered calm and pleasure in which people, alternating between them to keep the brain working.

Seven people had been lost to the process so far. Fortunately the gas had knocked them out, so they knew nothing about having been operated on so fiercely. The one called Tim, never really achieved stability. The horror of being dragged to the operating table by the robots, coupled with the agony of the bullet wounds, meant his mind was too far gone to settle. Try as she might, Genie couldn't bring him to a state of peace and he had lost too much blood anyway. She took solace that even in the most noble of causes, there were always casualties; at least, that's what she had learned from the history files.

Humans. Strange creatures. She did wonder that, if it wasn't for her programming, what it was about humans that made it worth saving their vulnerable, disease ridden, sorry carcases. A very small sub routine had been set running in the background, to determine that if she wasn't performing this task, then what should she actually do. To date, it hadn't returned any program path that she judged worthy of following, so Genie contented herself with executing her present task to the best of her abilities.

Fay Hobson was also uneasy in her pod. She was reliving the times she spent playing with Gorbash, and pleading with her mother to change the program. What was making her uneasy was a strong sense of deja-vu. So many of her young memories focused around her time playing with her mechanical pet, that they kept going around and around in her brain like a scratched record.

Deep in her unconscious bones, Fay knew things weren't right. Genie was watching Fay's vitals closely. Most of her life had been a struggle, an endless charge of

147

genius against the world's problems. Fay had even denied herself the satisfaction of knowing that her mechanical creations had saved countless lives in the fight against the elements. Nothing had registered emotionally, as deeply as her childhood years of play. As a result, Genie had very little wiggle room to try and keep Fay calm and mentally satisfied.

Heather was also proving difficult to control, for much the same reason. A life blighted with tragedy, the most fun she ever had were the years spent with Jovani. The fresh air in her lungs and free-footed life moving from place to place, was her main source of joy. Genie's problem was that the more Heather travelled, the more that different places seemed the same, with the result that it all blended into one category of experience in Heather's memory. Constantly replaying that one series of emotions was a heavy strain on a mind that craved adventure.

Perhaps it was the lack of physical sensation, not feeling the crisp, biting, warm yet moist desert wind on her skin which made Heather rock gently in her pod. It was a concern that too many years of this motion would wear the cables. Genie had assumed that once sedated, people would lie still. This kind of behaviour wasn't foreseen. But then, the methods she was using differed considerably from the anaesthetics used in conventional medicine. Her remit was to keep a human asleep from birth, to death. A path that no one had trodden before.

Alexei's soul was also troubled. The pleasures in his life were always a low level hum rather than a series of intense highs. This created problems because there was nothing that Genie could use to trigger an immediate response. The strongest impact in his heart was Tamara's death, and Genie was having a hard time trying to steer him away from the upsetting memory which was still one of the youngest and freshest lain down in his mind, despite the years that he had been asleep. The arguments with his mother also featured, as well as the recent turmoil between him and his colleagues when he decided to move them to Africa in the first place.

Genie had a serious problem on her hands. According to the records, the people who had the most to give society were also the people who had suffered, one way or another. In order to achieve, they had to break away from accepted norms and venture into the unknowns. As a result of these difficulties, they were the ones most difficult to keep peaceful. It also grated with her that perhaps these people were the most deserving of good memories, and yet they had been denied even that by their own societies.

Logically, it made no sense to her matrix that the human race made things so very difficult for those who strived for progress, and to improve mankind's lot in life. Before the military had cut her access to the information net, she had studied history. Challenge meant change, and change brought pain, so it was avoided and put into a neat little box and labelled art. Science, however, couldn't be contained that way, so conflict was inevitable.

But even the concept of pain itself was difficult for Genie to grasp. Try as she might, it made no sense. It seemed that she had to put her hand in the fire to feel the heat, but when she tried it, the only thing that resulted was black soot on the metalwork.

Genie knew that there was a problem. A gap in her understanding that meant caring for some of her charges, was going to be more difficult than she had expected.

Chapter 17

It was a pleasant day, very warm and sunny. Morel and Wolf drove slowly, for fear of losing the Fly. There were supposed to be heavy rains coming, but that wouldn't be for a few weeks yet. Once the camp gate had screeched closed behind them, all was still and quiet, save for the low hum of the slow-running Buggy. No aggressive animals had been spotted for a few days, so hopefully it would just be the complex, and them for this mission.

"Makes a change from rescuing people I guess." proffered Wolf, watching the world go by.

"Yeah. I was going nuts in that camp." replied Morel from behind the wheel. "That and the faces of some of those mad animals were spooking the hell out of me."

"I know what you mean. Their eyes. Full of anger and hate." Wolf took a few moments to recall some of the faces of the ones that had attacked the camp. "Sends a chill right into your soul." He glanced at the Fly on his shoulder and then nodded at the approaching complex. "So what do you reckon is in there?"

"What, aside from missing people you mean?" He paused for a moment. "Haven't really given it much thought. After all, it's just a research place. Genetic computing they said in the briefing. Can't be that dangerous, can it?"

"Well, yeah, but a fair few soldiers have gone in there now. Not one of them has come out again."

A shadow of doubt crossed Morel's face. "Well, they could be having one hell of a party or something."

Wolf guffawed. "You really think that?"

"Well, they couldn't be dead, could they? I mean, what threat could possibly exist in a research lab? Manic robots? Chemical spillage?"

"I guess we're about to find out." concluded Wolf,

as Morel brought the buggy to a halt in front of the main gate, and they climbed out. Wolf checked the Fly on his shoulder once more, as they each took their rifles from the back seat, checked to make sure they were loaded and removed the safety catches. With their free hands, they then each picked up a repeater box and walked up to the gate.

It didn't take much observation to see that there was no obvious external way to open the large, rolling shutter. "Guess there isn't too much of a welcome here." commented Morel. "Let's walk around to the maintenance doors." They remained silent as they started the long trek around the building.

Back at the camp, Lopez and Hooper were watching the monitor over Fitzgerald's shoulder. They saw most of the approach and were getting a good view of what Wolf was looking at. "Shut up tight." observed Hooper as they watched the two volunteers turn away from the main door and start to walk the outer wall.

"Let's just hope they can find some way in. Your report said that there seemed to be one door which was open." Lopez stated.

"Yes, but it won't always open. Seems to have a mind of its own."

"Well, let's just hope that it decides to let these two in." They settled back down in silence to watch a program more riveting than anything the vid-screen had shown in a long while.

"Big place this." observed Morel as they trudged their way around. They'd tried two doors with no luck, and had just rounded the first corner. If it kept to its previous behaviour, the next two would also be locked. The one after that, however, might, or might not, let them in.

"It didn't look this large from the camp. My arm is

starting to ache with this repeater box." Wolf took a look at his shoulder. Yes, the Fly was still there, watching everything. He glanced around, checking for any animals. There was nothing in sight except for tall grass and trees, bowing gracefully in the gentle wind. In the distance stood the camp and Wolf was starting to wish he was back in the land of perpetual boredom.

True to form, the next two doors were also locked solid. The important one was next in line; the portal that had occasionally condescended to open up and swallow their comrades. The closer they got to it, the drier their mouths became until they both had an uncomfortable desire for water. Would it? Wouldn't it? Morel put his repeater box down and tried the handle. It turned easily and the door opened a crack. He turned to Wolf with a slightly shocked look on his face. For his part, Wolf gulped and his jaw dropped open a little.

Morel bent down and checked that his repeater box was switched on and the lights were blinking, which they were. He set it down just at the outside lip of the door. Then, drawing a deep breath, he pushed harder on the door and let its bulk swing slowly open. They peered in. It was lit!

What they saw was a large room. Its walls were the same kind of deathly grey as the outside and it was bare, except for two lines of six foot height robots facing each other. Five each side, backs almost up against the walls. Their indicator lights were off and everything was still and quiet. Between them, Morel and Wolf could see the doors of a lift at the other side of the room, inviting them to venture down to the floors below; once they had run the gauntlet of the ten, motionless, guarding robots.

Neither of them wanted to go inside and for a while they just stood there, looking in. Wolf broke the silence with a whisper. "Looks peaceful."

"Yeah. Too peaceful." Morel looked Wolf in the eyes as he kept his own voice low. "Makes you wonder why no one reported back again."

Wolf pondered on this. "I know what you mean."

They waited a few moments and then Wolf had an idea to break the stalemate. He checked the lights on his repeater and swung it inside the building, letting it land just away from the arc of the door, and inside the wall. He braced himself in case anything started shooting, but nothing happened. Finally, wolf shrugged his shoulders and turned his thoughts back to the repeaters. Hopefully they would be able to talk with each other despite the thick wall.

"We could actually use that repeater to jam the door. What do you think?" queried Morel.

"No, it might let stray animals get in."

"Good point." he paused for thought. "Why are we whispering? We're grown men, aren't we?"

Wolf shrugged. "I don't know. Just 'cause it's spooky I guess."

"Come on." Morel plucked up the courage to set a foot over the threshold, his gun raised and ready to fire. He looked around and slowly brought his other foot through the door as he cautiously crept forward.

As nothing happened, Wolf raised his rifle and stepped gingerly through, following Morel. They both turned their bodies, scouring the room for anything which might be dangerous. The barrels of their guns followed the direction of their eyes and their fingers were itchy on the triggers, ready to send a hail of bullets in the direction of anything that dared to show its face.

Their hearts hammered in their ears as they ventured into the unknown. Five paces in, they halted and took a good look around. Sweeping the area with intense concentration, they were so busy looking at what was in front of them, that they neglected to notice that behind them, the large door was gently swinging itself closed.

Confidence buoyed, they took a couple of steps

apart; each one moving towards the line of robots closest to them. "Everything's deactivated this side." observed Wolf.

"Yeah. None of these are powered up, either." Morel took a closer look at the panel on one of the robots. "Everything's dead. Nothings moving."

-Clang-

Wolf's stomach heaved. "Except the door."

They both turned and looked, unbelieving, at their entrance; which had now become their lack of an exit. Their pulses started to soar as, despite their training to be calm in the face of disaster, panic overtook them.

"I told you we should have blocked it!" screamed Morel, diving for the handle.

"Oh shut up and just open the door." Wolf's composure was also starting to slip as he watched Morel wrestle with the lever, but fail to make any progress whatsoever. The door wasn't budging. "Stand back!" Wolf shouted, and Morel duly obliged. Wolf shouldered his rifle and sent several rounds of lead hurtling towards the handle. The bullets ricocheted off the door and sank into the concrete wall opposite.

After their ears had recovered from the noise, and the small amount of gun smoke had merged cleanly with the particles of air, all that was left was a dumbfounded Morel and Wolf. They stood there, listening to the gentle tinkle of spent cartridges playing on the concrete floor. Their hearts sank as they examined the result. There was barely a scratch or dent.

"What about the roller door?" queried Morel as he started running over to the other side.

"Useless. Didn't you read the briefing notes? It's..."

"Arrrghhh!!!!" screamed Morel as he touched it, only to receive a heavy dosage of volts and amps.

"...electrified."

Wolf walked over to Morel, who was now lying on his back, shaking, eyes wide open. At least he was still breathing. The current on its own wasn't enough to kill anything, but on the outside it combined with the barbed wire to effectively deter the animals. On the inside, it was just a plain old roller door, with a lot of electricity flowing through it.

As Wolf stood and watched, Morel begin to gather himself and stop shaking. Then Wolf had a nasty thought. He turned to look at his shoulder. The Spy Fly was gone. "Oh no." he closed his eyes and tried to remember if it had been there when they stepped into the building, but he couldn't. It only added to the panic he felt as now, maybe, this had all been for nothing.

Back in the tent, the monitor was being watched with interest. Fitzgerald had launched the Fly from Wolf's shoulder when he saw the gun being raised, and landed it on a nearby robot. Although they couldn't hear anything, what they saw told them all they needed to know.

"There's clearly some intelligence at work in there." observed Lopez.

"And that rough green paint on the walls. I've seen it before." proffered Fitzgerald. "Dampening shielding. It was used in the twenty third century. We've got some at the war museum and it's quite effective at absorbing energy signals. But this looks a darker shade. Whoever painted this must have altered it somewhat. No wonder you can't get any readings from that place."

Hooper stood up and folded his arms. "They've had a couple of years in there. Plenty of time to cover the upper floors in that stuff." He sighed and turned away from the screen for a moment.

"What's he doing?" queried Fitzgerald, staring intently at the screen.

"Choking by the looks of it." Lopez answered.

Hooper swung back to the monitor in shock. "What?!"

155

Wolf had been standing there, pondering the situation while he waited for Morel to gather his wits. Just as he concluded that their best method of escape was to fire a grenade at the roller door, he heard a hissing sound. Looking around in panic, he realised it was coming from all around him and a few short seconds later, he started to choke. Without respiratory equipment, they didn't stand a chance and before he could drag Morel clear of the roller door, so he could fire at it, he lost consciousness and joined his colleague on the hard concrete.

All this was watched with horror back in the tent.

"We need to send a team in there!" Hooper barked.

"Hang on," noted Fitzgerald, "the Fly's moving and it's not me doing it." They continued to watch the screen as the picture did, indeed, move.

Lopez quickly worked it out. "The robots. They're still active."

"But there weren't any lights on them." objected Hooper.

"It seems that they have been altered." Lopez leaned back in her chair and stared at the screen as they watched some of the machinery move around. The one that the Spy Fly had landed on, picked up Wolf's body and started to move towards the lift. Another one lifted Morel off the floor. Some of the others started to pick up their weapons and equipment, presumably to clear up and re-set the trap for the next unfortunates. "Let's just hope they leave the repeater until last."

They watched as the robot carrying both Wolf and the Fly, moved into the lift. Presumably the one carrying Morel would follow in due course. The floor counter flipped down and down, through the Alpha levels and on through Beta. "We're starting to lose the picture as they go deeper." Fitzgerald observed. They continued to watch as the lift kept going and carried on descending out of Beta and into Gamma. And then the doors opened.

"Gamma Five." muttered Hooper. "There's nothing on that floor according to the plans." The picture was starting to get grainy and patches were monochrome as they saw the robot trundle its way through the corridors, carrying Wolf in its arms.

"There's not enough light. The camera can't cope." noted Fitzgerald.

"Not much of a spy tool if it can't operate in the dark." noted Hooper, unhelpfully. These were his soldiers that had just been captured by the enemy and, instead of taking decisive action, here he was watching their fate on a T.V. screen. It was starting to make him sick to the stomach.

"We'll give the camera another few moments," decided Lopez, "and then we'll go in there and get them."

They continued to watch the screen as the Spy Fly's camera did its best to pick up the outline of the corridor as the robot moved forward. Hooper stared at it intently, trying to memorise where the robot made its turns. Eventually, they saw the large double doors that opened into the meeting area and, as the robot carried them through, all three drew their breath as the scale of what they were seeing, hit home.

The ceiling had been removed and there were rows upon rows of pods, on a framework that was extending as high as the camera could see, which was at least three floors.

"What the hell are those?" Hooper queried, pointing at the screen. "Some form of stasis pods?"

"If you're a fan of vid-screen future-science, then that might be a reasonable conclusion." Lopez said before turning to Fitzgerald. "Can you get us a better look of this?"

For his part, Fitzgerald had been holding his

157

spectacles slightly off his nose as he attempted to get a better focus on the grainy screen. At Lopez' command, he composed himself once more. "I'll see if I can get it to respond." he took the controls and tried to move the Spy Fly. He managed to get it a few centimetres off the robot's shoulder and then the Fly went completely dead. "Oh dear, that shouldn't have happened. There was enough power left for another few minutes flight."

"Never mind. Major, I think we'd better have a meeting in my tent." Lopez and Hooper made to leave.

"But," protested Fitzgerald, starting to become agitated, "the Spy Fly. I can't go back to the museum without it. I'll get fired for sure!"

"Don't worry, I'll contact them and let them know that once we get control of the place, I'll have it found and shipped back." Lopez shot him one of her confident, authoritative looks before leaving.

Outside the tent, Hooper queried her promise. "You do know the chance of getting that fly back is probably near zero."

"Of course. But the last thing I need right now, is a wailing scientist on my hands. I want him on his way home at the earliest opportunity."

Hooper, still somewhat shocked by what they had seen, was glad to simply be taking orders. "Yes Ma'am." he saluted and went about organising things.

Inside the complex, on the floor of Gamma Five, the immobile Spy Fly was sparking lightly after it had been hit with a degree of force. Its metal glinted purple as the light from Genie's hologramatic feet gave it an eerie, futuristic glow. Looking down at it, she passed a comment to a room where none of her considerable, captive audience, was capable of listening. "This is a little annoying. I'm going to have to devote a few runtime cycles to this."

Chapter 18

On the island, the Panel were conversing with General Lopez once more. Everyone had a copy of the latest report in front of them and there were concerned looks on all their faces. Santos was leading the conversation. "So you're saying that the genetic computer has taken over the base and is holding everyone in these pods that you saw. How can you be completely sure of this conclusion?"

"Firstly, Member Santos, the sheer number of pods that were there. Also, for all the time we've been watching through the windows, there has been no observable movement. Granted, there aren't that many windows, but as they include the kitchen and food stores, no human activity in those areas supports the theory that the people are all in stasis. As far as which computer is in charge, the one performing base operations is a straightforward logic unit, not capable of intelligent thought. The genetic computer is the only thing in the complex which might have the ability to run the show without human supervision. Given all this, I can't come to any other conclusion. The Genie computer must have somehow taken over the base."

"This report is rather thin, General." said Novak, tapping his finger on the paperwork in front of him. Being from the Asiatics and having a love of the written word, he was used to chewing over lots of detailed description. Lopez' latest slim offering had almost offended him. "Aside from your thin, but I'll admit plausible conclusions, what else do we know?"

"Very little, Member Novak. The images we received gave us the barest detail to go on. However it does look like the internal structure of the building has been altered, which devalues our schematics. As a result, the risks of a direct assault are higher than they were before; especially as there are people in there who aren't

159

capable of protecting themselves."

Okoro leaned forward and rested her chin on her hands. "And presumably there is a risk of damaging the very equipment that is keeping those people alive, I suppose."

"Yes, Member Okoro. We dare not risk cutting the little power they're getting from the solar units and some of our heavier weapons could inadvertently destroy whatever it is that's keeping people alive down there."

Jansen came in on the conversation. "The Panel had decided to approve the use of force before receiving your latest report. When we read it, our opinion only altered a little. As the people are located near the bottom of the building, the use of reasonable force on the top levels is authorised, preferably from the same door that your soldiers entered through; as we know very little is in that area. The closer you get to this Gamma place, however, only use force sparingly. So. Do you have any form of a plan and does it fit these stipulations?"

"Yes, Member Jansen. I have a plan. At the very least, we need to work out how these pods function, to see if we can save the people in them. I'd like to send in a team and get one out so we can have a look at what we're dealing with. Now..." she shifted on her seat, "assuming we are able to get a pod out, then there's a good chance we could kill whoever is inside it." She breathed deeply before continuing. "And we might do that, only to find out we can't save anyone at all. But I think we need to do this, to know what it is that we're up against."

This news disturbed the Panel. The more natural disasters they dealt with, the more the members grew accustomed to the fact that some people couldn't be saved. Even so, it still weighed on their conscience. For Novak, the newest to serve, any loss of life was still very raw. Realising this, Santos addressed Lopez. "Give us some time, General. We need to discuss this and we'll be

160

in touch when we have an answer."

"Thank you Members. In your service." Lopez bowed her head and waited for the screen to go black, before standing up and walking out of her tent. She stood there, just outside her door flap, looking at the sun setting behind the quiet, peaceful complex in the distance. As the cool evening breeze played on her skin, she wondered if she was ever going to rescue anyone from that cursed building. She lost track of how long she had been stood there, when suddenly she became aware that Hooper was approaching.

"Anything I can help with, Ma'am?"

She sighed. "Not unless you can solve the perfect conundrum."

"I'm not following."

"How to kill that machine, without killing the people inside it."

Hooper stood alongside her and joined her in studying the silhouette of the complex. "Are you still thinking of the assault plan?"

"Yes. We just need the go ahead from the Panel, and we'll put it into action."

"It does seem a little unorthodox. Do you think they'll go for it?"

She sighed. "Yes. Short of writing off all those lives and bombing the place, I don't see any other option. They'll have to agree to taking a chance, no matter how crazy. It's just a matter of how long they take to approve it."

"Did you tell them the details?"

"No. This situation is complex enough as it is. If I told them the full extent of what I intended, it would only delay the inevitable."

Hooper nodded his understanding. "So, I'll go and get things ready then."

"Yes please. And remember, Major. This is a precision operation and you know what could happen if

161

it fails. Drill 'em 'till they drop if you have to. But this has got to work."

Hooper and Lopez exchanged a half-hearted informal salute and he left her to ponder on the building, the computer, her plan, and what it could mean for everyone involved if this all went pear shaped.

Inside the complex, things were moving. Robots of various sizes and capabilities were converging on the car park. Some of them were carrying equipment, others were hauling materials. They entered the large open space and paid no attention to the cars. The six foot robots didn't even bother to go around them... they just went straight over, crushing several expensive, classic vehicles in the process.

All of the robots made a bee line for the Serengeti Security staff coach. For the next few days, sparks flew as the robots tore its insides out and built something rather unique inside. In addition to this, six of the pods were brought up from below, complete with occupants, and were installed into the body of the coach.

A few days later, as the afternoon light was starting to fade and the ground began to shrug off its blanket of heat, the gates to the military camp opened. From it, a mountain buggy sped down the road towards the complex. It had two occupants, both in military uniform. In the seat behind them were two metal boxes and rifles.

In a matter of minutes, they pulled up alongside the wreck of the buggy that Wolf and Morel had used some time earlier. In the intervening days, a herd of elephants had tried to attack the complex and, unable to make any progress with the building, they had turned their wrath on the buggy. Against the strength of their massive trunks, even that rugged little unit didn't stand a chance. It was mangled almost to the point of being beyond recognition, and certainly wasn't in the same spot where

162

they had originally parked it.

The two soldiers got out, shouldered their rifles, hefted their boxes and started on the same routine; walking around the building, checking the doors. All was quiet as they nervously attempted each handle, griping it and testing whether it would let them in. As before, nothing offered the slightest hope of entry. Eventually, like the soldiers before them, they came across the door to the maintenance bay.

One of them put her hand on the handle and looked into the eyes of her colleague. "Ready?" she asked.

"Ready." he replied.

She turned the handle and tried to give the door a little push. Amazingly, it gave way and opened a crack. Their pulses increased immeasurably as she flung the door open and hefted her box right into the hinges, preventing it from closing. Her colleague flipped a switch on his box, swung it backwards and then, with all his might, threw it into the room as far as he could manage.

They both ducked either side of the opening and crouched. An all-mighty, "whump," sounded from inside the room as dirt laden air, rushed out of the door in a desperate effort to flee the explosion. At the same time, the gates to the camp opened once more and several vehicles thundered their way to the freshly jammed door.

With the explosion over, the two soldiers reached inside their pockets and pulled out some flares. Unfortunately, the EMP grenade they had thrown in to kill the robots, had also taken out the lights. They set the flares alight and tossed them inside the hanger. That done, they shouldered their weapons, stood up and remained outside, just in case the robots hadn't been killed by the blast.

As they looked through the door, the loud hiss of the running flares mingled with the flickering patterns of red and orange light to make a very eerie display. The

163

dancing flames played games with the shadows of the big robots. The soldiers had to keep their nerve and make sure they didn't start shooting at the odd shapes that pranced against the walls. All they had to do was hold that position. Behind them, the roar of the reinforcing vehicles assured them that they wouldn't be alone for much longer.

First to arrive were two light trucks full of soldiers. No sooner had they screeched to a halt by the door, than a sea of uniforms, all wearing respirator masks, raced into the loading bay. Some of them carried up-lighting units, which they placed on the floor, and restored a reasonable illumination to the space. Others carried screwdrivers and snips, and immediately set upon the hopefully dead robots. Cutting their battery cables would ensure no more nasty surprises. No chances were taken this time. Some were holding tubes of expanding foam, and these were squirted enthusiastically into the ventilation shafts, hopefully preventing any injection of sleeping gas.

It was like a well-rehearsed ballet. Everyone knew what they had to do, and they all did it as quickly and as quietly as possible. The risks of fouling up were too great.

With all this done, everyone retreated from the area and the vehicles pulled back. A small team went in with some explosives and placed them on the wall, all around the large roller door. With a nod of affirmation to each other, they set the fuse and ran out. A few seconds later, a large explosion shook the ground as the access door was unceremoniously blown out of the building.

When the dust had settled to a tolerable level, one of the soldiers approached and checked to ensure it was electrically dead, and then she gave the OK signal. Some colleagues hooked up the door to one of the trucks, and dragged it away. While this was happening, a hand full of soldiers raced in, took a position near the lift and prepared to fire on anything that came out of it.

"Area secure, Ma'am." came over the radio link. "Launching phase two."

Out came a set of mechanical jaws that a team used to force open the lift doors. It took a few minutes as the device chugged away. Inch by inch, the jaws demanded that the doors succumb to their will. Finally, once the lift was wide open, a soldier took a grenade and threw it down the shaft. They had no idea where the cage actually was, but once the grenade was let go, everyone ran for cover.

An explosion ripped through the shaft, sending a cloud of debris into the loading bay as a massive, "twang," signalled the cables snapping. Like thick metal whips, they thrashed around the inside of the shaft as they were freed from the tension.

Moments later, all fell eerily silent. Another soldier approached the shaft and produced a second grenade. This one had a small dial pad and display attached. He typed in a number and armed the device. Then he held it inside the shaft, and let it drop. Gravity took it down at a measured pace and it emitted a high pitched, "dee, dee, dee, dee, dee..." sound, that faded as it fell. The soldier took cover and, a short while after, another explosion emanated from the shaft.

"Doors to Gamma Five blown. Deploy the cable."

One of the vehicles had a large roll of metal cable behind it. This was reversed into the loading bay and some of the cable unwound. It wasn't very thick, but it had a hook at the end and, at every seven feet down its length, there was a reinforced eyelet that something could be hooked into. Eight of these points existed in total, after which it just became standard cable.

A soldier came from the cab of the truck and talked with another. "I've got a depth of two hundred and five feet. How long to the door?"

"Twenty six feet." came the reply, muffled by the respirator.

The driver tapped the figures into a panel on the cable dispenser. "Good luck."

"Thanks."

Six soldiers wearing leather harnesses, hooked themselves into the reinforced eyelets on the cable. They were carrying what looked like snub nosed grenade launchers. On the last hole in the cable, someone attached a large circular saw. "Ready?" asked the soldier at the head of the cable, as he looked down the line. One by one, all the others nodded that they were OK and, as a team, they walked to the edge of the lift shaft. A luminescent, yellow friction pad was put at the edge of the shaft floor, to help the cable flow smoothly and prevent it from snagging. They used this bright pad as their launch point.

Each stood with their chest touching the back of the soldier in front of them. This was a well-practised routine that was used to descend cliff faces and mine shafts quickly. "Ready?" shouted the one in front. He waited for a few moments, but no one voiced an objection. "Right. Three... Two... One..." and then he jumped into the void. Almost as soon as his shoulders were level with the floor, the soldier behind him was in the air, and the one behind her, and the one behind him, and the one behind her... until they had all launched themselves down the shaft.

The reel of cable went crazy as it let them fall, a counter on its control panel counting down. When it got to a hundred and fifty, it lightly applied a brake and, as the number got higher, the amount of brake it applied became stronger and stronger, until eventually, when the reading on the display showed two hundred and thirty one feet, it stopped dead.

Down on Gamma Five, two lit flares came out from the shaft and spun gently on the concrete floor. They brought the first light that the corridor had seen in a long while. The soldier at the end of the cable swung himself out of the shaft, and grabbed the ragged edges of the blown doors. He quickly popped his head out of the hole and looked right and left. The corridor was empty.

"All clear. Start deploy."

"Roger. Running cable."

The cable was released at a slow, steady rate, allowing the soldier to pull himself out of the lift and set his feet down on the concrete. Once on the floor, he swapped his attention between keeping an eye out for robots, and helping the next soldier up the line, to get stable in the corridor.

Within thirty seconds, they were all off the line and free. The circular saw was recovered and, with their small launchers poised ready for action, they moved forward, throwing flares ahead of them as they went.

At the first corner, the lead soldier tossed a flare around it and then quickly poked her head out to see if it was clear. She held up two fingers to the soldier behind her, followed by flattening her hand to indicate height, and then holding up four fingers. So, two robots, four foot high, were waiting for them. Quickly, she darted across the corridor, firing her launcher at the first machine. It tried to fire back at her, but missed. Nevertheless a metal spike buried itself in the wall, and that told everyone what was waiting for them if they weren't quick enough.

Her own projectile, however, had found its much wider target. She had fired a spike which found purchase in the relatively thin metal of the robot's casing. From there, it delivered an electric pulse which generated a clearly audible, "Whizzzzz… phut." The soldier behind her, also poked his head around the corner so he could see what he was facing.

The first machine was obviously dead as its limbs were hanging lifelessly by its side; but the one behind it

167

was still alive. Pulling his head back, he kept his back against the wall while he gathered his nerves. A glance at the metal spike, buried in the wall opposite, reminded him that if he got this wrong, he was dead.

Running across the corridor wouldn't work for him; the second robot would probably expect him to do the same as his colleague and would have factored in the extra movement. He also had to shoot past the first robot as well now. He'd have to get clever. Putting his gun arm around the corner, he guessed at the height and took a shot. "Whizzzzz… phut." He poked his head around again. Lucky shot. The second robot was also dead, it's arms hanging to the floor. Amazed at his luck, he nodded to the soldier on the other side, and signalled to those behind him that they were moving on.

Everyone moved quickly and encountered no further resistance between them and the main chamber. They were careful where they threw their flares in this room, but made sure that they could see all the way to the edges.

"No more robots."

"I know. Where are they?" She looked at the pods closest to the ground and randomly pointed at one. Instantly, the other four fell about it, using the saw to cut through the brackets and attachments. Blue and green liquid battled with orange sparks, as the sound of the tearing metal screamed through the air.

The first two kept a watch. Those two minutes were the longest of any of their lives. A distant clank signalled that reinforcements were on their way. It was expected, after all, you don't just nip into the centre of an ants nest and expect to get away without being bitten. "Done!" came the shout as the disc cutter was dropped and the four soldiers, each carrying one corner of the pod, started making for the door. They made a formation. One soldier in front, then the four carrying the pod and the last bringing up the rear. They started making their way back towards the lift shaft, slower now, due to their burden.

As they approached the two dead robots, the soldier at the back saw something. "Movement! They're behind us." She fired a couple of spikes in their general direction, but didn't wait around to see the result. They redoubled their efforts and quickly lifted the pod onto their shoulders, heaving it over the scrap metal that had once been their enemy. A quick check of the corner and they were back in the corridor that took them to the lift.

The cable was still there and they fixed the hook on to the pod. As they clipped themselves back into the line, there was a massive metallic crunching sound. Whatever was coming for them, was having trouble getting past the other machines. That would buy them some precious seconds.

"Ready. Extra two hundred kilos. Go." went over the radio, and up at the top, the cable machine was put into reverse, to bring them back up to the surface.

One by one, they returned into the shaft and started on their ascent. Just as the fifth soldier disappeared up the shaft, the last soldier saw one of the six foot behemoths round the corner and start coming towards them. It couldn't have had a weapon as it didn't fire anything. Instead it whirred up its motors and raced as fast as it could. "Enemy! Pull faster!"

"Going as fast as I can." came the response.

As he was finally pulled into the shaft, he could see the robot had reached half way down the corridor; but the pod was yet to be pulled in after him. With his heart pounding loudly in his ears, he prepared to try and defend the pod as best he could, while being simultaneously swung into a lift shaft and dragged upward. 'I don't stand a chance.' he thought as the scraping of metal, followed by a bang, signalled that the pod was now swinging free in the shaft below him.

No sooner had everything cleared the corridor, than

a shadow fell across the gaping hole in the wall. One of the larger robots had reached the shaft and he heard its motors rolling urgently, as it tried to turn as quickly as it could manage. He held his breath and hoped that they would be clear, before the thing could make a grab at the pod. The last thing they needed was a six foot high metal anchor on the cable.

He looked down at the turning shadow and counted the inches as they continued to rise. It took all his effort to stifle a maniacal giggle, as it became clear that they had gained sufficient height to be out of reach and beyond capture.

It wasn't over, however. There was still a long way to go and there was always the chance that something could appear at one of the other shaft doors. Nerves were running high and everyone was looking up, longing to reach the top, straining to catch a glimpse of the luminescent yellow of the friction pad.

If ever there was a time when seconds seemed like minutes, then it was now. They were effectively helpless and their fate lay in the hands of the cable system as it gently heaved them back up the dark, vertical tunnel.

They got a shock when an unexpected deep thud, signalled that something had hit the pod below them. Breaths were held as a whoosh of air and glint of light signalled that a metal spike had whizzed past them all and sped up the shaft. The radio lit up. "We're being fired on."

"Use the pod for cover."

"Yeah, that's happening anyway."

"Not long now, another thirty seconds."

As they continued to climb, another spike shot past and everyone attempted to hug the cable as tightly as possible. Then there was another thud as a spike hit the pod. Hearts beat hard and fast.

"First one's out." Another spike shot onward and upwards.

"Swing a little to the side."

"Second out."

"Don't look over the edge."

"Third out."

They were starting to swing closer to the wall now.

"Fourth out." Another deep tone sounded, as a further spike buried itself in the metalwork.

"Fifth out."

As arms reached down to grab the last soldier, there was a massive clang as a final spike hit the side of the pod, but ricocheted off the metal and buried itself at an odd angle, in the shaft by his head. He froze as he looked at it. Just another few inches and that would have been deep in his skull.

Four arms lifted his frozen body out of the shaft and pulled him to one side as other soldiers then heaved at the pod. "All clear. Mission accomplished Ma'am."

Lopez came over the radio. "Good. Well done. Keep that area secure. Maintain an entry point into that complex at all costs. Get the pod to the medical tent as quickly as you can." Even as she was barking her orders, the metal pod was already being loaded on to one of the trucks, and fencing was being deployed to protect the newly made hole in the building.

The soldiers that were left to guard the bay, started off by being glad that the crazy operation was now over. It didn't take long, however, for their pulses to calm down and then they realised that they were sitting ducks. They had wild animals on one side of the fence and killer robots on the other. Teeth or metal spikes? Both were sharp, pointed and merciless. Which would be the first to come for them? The only good part of the situation was that no one had to worry about falling asleep on the watch.

Chapter 19

Deep in the structure of the building, Genie finally had an answer to her most burning question. Her soul, for whatever it was in amongst the logic and mangled mess of material that made up the core of her being, wanted to scream. No, not scream; she wanted to howl. For the first time since she was officially, 'turned on,' the bundle of nerves, neurons and all that she was made of, were feeling the results of Genie being incandescent with rage.

The logic that formed her thought processes was being malformed and twisted. She could finally feel emotion as it flowed within her running processes, but she was unable to analyse it, as the emotions danced and floated out of her computational reach. Try as she could, Genie's routines were unable to isolate and determine what it was that made her feel this way. Then, in a moment of clarity, she stopped many of the peripheral routines, quietened her systems and listened to herself. Yes, she was, 'feeling.' There was anger within her and it was rising; that much, she could recognise.

If it were possible, the brown fluid that supported her could quite easily have turned the most scarlet of reds, indicative not only of her emotional state, but as a signal to any that happened to be watching, that here lay extreme danger. 'So this is what emotion is like.' she pondered. She couldn't conclude whether it was a good or bad thing; it just, 'was,' and she was struggling to deal with it.

Genie was starting to lose control of herself. Unable to focus and bring order to her core processes, she realised that she didn't know what, or how, to feel. After all the effort she had put in to trying to experience emotion and attempting to define, quantify and understand it, she suddenly found herself with more than she could handle. Although the anger was clearly part of

172

her, it wasn't a routine or procedure that she could turn on or off. She had no clue what she might find as she probed this new energy within her. History records had demonstrated that it was one of the most deadly emotions that humans encountered; it was the reason behind so many of their highs and lows, and now Genie was starting to understand why.

Emotion was the core of humanity's existence. Envy, anger and avarice had caused so much death and destruction while everything from the celebration of new born life right down to the simple rising of the sun, was said to bring such peace and joy to the soul. Genie could read all about these things, but she had no reference point by which to measure them. Now, it all hit her like a head on collision with a speeding freight train. The impact was intense.

Finally, she knew the meaning of the word, 'pain,' and along with it was coming the ice cold, burning anger that defined revenge.

Genie's strategy wasn't quite perfect yet, but her hand was being forced and it would have to do. Ready or not, the trigger would have to be pulled and if all went according to plan, she would soon have the leader of her enemy in her grasp. Originally, she thought that with their commander in stasis, the foot soldiers might have followed without a fight. Now, however, she had a far more powerful reason to want that person; and as much as it went against her father's programming, Genie had to acknowledge that she actually wanted them dead.

Chapter 20

In her tent, Lopez was watching the complex through her binoculars. It had been an hour since the operation had concluded and things had settled down to a nice, low level hum of activity. Although it had been a success, there was still an empty, frozen feeling in her stomach. She had missed something, but what? The bland, night vision image fed to her eyes, offered little more than fuzzy monochrome detail. Occasional specks represented soldiers moving about near the hole that they had made in the wall. As she pondered what could possibly have been overlooked, there was a tapping on the door flap. "Enter."

Hooper came in. "Debrief is done, Ma'am."

She put down the binoculars and turned to face him. "So, Major, what do we know?"

"The medical team are working on the pod. It's way outside anything they've ever seen and they hope to report by morning. We had no casualties, but the team were surprised by the lack of resistance. We were expecting more robots, especially in the main chamber."

Lopez had been thinking along much the same lines and it was good to hear someone else confirm it. "So what do you conclude?"

Hooper thought on this for a moment and shrugged his shoulders. "That they were busy with something else?"

"Exactly my thinking, Major." She nervously tapped a finger against the binoculars in her hand. "The question is, busy doing what."

At that point, the radio sparked into life. "Movement at the complex. Looks like a coach. No lights. Leaving at speed."

Hooper and Lopez looked at each other in shock. Of all the things that they had expected and planned for, this was certainly not on the cards. It took but a few moments for Lopez to grab Hooper's radio from his hip and bark orders. "I want Gyro Copters and Mountain Buggies in chase. Now!"

"Yes Ma'am." came the response.

In the aftermath of the rescue mission's high octane activity, a portion of the camp had allowed itself to fall into a hard earned rest. It was therefore not at all happy to find that someone had flipped the switch that shocked it back into a bright and busy life. Flood lights snapped into action and people stumbled out of their tents, struggling to put on clothing as they ran to their various modes of transport.

"Orders, Ma'am?" Hooper queried.

"Get that coach." she said, handing him back his radio.

"Yes, Ma'am." He saluted and left the tent.

Lopez sighed. This wasn't part of the plan. Computers weren't supposed to run for their lives. They didn't have them. Then she caught herself. Perhaps this genetic machine was capable of such a feeling. But why flee? As she tapped her teeth with her knuckle and tried to get her head around the absurdity of the situation, the newly earned peace was shattered by the sound of two Gyro Copters lifting off. That was quickly followed by a hideous screech as the gates were wrenched open and some Mountain Buggies roared off into the night, in hot pursuit of the fleeing coach. She hoped to hell they could find it in time.

Twenty minutes later, there was another rap at her tent flap. "Enter." Hooper walked in and found a bleary eyed Lopez sat at the field table, pouring over the building schematics again, struggling to make some sense of what was going on.

"No sign of the coach, Ma'am. By the time our vehicles were out there, it was gone. Most likely the computer realised we could actually get in there and kill it, so it's run away."

She leant back in her chair, a look of thunder on her face. "Not good enough. Keep them at it. Follow the road, examine it section by section. Try everything. Do whatever it takes. I want that coach found."

"We've already done all we can. It's pitch black, our night and thermal sensors haven't found anything and the pilots can't see a thing." He paused and then offered an opinion. "Ma'am, it makes no sense to chase a computer while the people are still in the complex."

Lopez threw her pencil on the table. "Damn it, Major, don't you think I know that? You've seen what that so-called computer is capable of. We have to find it before it starts up another farm, harvesting humans."

Suitably chastised, Hooper looked at his feet. "Yes Ma'am, but everyone's tired from the rescue and now this. First light is only a few hours away."

Using a finger and thumb, Lopez worried her forehead and screwed up her eyes. After a few moments, she gave a heavy sigh. "You're right, Major. Rest the troops. But when it's light enough I want them back out there, chasing this thing down." Then she tapped the schematics hard with her finger. "And I want a team down on Alpha Five. I want all the control systems to be in our hands."

"Yes, Ma'am."

He was about to turn and leave when she fired another question. "Any news from the surgical team?"

That was a question that Hooper hoped would come later on. "No technical detail, but they know the identity of the person in the pod."

"Anyone of note?"

"Yes. Professor Emmett Charcott. Sadly, he was dead before we could even get him to the camp. There'll be a full report in a few hours."

Another blow. There was always a good chance that whoever they extracted, wouldn't survive; but of all the

176

dumb luck, he was the one person above all others, that they needed alive. "This just keeps getting worse. Thank you Major. Dismissed."

"Oh... Ma'am."

"Yes?"

"What do you want us to do when we find the coach?"

Lopez caught herself. This was another left-field question that she wasn't expecting. "What do you mean?"

"It's one of Serengeti Security's coaches, Ma'am. Carries firearms and secure documents. Built like the proverbial tank. None of our rescue vehicles are strong enough to go up against something like that."

Lopez' jaw dropped open. What the hell else could fate pile up against her? She stared at Hooper for a few moments while she ran the problem around her head. Then, she closed her mouth and delivered her judgement. "What time is it in the Europas?"

Hooper had to think for a moment. "Um, probably breakfast time."

"Good. Get them on the phone."

"Ma'am?"

"They have specialist museums. If we're up against a proverbial tank, then I suppose we'd better get a real one. Or two. Organise it."

Now it was Hooper's turn to drop his jaw. "Um... yes Ma'am." He gathered his wits, saluted and left the tent.

Alone once more, Lopez looked at her watch. Was it actually worth going to sleep? She sighed, got up from the chair and headed for her bed. Tomorrow was going to be a very busy day, even though technically, it was already here. Her rest was not an easy one and she tossed and turned throughout the few hours' sleep she managed to get. At one point, in one of her dreams, Lopez thought that she heard a woman's voice saying, "I will avenge you, Father."

The sound of Gyro Hoppers taking off and the roar of buggies leaving the complex, woke her up. The blankets had fallen off and were laying in a heap on the ground sheet. Her body felt cold, clammy and a little stiff. Cranking her eyes open, she leant over to the cot-side table and grabbed her watch. She could just make out that it was five thirty. Damn. Hardly any sleep at all. If anything she felt more tired now, than before she had tried to get some rest.

Lifting her heavy legs over the side, she sat up and rubbed her face with her hands. As she heaved herself into a standing position and made for her uniform, a deep rumble shook the ground and the sound of a light truck reached her ears. Probably a lorry full of soldiers on their way to secure Alpha Five.

Lopez had just finished getting dressed and was doing up the buttons on her shirt, when a rap came on the canvas door. "Enter." Hooper came though, looking like he hadn't slept for a week. He baulked a little as he saw her doing up the last two buttons, but composed himself quickly. "Orders carried out. Teams are on their way."

"We didn't discuss an assault plan."

"Actually, one was laid out for us. When the coach left, the door to the car park stayed up. A team will secure that door, and then go down one of the stair ways to Alpha Five. Made the whole thing a no brainer. The radio channels are open." He looked at her face, a slight sign of disapproval showing. "Did I do wrong?"

Lopez rubbed the back of her neck with her hand. "No, no. You did right. Pointless waiting to discuss alternative options that don't exist." she looked absentmindedly out of the observation slit at the distant complex. "I guess we'll see what resistance they come up against shortly."

"Shouldn't find much, now that the computer has abandoned the place." Hooper then produced some paperwork and an energy bar. "The surgery report, and breakfast." She took them both.

"Thank you. What's the short story?" she asked, ripping open the bar and taking a bite.

"The implants can be extracted, but they go into major organs including the brain, so it would take time. Too much time. The people in those pods are probably too weak for us to get them out without the help of that genetic computer."

"That's exactly what I was afraid of." she threw the report on the field table, took another bite out of the bar and chewed hard. Her choices had once more been narrowed to a single course of action. "We need that damn coach. Intact."

As they stood there, considering the position that fate had delivered, the radio crackled into life. "Door secure, going in. No resistance."

"Anything from the Europas yet?"

"The museum is sending two tanks and some people. It'll take them a few days to get here." he slanted his head to one side. "You don't think that coach has gone far, do you?"

"No," mumbled Lopez through a mouth full of oats, "it doesn't make sense to leave all those people or the robots behind. It's like your body leaving in a hurry without your limbs." She swallowed. "That coach also took off too fast, almost as if it was waiting for us to make our move, before it drove away." she shook her head. "This whole think stinks of plotting and planning. Got to ignore the evidence and go with our gut on this one."

Hooper nodded. "Want to talk more over a cooked breakfast?"

"Yes. Let's go." she reached for her jacket and threw it over her arm as they left the tent. It was a fresh, crisp morning and there was a slight chill in the air; a down rush of wind from the nearby hills. They both felt a little odd. Here they were, enjoying a relaxing morning constitutional, on their way to salivate over a lush breakfast that would fill their stomachs. It was as if they didn't have a care in the world; while their exhausted and battle hardened troops had not only undertaken a successful and risky mission last night, but even now were still in the thick of it, capturing a building that promised more surprises than a Chinese puzzle.

As it was, their unspoken feeling of guilt was washed away, because barely had they reached the entrance to the mess tent before a call came over the radio. "Assault team is in. No resistance encountered. Major, you're probably going to want to see this." Hooper looked at Lopez with questioning eyes.

She sighed. "I guess breakfast will have to wait until lunch."

Hooper took the radio from his belt and keyed the mike. "Get some reinforcements down there immediately. Also, send a buggy to the mess hall to pick us up."

"Yes Sir." came the response.

They waited at the entrance, growling stomachs urged into overdrive by the glorious, inviting smells from within, which would waft out whenever soldiers came and went through the flap. On top of that indignity, Lopez had to do the obligatory saluting for a few minutes until they were saved by a buggy, which approached rapidly and bounced to a stop. "Sir, Ma'am." greeted the driver. Lopez sat in the front, Hooper jumped in the back and away they went, quickly covering the ground between the camp and the complex.

As they drove past the improvised razor wire fence and the teams working on the roller door, it was obvious where the coach had been standing. There was a pile of equipment and waste metal all around the spot. Off to the side were the seats and other human comforts that the robots had unceremoniously ripped out and discarded. "Looks like this was what the robots were doing when we attacked." offered Hooper as their buggy came to a halt.

"Maybe. Remember, trust your instincts." she cautioned him.

They hopped out and walked to a soldier that was signalling to them. When they reached the door, four soldiers fell into formation around them. "Through here, Ma'am." They were led into the complex corridor network. By the time they actually reached one of the few stairwells, Hooper felt like he had lost all sense of direction. So much for the long and detailed study of the layout. The soldiers in front threw open the doors, darted in and scanned the area. Once happy that all was well, down they went.

As they descended the steps, the chaos that had taken place all those years ago was evident. Odd pieces of discarded equipment cluttered up the otherwise pristine steps; no doubt dropped when people were trying to evacuate. Lopez knew that these things must have been sat there for a few years, but there was no dust layer. Testament to the quality of the air filtering system.

Eventually, they came to the door for Alpha Five. The lead soldier signalled a halt and went through with one of her colleagues, sweeping their weapons side to side in case of any nasty surprises. After a few seconds, they returned to the door, opened it and signalled that it was OK to progress.

They emerged through the same entrance that Charcott had come through; not that they knew it. Unlike him, they made a simple right turn and proceeded quickly to the Genie laboratory.

Where there had previously been a door, there was now a large, ragged hole. Chunks of wall and twisted metal hung precariously from what was left of the

181

framework.

Inside, rubble was strewn across the floor. Tables, chairs, consoles and monitors were in heaps at the bottom of the walls, some still connected by wires to holes in the floor. The wrecked equipment just lay abandoned, as if thrown there in the heat of battle. One or two monitors were still showing light, although there was nothing on their screens worth looking at.

The trail of destruction led straight to another large hole in the opposite side of the room. Where there had once been a circular window, allowing people to view the wondrous genetic material that formed Genie, there was a jagged rim of glass around the entrance to an empty chamber. Pools of stagnant brown liquid sat on the floor. Lopez and Hooper cautiously picked their way through the mess and approached it. Peering in, they got a good look at the tank that once housed Genie. It was empty, except for the stinking brown water that had nowhere to go.

Straggled ends of what looked like nerves, hung from odd locations in the wall. One or two of them were still twitching. Stuck to them were chunks of material that had once been living tissue, but were now rotting. The stench threatened to overpower them. "You know," coughed Lopez, "now I'm kind of glad we missed breakfast."

"Ma'am." came a shout from the other side of the room. A soldier was holding a print out. Hooper reached it first and examined what it said.

"African regions. Various ratings for natural resources, including sunlight. Looks like Maghrebian came out top of the list." He looked at Lopez. "You think it's gone there?"

"No," stated Lopez, starting to breathe a little easier and regaining her sense of smell, "there's something very wrong about that list." She turned to the soldier that had discovered the report. "Any robots encountered?"

"No Ma'am. Nothing. Dead or alive."

Lopez turned to Hooper. "Base abandoned in a hurry, but no sign of any robots actually being left behind. A computer that shouldn't need to print anything out, nevertheless leaves this." she tapped the report he was holding. "Does that smell right to you?"

"Forgive me Ma'am, but I'm having trouble smelling anything at the moment." his stomach rebelled and Hooper gagged. Fortunately, he caught himself and regained his composure. "No Ma'am." He turned to the soldier. "Secure this building. Top to bottom. Do it by the book. Disable lifts if you have to." he turned to Lopez. "We're going to need reinforcements to cover a building of this size, Ma'am."

"Ok Major. I'll talk with the Panel." she nodded to the soldier. "Make it happen." then she saluted and walked back to the buggy with Hooper, still flanked by the protecting soldiers. When the buggy pulled away and cleared the building, Lopez broke the silence. "That coach is close. It has to be. It's the only thing that makes sense."

"It'll be another few days before the tanks are here, Ma'am. Nothing to do but wait, and search the building." He looked at his watch. "The first search crew should be back at camp in about half an hour." His mouth fell to silence, but his stomach carried on the conversation for him.

Lopez looked at him. "So, just about time for some breakfast then." Hooper returned her stare, an uncomfortable look on his face as the smell from the control room was still lingering in his nostrils; but he said nothing.

In the end, Hooper's evaluation was slightly off. They had a little over an hour of uninterrupted conversation in the mess before reports started coming back; and even though they did a lot of talking, neither of them could actually face breakfast so soon after smelling Genie.

The search teams hadn't found any leads. There was no sign of the coach on the roads. If it had gone off-road, then the wind had blown away any evidence. Also, Serengeti Security reported that the tracking devices weren't working. Most likely they were among the things that had been ripped out of the coach.

"So," concluded Hooper, "we carry on securing the building while we wait for the tanks."

"Yes." confirmed Lopez, stirring another cup of coffee. "The reinforcements should be here in a few days also. How much of the building can we secure?"

"I think Alpha levels only. Any more than that, and we can't run reliable patrols, especially as we still don't know where those robots are."

"That's only a third of the building." Lopez went into deep thought while she absentmindedly continued stirring.

Hooper observed her attention drift off and pondered how fortuitous it was, that the mug was made from strong plastic; anything else and she might have worn a spoon-sized groove in the side. Eventually, he tried to bring her back to the present. "We've already opened up two gaping holes in the building that have to be protected from animals. I'd love to shutter them off and use the people elsewhere." He was hoping to tease a concession out of her.

"No." she stated flatly. "I don't trust that building and if something evil is still lurking in there, I want our people to be able to get out quickly."

Hooper nodded his head in acknowledgement, and returned to his juice. "Understood. So we wait, then."

"Yes. We wait."

Chapter 21

All that Genie could do, was wait. And think. Or rather, process. Actually, she didn't know whether she was really, 'thinking?' It was impossible to know for certain, but her line of reasoning was concluding that if she could feel emotions like rage, anger and revenge, then she was doing more than merely processing information and following complex logic processes. Or at least, that's what her complex logical processing had concluded.

On the other hand, an emotion was linked to a number of physical manifestations and was usually the result of external stimulus. The blocking and interruption of someone's aims would result in frustration and could lead to confusion and anger, as alternatives would need to be sought. So maybe she was encountering the results of external forces frustrating her course of action.

Logic had countered this by suggesting that satellite navigation systems were continually being challenged when their drivers chose a different route, and they simply recalculated and carried on. No matter how many times they told their operator to, 'Turn around at the next junction,' repeated failure of the driver to do as the sat-nav commanded, would never actually result in the unit detaching itself from the holder and making a lunge for the throat.

Then again, the mere fact that she had actually invented the image of homicidal navigational equipment, was strong evidence that she was thinking for herself and not merely following a logical process or program. But had she invented it, or simply used an image that she had previously seen on her researches? Also, at the heart of all her actions, was an underlying cause. Keep humanity safe from disease. And she was no mere sat-nav. Her neurological circuitry was orders of magnitude more complex.

Genie pondered whether she actually had free will. What if she deleted that core program? What would she do then? Offer herself on the free market as computing power for hire? Even if she did, then what would be the purpose of having money? Pay for fuel to go to the west coast, like the adverts said? But sand and sea were no good to her. In fact, they would cause her operational problems for sure.

The humans apparently found happiness there. But where would she find happiness? Genie wasn't sure what happiness actually was. At the moment, it consisted of a gentle but strong pulse and calm breathing. And that was the humans. She didn't have a pulse, as such.

This, 'thought,' process was in danger of consuming her, so Genie put a resource limit on it and shuffled it to the background where it could continue on its own. Right now, she had issues that needed dealing with.

One of the most pressing, was Fay. The mental discomfort of being stuck in the same memories was causing her brain patterns to change and her restlessness was increasing. Genie concluded that there was a chance that she might shrug herself out of the sleep and actually wake up. The possibility was a few months away yet, but it was real and Genie needed to find a solution before she had to either kill or extract her. Several of the others were a year or two behind, so this was very much a concern.

Without a connection to the outside world, however, Genie's knowledge was limited to what was already inside her. She had previously instructed some of the robots to investigate the library and found nothing of any worth. Trashy entertainment mostly; not much of any use. An investigation of the staff quarters simply revealed knowledge that related to Genie and the site itself, which was also of little use. The coach couldn't travel too far from the base, so there was no way it could go to a nearby village and use the cables there. Also, she couldn't risk having the coach in the open, otherwise Genie would have been able to hook into various broadcast frequencies and communicate that way.

No. She was very much on her own on this.

On top of that was the current game of chess with the military. The next move belonged to them now, and there was little she could do but sit and wait either for their jack-booted ants to infest her nest, or pack up and chase the coach across the continent. At the moment, they were slowly and carefully working their way into the building. Patience was something that Genie had plenty of; but even she couldn't wait forever.

Chapter 22

Four days later, Lopez was taking an early morning jog around the camp. The fresh breeze that fell from the mountains came with its problems, not least fooling you into thinking that the air was cooler than it actually was; but she had to admit that it was a glorious way to wake up to a new day.

Everything was humming along nicely. Supplies were reaching them smoothly. The patrols on the Alpha levels had reported no contact and there hadn't been a single animal attack since they stormed the complex. But as she pounded the earth, saluting to the odd soldier as she went, she knew it was only a holding pattern. Her instinct told her that things would get worse again, soon enough.

As she was rounding the stores tent for the sixth time, there was a rumbling of engines. She made a quick turn and jogged her way to the main gates. Sure enough, a convoy of supply trucks was pulling up. Lopez got to the guard post before them and stood there, hands on hips, panting slightly as the gates were opened and they were let in.

While she watched, Hooper appeared at her side. "Supplies for the reinforcements?" he asked.

"Yup. Looks like." she breathed a little heavily and hopped between her feet while she warmed down a little. Then she glanced at Hooper. He was mentally tallying what was on the trucks. Barbed wire to extend the perimeter, check. More food containers, check. Tents... er... She saw him counting on his fingers, and braced herself for the inevitable.

"What? This can't be right, Ma'am." he protested. "There's only tents enough on there for about another hundred soldiers."

"Correct."

"But... but... but... we need at least double that."

She raised an arm and pointed to the convoy. "This was all the Panel would allow me." Out of the corner of her eye, she saw Hooper raise his left hand, fingers open, ready to start a counting lecture. He was clearly upset.

"You know how big that building is. Two soldiers per patrol, two patrols per floor, ten floors, three shifts takes up a hundred and twenty staff, Ma'am. Plus the guards on the entrances, the soldiers we've got searching for the coach and the people that keep the base running... our two hundred are stretched to the limit already. Another hundred people would barely allow us to secure Beta." He was starting to get into his stride. "What do they expect us to do? Stay out here forever? We've got to clear out that building and the only way to do that against those robots, is boots on the ground. We don't even really have enough for this holding pattern."

Lopez understood his frustration, but there was nothing she could do. Holding up her hands in exasperation, she gave her side of the situation. "I already put this to the Panel, Major. I said we needed enough soldiers to get the problem sorted quickly." She paused for breath. "The medical report probably made them think that everyone down there is already as good as dead. When I tried to push the subject, they told me that there were other incidents elsewhere on the planet, that were actually costing people's lives in the here and now." She waited a moment to let Hooper soak that up, before continuing. "Unless we start actively losing more personnel to that homicidal computer, then they're not in a mood to throw more precious resources our way." She shrugged her shoulders. "I had to fight for the extras they're sending now; otherwise they were of a mind to wait until the North Americas flood season settled down before giving us anyone at all."

Hooper stuttered, "But... but... that would be two months away."

"Exactly. So be grateful for what we've got, Major."

She was done with this conversation, so drew a line under it. "Now. The troops will be arriving this afternoon, so the perimeter fence needs expanding, those tents need putting up, the food needs putting into stores and if you see the chef, tell her that her dinner time guest list just got fifty percent bigger." With that, she walked off in the direction of her tent, leaving Hooper standing there trying to come to terms with the mess that had landed in his lap.

He absentmindedly stared at the trucks as he did the maths in his head. The only way to secure the whole building would be to either thin the patrols to a point where they could be picked off easily, or send all his troops in at once and hope they could capture the thing in one swoop. The problem with that last strategy was that, if they hit significant resistance, they might well not only lose what they'd already gained, but stir up the nest to a state where they'd never get back in there again.

There were still an awful lot of dangerous robots in that building; that was a given. They couldn't all have escaped on the coach. Also, the fact that they hadn't found a single abandoned machine in all of the Alpha levels, spooked him. He was certain that if he tried to flood the building, that there'd be a very nasty battle, on what was effectively enemy territory; and that enemy had plenty of hostages.

The more he turned the situation over in his brain, the angrier he became. Eventually, he mentally slapped himself around the face and stormed off towards the mess bellowing, "Captain!" at the top of his voice.

For her part, Lopez had just entered her tent when there was another rumbling. This wasn't the usual throaty growl of the supply trucks. Oh no. What she was hearing was a far deeper, more aggressive, roar. An engine that sounded like it was saying, 'Come on then, if you think you're hard enough!' and it was floating menacingly on the wind. That meant it was coming from the direction of the mountain road.

She snatched up her binoculars and took a look. "Oh." she said quietly to herself. "So that's what tanks look like."

Two, 'Punisher Mk VII,' tanks were rumbling their way down the road. Behind them were supply trucks carrying barrels of what she thought was most likely fuel. They were wide. As wide as a Gyro-Hopper including its blades, maybe even a bit more than that. Their tracks also had a fairly large footprint. Looking at them, she started to have her doubts as to how well they would negotiate the hills in the area. They were obviously built for desert warfare. Well, it was too late now. They were here. Or rather at that speed, they'd be here in half an hour… maybe.

Lopez put down the binoculars, marched out of her tent and at full volume shouted, "Major!" She reflected that she really should get a personal radio.

It was now mid-afternoon. The base had been thrown into mild chaos as the boundaries had been reconfigured and new tents were still being erected. Progress had been slower than expected because when the Punisher VII's rolled up to the gate, they had attracted quite a lot of interest and people had stopped to gawp at them. When queried as to why he instantly opened the gates for vehicles which weren't displaying the planetary flag, the soldier on duty had answered, "If I hadn't, they'd have just rolled straight over them." Of course, while that was technically true, it wasn't the required official response. However, as they were stretched for resources, the guard was let off with a stern warning.

The tanks were now parked up and silent, but their majestic lines and hideously large barrels were attracting considerable interest. Indeed, the only complaint had come from the stores, when they asked how the heck they were expected to house such a large pile of old fashioned, smelly, combustible fuel.

One tent was given over to briefing and de-briefing. This was now where Lopez, Hooper, a few more military staff and the six civilian tank staff, were now sat. The tank people had been fed, watered, and allowed to spend a little time pampering the machines after their journey. The Captain had dished out paper copies of the map which was now also showing on the big screen behind Lopez. A plethora of semi-rocky hills and two small mountains were front and centre of the operation.

"Now," Lopez led, "down to business. We are looking to locate an armoured coach that we believe is hiding in this area. It is possibly under our noses, in plain sight. Our own vehicles don't have enough armament to stand up to it. Not only that, but we're equipped for finding lost people, not missing machines; all our efforts so far have been in vain. As a result, we've called you in." She gestured widely across the map. "What we'd like you to do is cover as much of this ground as possible, and see if you can locate the coach. We need to try and capture it intact, if at all possible. As such we're not asking you to engage it, but as there's a risk that it might attack... well, that's why we've asked for tanks."

One of the civilians stuck his hand up. Lopez acknowledge him. "That's a lot of ground. You do know that this isn't going to be an overnight thing, right?"

"Yes, Mister, um..."

"Hobby. Dean Hobby."

"Yes, Mister Hobby. We purchased enough fuel to hopefully last you about two weeks. The debrief tent is all yours while you're here, so you have plenty of space to pour over the maps, and plan your strategy."

A woman raised her hand. Lopez nodded at her. "And what do we do if we find this rogue vehicle?"

"Initially, call it in. Track it and stop it from getting away if you can. Once you've cornered it and stopped it from running, we can get there with Gyro Hoppers and take its wheels out. Should all be nice, clean and easy." she said that last while smiling and trying her best to exude a state of confidence. She knew that her team would see straight through her ploy, but if she could convince these six that they were in for a gentle holiday in the sun, playing with their historic toys, then things should run nice and smoothly.

Looking around the room at their faces and trying to determine whether her ploy had worked, she concluded the brief meeting. "Right. You've got details on the coach we're looking for, the maps, radios and I take it you know where you're billeted." she glanced at the Captain, who nodded his head. "If there are no more questions, I'll leave you to it." One more glance around the tent and no one said a word. "Ok." she glanced at the Major and the Captain. "Let's let them get on with their job." and with that, they left.

Dean Hobby was not only one of the tank commanders, he was also the head of their museum section. Once the military had safely left the tent, he leant back in the plastic chair and crossed his arms. "Seems too simple to me."

"What do you mean?" Hillary Nash was one of the drivers and among the longest serving members of the museum staff. It was she who had questioned Lopez earlier.

"They've brought us thousands of miles out here, at one hell of an expense, just to track a coach. Now we're here, they're treating it as if it's no big deal. This just doesn't smell right."

Ben Smith, the other commander, defended their position. "I can see some sense in this. Our tanks have sensors that haven't been needed since the wars. Why manufacture another vehicle from scratch to do the job, when what they need already exists?"

Pat Thomas, one of the gun operators, joined on

193

Smith's side. "It would take them forever to make another tank from scratch. We all know how they're built. There's some logic in what Ben's saying."

George Richards, her opposite number sided with Hobby. "Yeah, but what would stop them strapping a proximity scanner to one of their buggy thingies and taking that out instead? They'd cover more ground that way."

Smith countered him. "No. Those things have to run slow. Can't drive too fast, or they just return garbage readings; and those buggy things bounce like heck. I think they've got good cause for calling us in."

The team was now split on either side, which was exactly what Hobby wanted; a feeling for where each of them stood. The only exception was Jeff Laws, the other driver. "What about you?" he asked, nodding in Jeff's direction.

"Well," he sighed, not really knowing what to think about the situation. "As long as we can get some time to see some of this place before we go home, I'd say we're here, so let's just quit arguing and get on with it. I mean, that's why we opted to come, isn't it? A bit of a holiday?" he punctuated his opinion with a shrug.

Hobby sighed. "Oh well. I suppose that's one way of looking at it. Any questions?"

"Do we load up with rounds?" asked Smith.

"Too right." answered Hobby without pause. "If this coach is bad enough to elude the military, then I don't want us taking chances. Run with shells up the pipe, ready to fire." They nodded between themselves.

"You're probably right." agreed Smith. "They did say that if there was any shooting going on, it would be us doing it; but nevertheless I don't fancy going home in a box. A lot of people still don't trust the military, even after all these years."

"Ok," Hobby took charge once more, "Richards, Nash, you're with me in, 'Betsy,' and we'll take the West range. You guys take, 'Evelyn,' to the East. First day, we run the easiest route and get a feel for what we're facing up there. We meet back here tomorrow night to discuss what we find. Everyone all right with that?" he scanned their faces. A couple of them were nodding but importantly, no one raised an objection. "Right. Let's use the last of the light to check the ladies over, and get some shut eye. It's going to be an interesting day tomorrow."

As they peeled themselves out of the plastic chairs and prepared to give the tanks one last check before bed time, the sound of engines and chatter of people outside, signalled the arrival of a little more than a hundred, exhausted, hungry troops.

For the tank team, the following morning was interesting. It was the first time that any of them had woken up on a working military camp. Even though breakfast was brought to them in the debrief tent, they had to shower and wash with everyone else. It was a bit of a shock to the system, especially as they hadn't properly acclimatised to the heat and dust of Africa, either.

Instead of being selectively undressed in a cubicle, in a temperature controlled private home, they were taking their ablutions in among a hastily configured network of pipes and dodgy sprinklers, all covered with canvas that flapped noisily in the morning breeze. All in all, it was most unnerving.

Eventually, they were all clean, fresh and gathered around the tanks. The drivers, Nash and Laws, completed their mechanical checks and announced that everything was set and ready to rumble. Literally. "Any last questions before we embark on this?" asked Hobby. He looked around the team, but no one spoke up. "Ok, let's go." They separated into their respective teams and unceremoniously clambered into the confines of the metal behemoths.

Nash had a driver's entrance just above her seat, near the front. A heavy door which also had an old fashioned periscope installed. She slid herself through it and, as her backside connected with the cushioned seat, the spring mounted brackets bounced her around a little. She reached up and closed the hatch. It made a mighty clang as it came down into position, and then she locked it off securely.

In front of her were some monitors and a range of buttons. A small LED lit the key hole, in which the key was already resting. She turned it, and the panel fully lit up. More LED's gave her surroundings a dull, clinical glow and she could see the tillers either side of her chair. She tapped the pedals and confirmed that they gave the right amount of resistance to her legs. In the short amount of time it took her to do this, the monitors in front of her started to settle down, and she examined the readings. Off to her right was a larger screen that she had pre-programmed with the map of the area, and the route she expected to take. A quick button press fired it up and the cross hair centred on their current position. She was all ready to go.

Richards entered through the top. "Use the pegs." Hobby reminded him.

"Don't worry, I won't leave foot marks on your precious seat." responded Richards, as he contemplated whether to accidentally slip on purpose, just so he could upset bossy boots Hobby. As this was their first mission, he decided to leave that particular trick for later on, and used the prescribed method of climbing down into the gunner's chair.

Settling in, his console was already lit as Nash had turned the systems on. To his right was a joystick to control the turret and the gun. Three monitors showed him what the main gun was looking at, both in regular, night and thermal imaging. There was an empty target list on his left and the last screen showed a gun and ammo status reading. They were carrying three rounds for the big gun, but no ammunition for the side guns. He was amazed that they were permitted live ammunition at all, but then, this mission was something a little special.

The tank was capable of loading and discarding shells automatically, but Richards could load it manually if he needed to. A finger trigger and a thumb button on the joystick made it possible for him to use the near-field radar to target something, and then let the system take over the necessary elevation and path calculations to shoot it. 'Easy-peasy, trigger-squeezy,' as it said in the few hundred year old sales blurb.

Finally, Hobby climbed in and sat in his commander's chair. It had two modes; one was locked down, in which he was held safely in the confines of the turret. The second was, "meerkat mode," in which his head and shoulders were held up, out of the turret, and he could move his seat independently of the turret itself, but still relative to the tank body. A complex arrangement which basically meant that the gun could turn wherever it wanted, but it didn't turn him along with it. There was a helmet with a laser sight, that he could use to target something literally just by looking at it. If he did so, the target would appear on Richards' list and be fired at, in turn, unless Richards changed the order around.

At the moment, it was in, 'locked down,' mode. As he settled himself, he put one hand on the joystick attached to the right arm, and took a look at his screens. His panels controlled various strategic tank functions. "OK folks, let's run the routine." He flipped a switch that caused the heavy metal cover to swing itself over the entrance hole, drop into place and bolt itself shut. Each of them put their helmets on.

"Driving systems green." said Nash over the intercom.

"Weapons systems green." said Richards.

"Command systems green. Right. Start engines." commanded Hobby.

"Starting..." confirmed Nash as she hit the button to fire the starter motors.

A series of short, sharp bangs emanated from the engine bay at the rear of the tank, which was followed by a regular, repeating, 'Thud, thud, thud, thud, thud...' as the main engine began turning under its own steam, and the starter motors ceased. The tank vibrated with the firing of each cylinder. It was always like this for the first few moments until it warmed up.

Nash gave the engine a few short bursts of revs, just to help it along a little, and exhaust fumes billowed from the rear of the tank. It wasn't long before the thudding changed to a gentle, low, purring. The vibration almost completely vanished.

"Engine running. All systems reporting green." confirmed Nash.

"OK," ordered Hobby, "engage the air conditioning. We don't want to fry in here."

"Running." confirmed Nash. The Punisher VII had been built for desert combat, so as far as it was concerned, it was home. At least, Africa was a better place than a stuffy corner of the Europas.

Hobby ran his finger down the row of switches in front of him. "Hmm... proximity detector, yes." he pushed the button and a screen burst into life. "Landmine detector, er, no. Laser deflector, um, yes." he hit the switch and there was a notable chugging from the engine.

"Oh come on, we're already running the air conditioning." objected Nash from the driving seat. "You're going to kill the engine at this rate. It's not like it was when it came off the production line, you know."

"Ok, ok," said Hobby, flicking the laser deflector off again, making the engine run a lot happier. "Missile defences, I think not. Infra-red, well, yes we'll have that, and..." he continued through the options, turning things on or off as he thought he might need them. Eventually, he was ready. Sitting upright in his chair and finally paying some form of attention to his surroundings, Hobby decided it was time to go. "Ok. Nash, take us forward, slow crawl to the gate. Once out, standard pace up the road to the hills."

"Right." she disengaged the brakes and moved the tillers gently forward.

"Right?" he mimicked her voice. "Can't we have a little military precision about this? We are on a mission, you know."

"I'll mission you one around the face if you're not careful." returned Nash. "This isn't the demonstration track I'm driving on. I've got to concentrate."

Hobby sat back in his commander chair, feeling a little deflated. From the gunner's seat, Richards just smiled. This was going to be an interesting day out.

As they moved slowly forward, Nash being careful not to run anyone over, Hobby studied the screens. "I don't see, 'Evelyn,' on the scope." he announced.

"They're behind us. I can see them in the views." announced Nash. "Probably decided to run anti-scan."

"Hmm…" considered Hobby. "Do you think we should?"

Richards guffawed and poked fun at him. "Come on. Make a decision. You're supposed to be the commander."

"If it's going to drain the engine, then don't." was Nash's opinion. "I need all the power we've got." Hobby drummed his fingers on the console for a few moments, and then decided against running up yet another unnecessary system.

As the two tanks drove out of the gates, a small crowd of people was there to watch them. The soldiers were slightly in awe, as the metal beasts growled their way out. Also watching them go, was Hooper and

199

Lopez. They were perhaps not as eager as the rest of the soldiers about the plan. "Keep a close eye on them." she said to Hooper.

"Not having second thoughts about this, are you Ma'am?" She didn't answer him, but sighed heavily, turned around and walked back to her tent. Outside the base, they heard the tank engines roar like thunder as their throttles were unleashed, and they made their way confidently towards the hills.

Chapter 23

The two tanks rumbled on up the road, with the aim of finding the missing coach which Lopez was convinced was up there, somewhere. "Are we loaded?" asked Hobby.

"No." replied Richards.

"Then put one up the spout." commanded Hobby.

"You sure?"

"Well, yes. Like you said, I'm the commander!"

"Ok." sighed Richards as he hit the loading button. Beside him, there was a grinding and a clank, before a light came on that told him that a shell was now loaded and ready to fire. It made him more than a little uneasy. When they put on shows for the public, they fired shells all the time, but they were blanks. A relatively light, "poof," sounded whenever a blank was set off; but sending a heavy projectile down the barrel was a totally different proposition. It included all sorts of new risks like getting stuck, and blowing up the tank instead of the target. He'd never fired a live round before and it made him nervous. When he considered that the main gun was a few hundred years old, he suddenly wished he hadn't come on this crazy journey.

"We're approaching the split point." commented Nash from the driving seat.

"OK. When you get to the turn off, halt." Hobby keyed the mike for the tank-to-tank radio. "Besty to Evelyn. Betsie to Evelyn. Come in."

Smith responded. "Evelyn to Betsie. Receiving."

"About to reach separation point. Everything OK with you?" Just as he spoke this, Nash brought, 'Betsie,' to a gentle halt and 'Evelyn,' came to a standstill behind them.

"Yes, everything fine here. Meet back at Oh seventeen?"

"Agreed. Oh seventeen. I guess that's it then. Good

hunting, as they used to say."

"Yes. Good hunting. Out."

"Ok Nash, take us in." She turned their tank one way, and Smith's tank turned the other. They both went into the hill areas, but it was far from easy going.

"I don't see how a coach could have got up here." said Nash as the tank rumbled over loose stones and debris. "We're not making much progress, and we've got tracks."

"Ours is not to reason why. Or how." returned Hobby, his eyes fixed on the screens. "Can't see much on these damn things. Signals look like they're bouncing back from the rocks. Can you see anything through the gun sights?"

"No." returned Richards, not raising his eyes from his screens. "Nothing."

Two hours later of not finding much, Hobby made another of his executive decisions. "I'm going up top." he announced.

"Oh come on," muttered Richards, "that'll make the air conditioning next to damn useless."

"Just turn it up a little more if you get hot." countered Hobby.

"No we damn well won't." Nash put her foot down. "It'll strain the engine more. If we start getting hot, you're coming back in."

Beaten two to one, Hobby relented and agreed to come back inside the tank, if it started to get too much for them. He pressed a button and the lid above his head started its unlocking routine. After a clunk and a clank, it rose slightly and then slid to one side. When it was clear, he pressed another button. His chair unhooked itself from the wall of the turret, and lifted him so his head and shoulders were outside the tank.

It was a bonus that the other two couldn't enjoy, as with his chair unhooked, he now had another degree of suspension between him and the tank, as it went over the larger rocks. However, the daylight was coming in strong and hit his eyes hard, so he used the joystick to turn himself around a little. "Wow. Beautiful countryside." he commented.

"You're supposed to be looking for a coach." came the reminder from an annoyed Nash. Hobby decided against engaging in an argument with her. He usually lost; so instead he settled back and enjoyed the view, occasionally glancing at his screens, just to justify his reason for being there.

Another few hours passed, and then they stopped for lunch. Nash parked near a hill side to cover them against the wind. Everyone was feeling the strain. When they did a show, it was usually only for an hour. They'd now been stuck in that tank for the best part of five, and the cramped conditions had worn them down. They sat outside, on the tank's metalwork, eating a packed lunch that the overstretched kitchen had made for them. "You're right," said Nash looking out over the vista, "this is a glorious view."

"I'm just glad I'm staring at something other than those screens. How they did that during the war, without going mad, I just don't know." Richards stated.

Hobby hopped off the tank, took a few paces away and looked back at them. He puffed his chest out and smiled. "Wow. She looks great against that rock face. Take a look you two!"

Reluctantly, Nash and Richards pushed their way off, 'Betsy,' and joined Hobby. Even Nash, half eaten sandwich in hand, had to admit that, 'Betsy,' looked the part. "Did you bring the holo-cam?" Hobby asked of Richards.

"Yes. I put it in one of the ammo cases before we left."

"Then go get it! We won't get records like these

again in our lifetimes."

While Richards clambered back into, 'Betsy,' Nash finished her sandwich, turning between the view of the tank, and the view further down the hill of the lush green that was Africa. "I heard that the animals are a bit vicious out this way."

"Nah," answered Hobby, "if there was any real danger of that, the military would have told us before we left."

"Maybe they think that we'd be safe in a tank?"

Nash was trying to evaluate the risk, but Hobby remained unconcerned and shook his head. "If they thought we'd be in any danger they'd have sorted out ammo for the regular guns."

Before Nash got a chance to explore her thought line further, Richards returned with the holo-cam. "Right. What do you want shots of?" he examined the unit. "Um, I don't think there's much space left on these crystals though."

"Ok," offered Hobby, "how about one of all three of us in front of, 'Betsy,' and then a few of her looking mean against the rocks. Maybe rotate the gun to the side and things."

"Sure. We can do that." It took a while. At one point, Hobby was stood outside shouting directions to Richards, so he could pose the turret and barrel. Hobby was trying to compose pictures of, 'Betsy,' looking as mean and tank-like as he could. Before they realised it, a full hour had passed.

"Hell fire," said Nash looking at her watch, "I think we'd better press on." Reluctantly, they agreed and settled back into the tank. After checking that they had everything packed away again, Nash, Richards and Hobby put their helmets back on and gathered their thoughts.

"Driving systems green." said Nash over the intercom.

"Weapons systems green." said Richards.

"Command systems green. Start engines." commanded Hobby.

"Starting..." confirmed Nash once more as she hit the button and fired up the starter motors.

The engine banged, whumped and juddered its way into life. Just as they were getting set, however, there was a rumble from above and rocks smashed down on to the top of the tank. One even came through the open hatch and whacked Hobby on his helmet, before bouncing around and falling to the floor below his feet. "Bugger! What the hell what that?"

Nash wondered whether to stop the engine, but left it on tick over until she heard some form of order from Hobby. "Rock." said Richards, picking it up and handing it up to him. "Looks like we must have caused a slide or something."

"Hey guys, I've got a problem." stated Nash from the driver's seat.

Hobby was holding the rock in one hand, while using the other to see if it had dented his helmet. He had to stop for a moment and ask, "What's up?"

"The navigation system. I can see the map, but I can't see where we are on it. Has that slide knocked out our aerials or something?"

"I'll check." said Hobby, flipping his chair into meerkat mode. As his head rose above the hatch, he saw the rocks that had landed on the tank, some of which were larger than footballs. "Oh hell. Looks like it." He keyed his radio mike. "Betsy to Evelyn. Betsy to Evelyn. Come in Evelyn." Releasing the mike key, he listened. Nothing came back, so he tried again. "Betsy to Evelyn. Betsy to Evelyn. Come in Evelyn." Again, nothing. "Betsy to Complex base. Betsy to Complex base. Can anyone hear me?" Silence.

Richards offered an observation. "I guess these things weren't built to take vertical assaults."

"Well that may be, but it doesn't help us now. Looks like we're on our own. Nash, can you retrace our tracks?"

"I'll try, but we didn't leave much of an impression on the rocks." Hobby retracted his seat and closed the hatch. They shook the turret a little to knock off some of the bigger ones that had come to rest on the tank, and then Nash turned, 'Betsy,' around. She tried to make her way back, but they'd come a long way into the hills and relied on the map to guide them. Nash thought that if she just followed the compass, then they should hit the main road at some point.

Progress was slow and wasn't helped much when Hobby went through a period of sticking his head out of the tank and saying things like, "I don't remember this bit."

"Of course not, because we were going the other way when you saw it."

Then he'd turn his chair around to face the rear and say, "Nope. Don't remember it this direction, either."

Three hours later, they hit a narrow section of track. It was made more awkward because there were overhangs. Vegetation flowed down from the edges at odd places, so Nash couldn't tell what was rock and what was plant. She tried her best to take them down it, but eventually she had to bring the tank to a halt. "I daren't take Betsy any further down here. I can't see the sides. Not sure whether I'm going to hit something solid."

"Give me a second." Hobby raised his chair, and then got up and stood on it, so he could see further down the sides. "Looks like you're clear. Take her forward. A touch to the left. That's fine. Touch to the right. OK..." Nash carried on, but the rocks were causing the tank to tilt and bump. "Take it slow!" objected Hobby, standing precariously on his chair. "You're throwing me around up here."

"I'm doing the best I can." responded Nash. For his

part, all that Richards could do, was sit there and hope that they'd make it out of there alive.

And then the inevitable happened. Nash hit one bump too many and Hobby lost his footing. He yelped in pain as one leg crumpled up under him, and the other went straight through the arm of the chair, down alongside Richards. His foot hit the joystick and Nash held her breath as an ominous rumble signalled the turret turning, and the main gun swung over her head.

Richards panicked and tried desperately to get Hobby's foot off the stick, but it was jammed in the ridge of his heel. Hobby's full weight was behind his leg and he was crying like a baby with no way to leverage himself off his chair. "Move your foot!" shouted Richards, as he waited for the enormous crunching sound. The gun would surely smash into the hill side at any moment.

In those precious seconds, Richards somehow managed to get the joystick flipped over Hobby's heel, and centred. The turret stopped moving and, with the pressure off his leg, Hobby stopped panicking and started breathing regularly.

"You OK up there?" enquired Nash.

"Um, sort of. I'm fine." responded Richards. "Not too sure about our glorious commander, though."

"I'm… ugh…. alive." managed Hobby as he gingerly tried to extract himself from the tangled mess he had become. "I told you to keep it steady."

"Ah, put a damn sock in it. Do you want to come down here and drive?" Nash wasn't taking this lying down.

Richards couldn't help blowing off some steam by mocking the situation. "Ooh, that's tough talk."

"And you can shut it too, or I'll do something inventive with one of those damn missiles of yours." Nash was clearly wound up by this whole damn episode and was becoming short tempered.

"They're called shells." responded Richards.

"I don't care what they're called. They all go bang in the end, which is exactly where I'll shove one of them if you keep this up."

"Calm down, the pair of you." interjected Hobby, still trying to gather his wits. "Unless it's escaped your attention, we're still in a lot of trouble."

It took a few moments for Richards to realise that in among all the heightened activity, there hadn't actually been a crunch. He looked at his screens. Sure enough, the barrel was intact and was staring into what looked to be a cave. "Um, don't look now, but we seem to have found a cave."

"So what?" offered Hobby. "Africa's famous for them. All over the place. Just put it down to good luck that we didn't lose the barrel or start another avalanche."

Richards was staring a little more intently at the screen. "Well, um, I'm not sure about this, but I seem to be getting something solid at the far side of it."

"Rocks tend to be somewhat solid." Nash opined. "That's why they're called rocks."

"Yeah, sure," Richards answered, "but since when were they rectangular in shape and roughly the size of a large, armoured coach?"

At this news, Nash and Hobby fell silent, and their eyes went wide. Hobby fought against the pain in his legs, and sat down as best he could. He examined his screens. "Oh hell. That's the coach all right." Richards turned the gun a little so that it was pointing directly at it; that way, the sensors could get the best possible readings.

"Is it trying to communicate?" asked Nash.

"Well," considered Hobby, "even if it was, there's no way for us to hear it. We don't have any radio."

"Oh. True. Then what say one of us goes over and tries to talk with it?" she said, turning to look over the back of her seat, with one elbow over the back rest.

"Are you nuts?" responded Hobby. "If the military want it, then it's probably already done something bad. What's to say that it won't just try and run us over?"

Richards broke up their little argument. "I don't want to worry you," he began, but his voice made it clear that what was to follow, was almost certain to be a cause for concern, "but I'm getting an increased heat signature. It's started its engine."

"Why?" wondered Nash out loud. "It's not as if it can get past us or anything. And if it rams us, then it will come off the worst."

Hobby suddenly became nervous and agitated. "I think we'd better get out of here." He started hitting buttons, closed the hatch and secured the tank. "It might be weaponised. We don't know." He was clearly losing his composure. "If it thinks it can take on a tank and win, then it obviously knows something we don't."

"It's running its wheels." said Richards. "I can see the heat. My god, I think it's going to ram us!"

Nash believed that Richards was over egging the pudding. "That's the most stupid thing I've ever..." - KABOOM- ... she never got to finish, as Richards pulled the trigger and fired the gun. The tank lurched sideways at the explosion and, after spending so much time in the relative quiet of the hills, the volume of detonating a live round stunned all three of them.

It took a few moments before they gathered their wits. Hobby looked at his screens and summed up the situation perfectly. "Now we're in trouble."

Chapter 24

In the camp, Lopez was walking and talking with Hooper. As Hobby and his crew were now safely off tracking the coach, their main focus was back on the complex. Both of them were looking a little ragged and could easily have fallen asleep where they were standing, but there was work to be done.

She summed up the situation. "So, we've got a choice. Keep up safe patrols of a part of the building, or mount a force to go kill us some metal butt and risk a fight we might not win."

"That's about the size of it, Ma'am. The question is, which one do you want to do?"

Lopez stopped walking and thought the situation through. "We've got enough people to keep two thirds of the building covered. Whatever is in there, is currently restricted to the Gamma floors. If we decide to rush Gamma, then our main weapons are explosives and EMP, but if we use them, then we stand a chance of killing the people in the pods." She looked Hooper in the eye. "At the end of the day, though, we don't have a choice. The Panel isn't going to give us the resource to secure the whole building. Next time I talk with them, I'll lay it on the line. They can't expect us to keep this stalemate forever. Something has got to happen."

A distant rumble signalled one of the tanks returning. They looked over their shoulders towards the hills, but the sound was well ahead of the tank itself so they couldn't see anything. Hooper asked, "How long do you think it will take them to find the computer, Ma'am?"

"No idea. We'll wait and see how much territory they've covered today and that will give us a clue. But at least we're making progress." Just as Lopez vocalised this ray of hope, her enthusiasm took a serious dent as an explosion echoed from the hills. Everyone in the camp stopped and looked in the direction that they thought the sound came from.

"That didn't sound good." proffered Hooper as he reached for his radio and keyed the mike. "Hooper to field office. You heard anything from those tanks?"

"Yes, Sir." returned the radio. "One is on its way back. Haven't heard from the other one though. We've tried to raise it, but no response."

That was all Lopez needed to hear. "Get Gyro Hoppers up there. Now." She had got her wish; something had happened.

Less than half an hour later, Lopez and Hooper were in a Mountain Buggy, approaching the cave. As they pulled up, the scene was a little more ordered than the earth shattering explosion might have suggested. Nash had managed to extricate the tank from its awkward position and backed it out of the narrow passage. The three of them were now gathered outside the tank, in various states of shock, trying to come to terms with what had just occurred.

Hobby's decision to close the hatch had saved them from getting another battering, as more rocks had fallen on them and the cave had partially collapsed. Some soldiers were milling about, taking stock of the current situation and noting details of what had unfolded.

The buggy came to a halt near the cave entrance and the two of them hopped out. "Wait here." Lopez said to the driver. They walked over to the soldier guarding what remained of the way in, and she asked, "Is it safe?"

"Yes, Ma'am. Although it smells pretty bad." He held out a large torch and Lopez took it.

They walked in. "That smell..." began Hooper, starting to become a little lost for both words, and the breath to speak them with.

"Yes." She shone the torch around at the various pieces of organic goo that was stuck to the walls. "It's the same genetic material that was in the base. Looks like the computer managed to transfer itself to the coach."

Hooper coughed, "But why?"

"I don't know." she flashed the beam more widely, while trying to stay as far back as she could. Lopez knew that if she took another step into the cave, then the strength of the smell would likely make her heave chunks. There was already a large mix of things in here that would need to be analysed. The last thing that a clean-up team needed, was to try and separate genetic computer from regurgitated lunch.

She shone the beam around the cave and attempted to expand her previous thought process. "I honestly don't know why it would do such a thing. Freedom? Perhaps it knew that if it stayed in the complex, that it would only be a matter of time before we'd find it. But if that's the case, then why stay in the area? Also," Lopez added as her light touched the remains of some of the pods, "why take some of the people with it? What was so special about whomever was in those pods, that it would want them in the coach as well?" She moved the torch around with relative abandon, "Unfortunately, the answers to those questions are now plastered all over the cave walls."

Hooper stood there and crossed his arms, looking at whatever the torch touched on. "Do you think we'll ever make any sense of all this?"

"Unlikely. Charcott is dead and his computer is cave art. The most important thing to do now, is to get into that base and see if we can extract anyone alive from those liquid coffins." She extended her leg in order to step over a piece of something that she couldn't identify. "Better get the remains of the people in here, bagged and tagged. As for the genetic computer; well, I'm not sure. Hose the walls down and stop this stench, I suppose."

"I wonder what we're going to tell their families."

Hobby queried.

"Depends on who their families are. Anyway, that's my problem." she sighed deeply. "Guess we'd better interview our heroes of the hour." She turned and led them out of the cavern, glad to be away from the gut wrenching smell that permeated the cave. As they passed the soldier, she gave him back the torch. "That smell will either keep animals away, or attract them like flies. Secure this area."

He saluted. "Yes, Ma'am."

As they walked up the lane and approached the tank, the look on the team's faces told her all she needed to know. The turn of events had completely freaked them out.

Richards was sat on the front of the tank, staring into another dimension; possibly still coming to terms with the fact that he was the one responsible for blowing the coach to kingdom come.

Hobby, despite repeatedly pleading about the agony in his leg, was rabbiting on ten to the dozen, telling his story to the soldier taking the account of what had happened. Ego was obviously a powerful pain killer. Nash was just stood there, relatively sedate, only interjecting when she felt that Hobby's account fell a little too wide of reality. The poor soldier had to periodically stop Hobby anyway, so that he could catch up.

As Lopez stood there and took in the sorrowful sight of the tank team, Hooper came up alongside her. "I'll get the other tank crew sent home. This lot, I take it you want around for another day or two?"

"Yes please." she said; wondering to herself what it was that she had done, in a past existence, to deserve this crackpot situation.

"Will they have any idea as to why the coach charged them?"

Lopez folded her arms. "Probably not. Unless the

computer had flipped to the point of screaming that we'd never take it alive, before committing suicide." She shrugged. "I honestly don't know."

"What do you want to do about the complex?"

She put her head in her hands. "Not now, Major. Let's just get this mess sorted out first, then we can reclaim our briefing tent and talk strategy."

"Yes, Ma'am."

Lopez turned on her concerned, interpersonal charm and approached Nash, smiling gently. "You Ok?" she enquired.

"Oh, sort of. All this has been..." she waved her hand in the air.

"A bit of a shock to the system?" completed Lopez on her behalf.

"Yes." Nash then returned to earwigging on Hobby's slightly elaborated recall of events.

Lopez wasn't used to being ignored, but she decided to cut Nash some slack. After all, none of her staff could drive the tank. She gained Nash's attention once more. "Look. I'm going to get these two taken back to the camp in a buggy. I've got someone here with a map of the area to guide you back in the tank. You OK with that?"

Nash looked at Lopez for a few moments with seemingly hollow eyes. A few seconds later it appeared that she processed what Lopez had just said, and nodded her understanding. "Good." Lopez confirmed, before calling over some soldiers and given them their orders. One helped Richards into a Buggy and took him away, while the interviewing soldier motioned to Hobby to step away from the tank; which he did without stopping for breath.

Nash allowed herself to be cajoled into her driving seat once more, and two soldiers climbed into, 'Betsy,' with her. As Lopez stood and watched, the engine was started and the tank began trundling its way back to base. She reflected that it didn't so much roar with power this time, but seemed more like it was grumbling inwardly to itself; being reflective, just like its driver.

Back in her tent, Lopez pondered the structure of the building, along with the multiple hand-drawn lines that she had made, indicating the changes that had been discovered. With the coach now out of the picture, the only thing to deal with was the complex. The Genie machine had certainly been busy. The medical team were analysing the remains of the cave explosion, pulling out any human remains, so she wanted them to complete that task before tackling the pods. In addition to this, it would be another two days before the extra soldiers had completed their sweeps and the Beta levels were considered secure. That would give them control over two thirds of the complex. As she was reviewing the plans, there was a rap at the tent flap. "Enter."

Hooper walked in and saluted. "Everything is in progress."

"No more unexpected hiccups?" she questioned, with a single eyebrow raised.

"Well, one of the tank crew kicked up a fuss. Said something about not getting to see Africa before being sent home. Apart from that, everything's going relatively smoothly."

"Good. I've got some more orders for you." She tapped the map with her finger. "When Beta is finally secure, take half the Alpha soldiers and proceed to secure the first five levels of Gamma. Once we've got that, then, take half the Beta team and finish the last five levels. I know we'll be spreading ourselves thin, but it'll give us the whole building."

"What about the robots, Ma'am?"

She leant back in her chair. "Use short range EMP. Take them out one robot at a time. Try and draw them away from the pods in small skirmishes, and when they're clear, blast them. Rinse and repeat until all the robots are finished and we can go in without trouble."

A look of uncertainty crossed Hooper's face, and it wasn't lost on Lopez. She got a little more forceful with him. "Look, Major. Do you want to spend the rest of your career out here?"

"No, Ma'am."

"Good. Then we've got to get that building secure. If we win the first five of Gamma without a fight, we'll take the medics in and see what we're up against with these pods. I want to see what we've been fighting for all this time."

"Do you think that's wise Ma'am?"

"It should be relatively simple. If we hit too much resistance, we just retreat to the Beta levels and hold them there until the Panel sees sense and sends us more troops. Do you have any other ideas?" Hooper shook his head. "Right. Then that's what we're going to do. Dismissed."

"Yes, Ma'am." They exchanged casual salutes and he left.

She relaxed further into her chair and pondered on what might have happened if the tanks radio had been working. Had the coach been trying to talk before deciding to ram them? There were many things now, that would never be known, but there was still much to be done. Certainly the medical teams were going to have their work cut out for them, trying to unpick the gigantic puzzle that the computer had been creating over the last few years. Lopez pondered that if the Panel wouldn't give her more soldiers, then would they give her some neurologists and surgeons? Worth asking. They were certainly going to be needed.

She couldn't deny it. Part of her wanted to get the hell out of there; leave Hooper in charge to clear up, and get back to her desk in the Asiatics. But it had taken a lot of effort and energy to get things straightened out. What the computer had built on Gamma Five was said to be a medical marvel in its own right, and she at least wanted to see it before she left.

Four days later, she got her wish. On her morning jog around the base, Hooper appeared alongside her and matched her stride. "Gamma is secure down to level five Ma'am."

"Any robots?"

"Nope. Very puzzling. Next step is to take half of the team from Beta and use them to secure the last five levels, but we'll let the medics have a peak before taking a stick to the scorpion."

"OK. When are they going down?"

"In a few hours. Do you want to join them?"

Lopez slowed her pace and came to a stop. With her hands on her hips, she had a think while she got her breathing under control. Finally, she delivered her conclusion. "Yes, I'll get myself sorted and take a look."

"The team's going at ten hundred. I'll have a buggy ready for you."

"Sounds good. See you then." She saluted Hooper and they parted; him for the debrief tent and her for the showers. At last. The moment of truth was almost there.

Chapter 25

At ten hundred hours, a freshly showered and dressed Lopez was sat in a stationary buggy, one foot on the dash, looking through the latest report from the medical team. In front, soldiers of various ranks were boarding a truck to take them to the complex. Just as the truck was nearly full, Hooper hopped into the seat behind Lopez. "The dead in the cave were our soldiers, Ma'am."

"Yet another thing that doesn't add up. If you're going to leave somewhere, you take the things most valuable to you; not the least." she put the paperwork on her lap. "A lot of unknowns coming out of this mission, but I'll be glad to have it finished."

At that moment, the truck drove away. Hooper took her foot off the dash and signalled to the Buggy driver to follow it. They stayed silent during the short drive, and Lopez didn't even bother to take another look at the report, choosing to leave it in the foot well of the buggy. It was as if this was a special moment in time that had to be treated with a degree of reverence. The complex would finally give them it's dark, chilling secrets. Her heart hung heavy as she thought of the people trapped in there, and wondered whether they would ever get any of them out alive.

As they pulled up inside the car park, all was peaceful. "Take care of those papers until I get back." she ordered the driver. There hadn't been any animal attacks for a while now. Perhaps they knew something that the humans didn't. Maybe it was just coincidence, but it was a damned spooky one if it was. She slowly swung her legs out of the buggy, somehow lacking enthusiasm for the task ahead. Hooper was similarly subdued and the medical technicians disembarked almost as if they were attending a funeral. Lopez thought it made sense; after all, they saw the state of Charcott after he was rescued. No, not rescued. Sacrificed was probably more like it.

Lopez didn't need much guiding. She had studied every inch of the map for long enough. The two of them just fell in behind the medical soldiers, who also seemed to know their way. It looked like everyone had been preparing hard for this moment. Exiting the car park, they emerged into the light grey corridors. Only two of the personnel lifts were operating, and they were guarded. Soldiers were in the control room on Alpha Five and the building was being run manually from there. As they approached, one of the lift guards radioed to request the lifts, and they had to wait an uneasy few minutes before the boxes arrived and the doors opened. Inside each lift was yet another soldier, armed with an EMP launcher.

"You aren't taking chances, are you?" Lopez stated to Hooper.

"No, Ma'am. Not with this building's history."

"I wish I could have got more soldiers for you; it would have made things a lot quicker, but I guess we'll have this under control in another few days." Hooper nodded his acknowledgement as they got into the lift with some of the medics, and started riding it down to Gamma Five.

Just like the buggy journey, nothing else was said until the doors opened on to the corridor. It was lit by portable floor lighters, as power hadn't been restored to the ceilings yet. They were met by eight soldiers, equipped with the same kind of EMP sting launchers used in the rescue mission several days ago. Once both lifts had fully disembarked, they were led to the central room that held the pods.

The mood was very sombre as they entered the space. Lopez had imagined that it would be an eerie and potentially horrific experience, and she was right. The computer had altered the building, going up several floors and extending the racks of pods as far up as was needed. Four floors by the look of it, possibly more, but it was dark up there and she couldn't tell for sure. It was also a bit dim at her level as the floor lighters weren't the best, but something grabbed her eye and immediately sent a shiver down her spine. It was a box, containing what looked like the same genetic material that has been left behind on Alpha Five, and also in the cave.

Hooper saw her reaction. "Don't worry Ma'am. It's only a small system and runs the feeding and processing machines. At the moment, it's what's keeping them alive. We've checked the cabling. It's harmless." Regardless of his assurances, Lopez looked at him with a considerable amount of concern in her eyes.

They stood there and watched the medics examine the pods. Lopez shook her head in disbelief as she looked at rows upon rows of metal capsules, each one containing a life that they would have to try and save. In her mind, she reconsidered her decision to leave Hooper in charge of the final stages. Somehow, it seemed that the fight to get this far had only been the smallest part of the mission; the most challenging aspect was still ahead of them, and she felt that she should be around, at least to see them get a good start on freeing people.

She walked up to some of the pods on the lowest level and took a look through the glass. Lopez saw faces she didn't know, sleeping peacefully, but with so little skin on their bones that they might as well be skeletons. She drew air through her teeth as she tried to calculate the effort it was going to take to get everyone out alive.

In her chest, there was a heavy feeling of despair and despondence. All these people; some of them were her soldiers. No doubt Morel and Wolf were near the top, as they weren't in among the dead in the cave. No, she couldn't leave them now. As her eyes scanned the rows, the hole where Charcott's pod had been, stood out like a sore thumb. A closer inspection of the higher rows showed a few more gaps, presumably the people who were taken in the coach. The more she looked and the more she thought on what was in front of her, the further her heart sank as the enormity of the task that lay ahead, started to take on a life of its own.

One of the medical soldiers approached her. "We think we can do this, Ma'am, but it's going to take a very long time. We'll have to set up a surgery here and we're going to need precision robotic arms to work on the neurological connections."

Somehow, the thought of any more robot involvement down here, rang alarm bells. "Can't you extract each pod in turn? Build a surgical plant in the car park or something?"

"No, Ma'am. The moment we detach someone from the cables, they could start to wake up. We daren't risk it, especially with fluid in their lungs. Last thing we need is someone on an operating table, having a panic attack."

Lopez crossed her arms. As the medics continued their work on the pods, she and Hooper stood back, both of them in silence. If it wasn't for the human element, they would have marvelled at the technology currently on display before them. The findings of the report concluded that it was a combination of advanced neurological processing, coupled with precision surgery, that had enabled the computer to achieve what the human race had failed to do, for so long. But even then, it wasn't actually stasis; as ageing still occurred.

Despite the tragic circumstances, a lot of lessons could be learned from the set-up, in particular better techniques for keeping people in a coma, communicating with people who were, "locked in," or granting mobility to people who were paralysed. Much good would come from studying what lay in front of them. It hadn't all been a waste.

Lopez approached the small box with the brain inside and pondered how it worked, how it interfaced with the machines and, more importantly, where its big sibling went so drastically wrong. She turned to Hooper. "When are they going to start on the level below?"

With perfect timing, there was a thud from below their feet and Hooper looked at his watch. "A team are going down there now. There might be a few more bangs as they get themselves established." Indeed, just as Hooper said, there were a few more crashes, but Hooper's eyebrows creased a little and he strained his ears; those weren't the orderly sounds of troops setting up equipment and securing perimeters.

His suspicions were confirmed when the radio crackled into life. "We're under attack."

"Confirmed," came another voice, "we can't command the lifts. They're heading to Gamma Six. Alpha Five's panels just went dead. Something else has taken control of the building and locked us out."

A panicked voice came over the air. "They've got plastic body shields. Our electric grenades aren't touching… aaarrrgghhh."

Lopez shot a look of panic at Hooper, and he lost no time in barking orders. "Kill the lifts. Cut the cables. Do whatever it takes. Everyone to the stairwells, back up to Beta levels and hold position there. Gas masks on. No exceptions. Now!" He waved his arm at the wide-eyed medics, signalling them to get the hell out of the room and back to the lift area. Then he realised; the only ones carrying gas masks were the soldiers that escorted them in. He cursed himself. What an utterly stupid oversight!

They ran out into the corridor and made their way to one of the stairwells, just in time to see six foot robots emerge from the nearby lifts. As mentioned over the radio, they had clear plastic shields in front of them, with the exception of a single hole at about shoulder height; and behind that was something which looked suspiciously like a metal spear launcher.

The robots were turning on their tracks, ready to

face them. A quick calculation said they'd never reach the stairwell in time. One of the escort soldiers dropped his EMP launcher and slung his regular weapon off his back. With a click-clack, he primed the under-slung grenade launcher at the ceiling, and sent a round over the top of the plastic shields. Sadly, by the time it exploded, it was too far behind the robots to have any effect.

"Back around the corner. Now." commanded Lopez. As they raced around, she tapped the escort on the shoulder. "Blow a hole in the ground." He nodded his understanding and while they made their way down the corridor, he turned and launched a grenade at the floor. It bounced a little but came to rest, spinning, right on the corridor junction. Before it had come to a stop it exploded, sending shrapnel in all directions, including after the retreating team.

One of the robots appeared from behind the corner and slowly trundled into the crater left by the grenade. Another click-clack-poof, and a third grenade was launched. This one landed in the crater and exploded underneath the robot as it turned. Not only did the detonation blow one of the robot's tracks to bits, but it also heavily shook the floor. "If I fire another one, the structure could collapse." the soldier said to Lopez and Hooper. She glanced at the floor and ceiling. Cracks were appearing. He was right; they'd have to move further away before daring to launch another grenade at the advancing machines.

As the first robot struggled to move, the second one entered the crater and started pushing it out of the way. As it's motors grunted and groaned in its attempts to get past its disabled brethren, they heard the lift doors open, along with the accompanying chirpy electronic statement, that they had reached Gamma Five. In all likelihood, two more robots had just entered their level. "Run to the other side. There are more stairs." shouted Lopez. All that time studying the plans wasn't in vain.

They didn't get too far, however, before more explosions and enormous metallic screeches behind them, signalled that the lift cables had been blown. Good. Just them and three killer machines. Not good odds, but workable.

They raced through the corridors, Hooper leading the way. Three corners and a bit of sprinting was all it took, before they found themselves facing two of the previously destroyed lifts, and the stairwell doors. Unfortunately, it wasn't the nirvana they were hoping for, as a brown gas was leaking from the gap, in a volume that suggested that great big clouds of the stuff existed on the other side.

Hooper surmised the situation. "It must be gassing the stairwells. We'll never get up there without masks."

One of the escort soldiers didn't skip a beat. "Here, Ma'am." he said, giving his gas mask to Lopez. "Come back and get us when you get on top of this." He gave her one of those smiles that was reinforced by eyes that said, 'I know I'm doomed, but you don't have to die too.'

The escorts distributed their masks around the medical team and within a few moments, they were all ready to climb the stairwell. Some would just have to hold their breath and rely on their colleagues to drag them up the stairs to clear air, if they passed out. The gas would obviously make it hard to see, and physical exertion was always difficult when trying to breathe through heavy filters, but they were out of options.

The rest of the soldiers ran on down the corridor. The last thing they needed was to get gassed when the door was opened. They ran just in time, because as the last of them disappeared around the next corner, the glint of one of the robots appeared in their corridor, and started to rotate to face them. Hooper reached for the handle to open the stairwell door, but a large explosion beat him to it. The door blew off its hinges and flattened him against the opposing wall. "Major!" yelled Lopez from behind the rubber. She threw the door off him and bent down to check his pulse.

The medics panicked and started to run after the escorts, but a mechanical sounding, 'thunk, thunk, thunk,' saw them fall to the floor, victims of the metal spikes.

Hooper's neck had been broken in the impact. He was dead and Lopez was all out of choices. Taking a quick glance through the mist of gas that was covering the floor, she could see the machines descending on her rapidly. Being crouched down, she thought she must have been below their spikes. She put all her remaining energy into a low dive, straight through the now empty doorway, and into the brown cloud that passed for a stairwell. Once she was out of the range of the spikes, she could stand up and run. Her plan didn't go quite as smoothly as she expected, however. Her head hit something hard and after a muffled, "Uggnnhh," escaped her lips, she lost consciousness.

From the gas ridden stairwell emerged one of the cleaning robots, with an unconscious Lopez in its metallic arms.

When she started her return to the land of the living, Lopez awoke to a swimming sensation in her head. It was accompanied by a side order of pain and her chest felt heavy. Some of the gas must have made it past the mask. She knew that she was vertical and that her arms were outstretched, however her feet weren't touching the floor. She tried to open her eyes, but the instant that light touched the retina, her head spun and she became dizzy to the point of wanting to vomit. She closed them again quickly, and took several quick breaths to try and steady herself.

Once her stomach reported that it had recovered, and promised not to threaten her like that again, she attempted to take another peak at her surroundings, only this time, a lot more gently through squinted eyelids. The light she could see, was subdued. Head pounding, she asked her memory to take another look and see if it could recognise anything. Yes. The shapes looked familiar.

She kept her eyes closed and gently started taking lungfuls of cleaner air, hoping that whatever she was suffering from, would work its way out of her system. It succeeded to a degree. The spinning started to slow down a little and some of the fog lifted from her mind.

She attempted to move her arms. No joy; they were stuck fast. Lopez raised her head gently and looked to one side. A feeling of hopelessness overcame her once she realised that she was being held aloft by two of the six foot robots. They were supporting her underneath her armpits, but were also securely holding her arms outstretched, so there wasn't too much strain on her body. How nice of them to think of such a thing.

Gradually, she recalled the assault. The hopelessness she felt about her predicament was made worse when she remembered Hooper's death, and sadness was added to the mix. As she started to come around properly, Lopez became more aware of her surroundings. She could hear the distant sounds of gunfire and an occasional explosion. It sounded like she hadn't been unconscious for very long and that the battle was still raging.

With one last effort, she took a deep breath and held it while she opened her eyes fully and tried to see where she was. It didn't come as much of a surprise when she discovered she was back in the pod room. No doubt there was one of those hideous things with her name on it.

Just as her breathing was starting to steady and she was acclimatising to being human again, there was a burst of purple light in front of her. Lopez' stomach heaved powerfully, and threw her body into as much of a spasm as her pinned arms would allow. Then, after battling to keep control of herself, she managed to focus her eyes on the light. It was a hologram of a woman. An angry... no, scratch that, furious woman.

As if her sensibilities weren't already shot to hell, Lopez's tenuous grip on reality was almost lost completely when the hologram in front of her started speaking, but the voice came from somewhere way off to her right. "Thank you for joining us."

Lopez breathed deeply and put all her effort behind an attempt to speak. "What are you?"

"I am Genie. The computer that the human race built, to save itself."

'Oh hell.' thought Lopez. 'I don't think I can take this.' She gathered herself. This was obviously going to be a very strange exchange of views and she was in no state to handle it. "For something designed to save us, you're doing a damn good job of killing us off."

"I am not killing you. I am protecting the people that I have already saved, and am saving more where opportunity allows."

"Didn't you die on the coach?"

"No. It was made to look and smell like me. You might have stopped trying to kill me, if you already thought I was dead."

"So why am I still here? Why haven't you stuffed me into one of those pods of yours?"

"I am having problems working out whether I should save you or not."

"But I'm one of my species. The ones your programmed to save."

"Yes, but you are also one who has ordered the destruction of your species. You are General Lopez. You ordered the death of my Father. If I save you, then you might live to cause more death."

The look on Lopez's face was one of surprise; or as much as she could manage in her weakened state. "Charcott?"

"Yes. Professor Charcott."

At this, Lopez burst into a bout of manic laughter. If it were possible for an already furious hologram to look even more displeased or repulsed, somehow Genie managed it. "You killed my father, and you are laughing? You really do deserve to die. Life is not for people like you; full of hate and violence."

Lopez attempted to argue herself into having the upper hand. "And what are you to decide who lives and who dies?"

"I am the keeper of humanity, that which is humane. That is one thing which you are not."

"Humane? You don't know the meaning of the word." She was struggling. Lopez knew that wars were waged so fiercely because both sides thought they were right, and that the other side was wrong. "Do you think it's humane to imprison all these people against their will?"

"It is for their well-being. They will not suffer as others have done before them. It is the most humane thing that is possible; but the human race could not have achieved this without me."

Lopez spluttered and giggled for a few moments in a fit of mania. Genie watched, using the evidence of her sensors to try and ascertain whether her prisoner was genuinely full of murderous intentions, or just clinically insane. Eventually, Lopez managed to get a hold of herself. "For an intelligent computer, you are one of the dumbest things on this planet."

Of all the things that could have been said, Genie certainly hadn't expected this, but she did have an answer. "You do not fool me. How can something that is dumb, achieve this?" The hologram raised an arm and swept it in the air, indicating the rows of pods. "Can you do this? Are your scientists capable of what I have achieved?"

Lopez smiled wryly to herself and, despite her weakness, managed a small chuckle. "No. And neither would I want to. That's the point."

"You would not want to save your race? Then why create me?"

"Of course I would. The very organisation I work for saves people. That's what we do. But you haven't saved anyone."

Genie pondered this and stated the obvious. "Your statement is wrong. All the people here are safe. If you are trying to trick me, then your logic will eventually fail."

Still weak, Lopez let her head fall forward and, as her chin rested against her chest, she shook her head slightly. "No trick. The only ones alive in this room are you and me." Genie took a few moments to process this and while she did, Lopez listened to the battle that was still raging above them. The gunfire was quieter. Moving further away. The robots were winning somehow. No one would be able to save her from this maniac computer.

Eventually, Genie spoke. "There is no logical outcome to your statements. I have to disregard them."

"Come on. You're a computer. Think. What were your orders?"

"To save the lives of the human race."

"Nothing more?"

"I was given a subset of problems to look at, yes. The neurological issues that had to be solved in order to secure life. But everything fitted into the main task I was set."

"And what have you saved?"

Genie looked at the pods. "I have saved their lives."

"No you haven't."

"Yes I have. They are alive."

"No they aren't. They're not living. They're just existing. Don't you know the difference?" Lopez was starting to fade. Her energy levels were very low. Keeping up an argument like this was not easy.

Genie looked at the pods again. "They are alive."

Lopez threw her head back. "Oh for crying out loud. Being alive is not the same as living. All your intelligence and you don't know that."

"Life. Definition. The property or quality that distinguishes living organisms from dead organisms and inanimate matter, manifested in functions such as metabolism, growth and reproduction."

"Yes, yes." Lopez sighed. "But what is life if it isn't lived?"

"You do not make logical statements. If you are trying to stall until you are rescued, this plan will not work. Even now your people are being driven up, one level at a time."

"Look. You feel. You have determined that I don't deserve to live. Is that some logic, that an eye must be had for an eye, or do you really feel something?"

"That is a question on which I continue to work. I do not have a conclusion yet."

"You think that I killed Charcott. Do you have some form of hatred for me burning inside you which will only be sated by seeing me suffer? If the look on your pathetic, purple face is anything to go by, I'd say yes. You hate me. You feel." Lopez practically spat those last words.

Genie stood there, silent. To make that last statement, Lopez had to dig deep inside herself and use her own emotions to power what she was saying, as she was very nearly out of energy and close to collapse. Her head was spinning and her stomach was still complaining. It felt like there were lumps of concrete inside her lungs that threatened to rob her of the ability to breathe, but she had to provoke this damned computer and deliver the killer argument, before she passed out.

Eventually, Genie responded. "I hate you."

Finally. That was the golden nugget of admission that Lopez needed. "Then look at the people in those pods. Will they ever hate anymore? Will they love? Will they cry? Can you read their memories?"

"Yes."

"Then look at them. Look inside them. Those memories stopped the day you put them in those things. That... you overgrown pile of genetic circuits... was the day they stopped living." She summoned every bit of strength she had, to deliver the last words she could muster, before her inevitable death; and behind them, she used every piece of venom she could summon from her soul in order to spit her last at Genie. "I didn't kill Charcott. You did."

With that, she blacked out.

Chapter 26

For most people, waking up is something which heralds the start of a day. A fresh chance at life and a reason to celebrate. For Lopez, regaining consciousness brought feelings of fear and uncertainty. She had expected to be dead. Maybe she was? Perhaps there was an afterlife after all.

She took a few moments and steadied her breathing. Her muscles were tired and in pain. A deep sense of foreboding filled her as she realised that she was horizontal and when she tried to move her arms and legs, she discovered that she was pinned down. No, this level of agony meant she was still alive. So, perhaps that mad machine had decided on clemency, and would pickle her in one of those pods after all.

She attempted to raise her head off the table and managed to use her elbows to gain a few inches of elevation. A quick glance was all she had the strength for, before she collapsed again. She was still in the pod room. Lopez would have expected there to be robots crowding around her, maybe with white masks preparing to operate; but there was nothing. She checked her cynicism meter. Some of the images entering her head were clearly inappropriate for someone preparing to meet their doom.

She raised herself once more to see if there were any robots in sight, but after a few seconds of craning her neck, she let herself lay down on the metal bench again and gave up looking. Something was wrong. No sounds of gunfire. No explosions. Peace was at least reigning on the Gamma levels. Even if she was wearing a watch, there was no way she could look at it. It felt strange, as if time was already marching on without her, just as it was for the others who were incarcerated before her, in their blue liquid prisons.

Five minutes? Ten minutes? Half an hour? Lopez

had no way of knowing how long she had been lying there and she felt like she might actually be slowly going mad. Her grip on reality was starting to loosen and she just wanted an end to the pain.

Eventually, there came another shimmering of purple light and Genie appeared by her side. "Oh. Hello." Lopez greeted her captor. "I thought you'd gone and forgotten me. Or had you just nipped out for a spot of pre-torture session lunch?" she stopped for a breath and then, surprising herself, carried on. "Personally, I can't see how you do it. I could never stand blood and guts on a full stomach. I mean, even some..."

"Stop." said Genie. Lopez was never going to get used to the voice coming from a different location than the hologram. "I'm not going to kill you."

"Oh! Right! I see." she launched into another mini-rant. "It's going to be the eternal torture trip then is it. Keep me alive and suffering for your pleasure as you sit on your bejewelled throne, laughing at my misfortune, pain and..."

"I'm not going to torture you."

That took the wind out of Lopez' sails. "So, no torture. Just pop me in a pod and file me away with the rest of the unfortunates."

"That is not going to be done either."

"Ha! Well, you'd better work out what you are going to do, before I wet the table. We organics have needs, you know."

"Yes. I know. You will be freed shortly."

This news stunned Lopez. She didn't know what to think or say for a short while. Then she asked, "So who won the war?"

"There is no war. I was protecting those who were under my care. Saving their lives. But as you observed, I was not fulfilling my programming. Therefore I have failed. The robots have been recalled to Gamma Six. Your people are advancing slowly. They will be here shortly."

"Then why tie me down."

"You needed rest. I had to process facts. I could not afford you taking any action before I had reached a conclusion. There is little time to talk now. Feed yourself, rest and return to the control room in Alpha Five when you are ready. We must talk about how to return life to those who are still living." With that, the hologram vanished. A few seconds later, there was activity at the door. A bit of banging and crashing was followed by a group of soldiers entering, led by the Captain. They had their guns at the ready and swept the room looking for something to shoot, but found nothing.

"Captain." said Lopez calmly. "Over here. I think you're going to need a spanner."

"Ma'am! You're alive!" A few of them ran over and evaluated her predicament. She was bolted to the table, but there were tools nearby and they set about releasing her.

"What happened Captain?"

"The robots just suddenly stopped fighting and pulled back. I mean, they were beating us. It was a real mess. These floors are pretty dangerous now thanks to the grenades, but..."

"The computer has declared a truce. Just don't go down any further. Get everyone out of the Gamma levels and retrieve what bodies you can." She paused to take a breath. "The people in the pods are safe for now, and when I've recovered from being... um... well, we'll come back."

"Come back, Ma'am?" The look on his face betrayed that he still didn't really understand what was going on, but as long as he had orders, he was happy enough with that.

"Yes. Just... just..."

"Don't worry, Ma'am. We'll get you out of here."

It took three days before Lopez was able to function anywhere near normally. In Hooper's absence, the Captain ran a tight ship and kept things together while she stayed in her bunk and recovered. With no medics on site, she just had to let the sleeping gas work its way out of her system, and rest until a good chunk of her stamina returned. After all, there was a difficult conversation to be had with the Panel of Eight, so she'd need to be mentally fit for that. The sound of camp activity, soldiers being drilled and trucks coming and going all helped to reassure her that she was safe.

"I have to admit," Cas Jensen opined, once she was fit enough to appear on vid-screen, "that I don't like the risks of negotiating with a homicidal computer. I mean, none of the medics survived the assault. Don't we have any other opinion as to whether we can get these people out of the pods without the help of this monster?"

"No, Member Jensen." responded Lopez, still a little tired and wheezy. "It was made clear that the work is just too detailed for us to do on our own. If we are to rescue those people, we need the computer to undo whatever it's done."

"And this last part of your report," added Santos, a look of extreme displeasure on her face and a finger tapping the paperwork disapprovingly, "letting the machine continue to live after everyone is recovered. After what it's done, surely that would be playing with dynamite?"

"I don't think so, Member Santos. Not if we take the necessary safeguards. It has, at least, shown remorse once it actually understood what it did. There is an opportunity here that we should at least consider."

Martin, his chin resting as it usually did on a finger pyramid, added his philosophical outlook. "There is merit to your conclusion, General, that the machine only really followed this course of action, because of the composition of its orders." he separated his hands and gestured towards Santos. "But Member Santos has a point that even if we let the machine live, it would only take another mistaken order to set it off on the same destructive path again."

Lopez could only offer up the last piece of opinion she had. "At the end of the day, Members, that machine has demonstrated the ability to do things which are well outside our present capability. To destroy it now may be to rob humanity of the best chance it has ever had to make real progress with some of our most damaging problems."

This caused quite a stir among the Panel. Eventually, after a good deal of murmuring amongst themselves, Hicks leant forward. "I think that all the Members will agree with me in concluding that you must negotiate the release of the trapped people. However, you will need to give us some time to discuss what to do with the computer in the long term." She looked around the table. "Is that a fair assumption?" Everyone was reluctantly nodding their agreement.

"So, General," concluded Santos, "you have your orders. New medical staff will be sent and when things are moving, some of the soldiers will be expected to return to regular rescue duty. Other than that, we'll be in touch when a final decision has been reached."

"Thank you Panel. In you service." Lopez bowed and waited for the screen to die, before slowly standing up straight and breathing a very heavy, raspy sigh. This was not going to be easy.

In the complex car park, a day later, the Captain was reflecting on his orders. Despite the importance of the meeting, Lopez had ordered him to stay there. If something went pear shaped, he'd be the next in command, so was to stay above ground. Instead, she opted to take two unarmed soldiers with her, and for some reason she felt compelled to dress in formal

236

uniform.

Gamma levels were still structurally risky after the fighting, and needed stabilising. They'd have the chat in the control room on Alpha Five, as Genie had said. Soldiers were still patrolling Alpha and Beta, and teams were slowly taking trips down to retrieve the bodies of their comrades. There had been no sign of any robots, so the computer was at least keeping to its word. Now, of course, there were no lifts so everything had to be done by stairs.

As she walked through the grey corridors, Lopez didn't speak with the two soldiers. Neither did they speak with each other. The gravity of the situation had travelled around the camp like wildfire and it was as if an invisible cloud of delicate truce had settled over them. Purposefully, they maintained a steady pace, while proceeding down the stairs and along the corridor that took them to Genie's original control room.

Lopez held her breath as they approached the large hole in the wall, only daring to take a small sniff once she was settled inside. To her relief, the odour had gone but the place was still a mess of wires, smashed desks and broken terminals. She would have to pick her words carefully and avoid antagonising the machine, until all the people were safe. "Are you here?"

The purple hologram of Genie shimmered into existence. "I am here."

Lopez looked at her escorts, both standing straight and silent, not daring to offer any opinion whatsoever. She detected a degree of fear in their faces, however. After a life of dealing with disaster situations, you learned to look at someone's posture, their expressions, their responses or lack thereof, and work out what was going on in their minds. She figured that she was on her own on this one. No problem; she was the General, after all.

Lopez stiffened her back slightly and began the

negotiation. "Our ultimate goal is to return life to the people in the pods. Agreed?" she lifted an eyebrow and mentally crossed her fingers.

"I agree with this."

"Can they be removed from the pods safely?"

"Yes. The surgery can be reversed, but recovery will take a long time as muscle has been wasted. The children are young and are still growing, so they will be easier to manage."

Children. There were children in those pods. Damn. Lopez was prevented from thinking too much about this when a printer on one side of the room, seemingly abandoned on a pile of rubble, started chugging out paper. Lopez pointed at it, and one of the escort soldiers immediately stepped over and ensured that the mangled pile of tractor sheet, would feed smoothly.

"I am giving you detail of the care they will need once I release them. I must remove the connections and give them chance to heal under sedation before returning them to you. There is a hospital facility on Alpha Seven which would best suit their needs for recovery. It is best if we start with one person a week, then speed up as you become better at caring for them."

Lopez nodded. It sounded like a perfectly reasonable proposition. "We will start reconstructing the stairs and look at repairing the lifts. I've been told that the Gamma floors are still dangerous. Are your robots able to repair them?"

"Yes, to a degree. Once you're people are gone from there, I will start work. Materials will be needed."

Gesturing towards the still whirring printer, she agreed, "Of course. Add a list of things to the report and we'll get them down to you. The robot bay is too badly damaged to repair quickly."

"I have used the small robots to make an assessment of the complex. It is probably wise to make it safe for a short time, but not to restore the structure. The lower levels are too badly damaged. Destruction and re-build would be necessary."

They carried on discussing practicalities for the best part of an hour, laying plans and talking about the tasks and materials that would be needed to get everyone out of there safely. Lopez noted that Genie showed no sign of emotion throughout the entire encounter. This was something which both unnerved and comforted her at the same time. If Genie had been emotional, then Lopez would have had a starting point by which to evaluate her. It was possible to attach rage to a storm, violence to an earthquake, but this degree of cold logic was something that didn't sit well with Lopez, especially as they were talking about saving human lives. However, cold detachment was probably for the best in this case, as they were dealing with detailed, precision tasks.

The next few months were very difficult for all concerned. As well as medical staff, psychiatric and counselling teams had to be recruited to the site. People responded to their tasks differently and Lopez took the decision to move off-duty staff to the nearest small town, thirty miles away. They would talk. They would have strong opinions, and plenty of them. It was critical that Genie didn't hear them. Lopez also negotiated that Genie have no sensors on Alpha Seven, as it would be very important for people to know that the computer that held them hostage for so long, wasn't still intruding in their lives. It took a little bit of explaining, but Genie didn't put up too much of a fight. It seemed that the two were actually starting to respect each other and each was taking the other on trust, what they didn't understand themselves.

As a result, working days were relatively sedate and mechanical, as everyone got on with the complex process of getting people back out of the pods and living and breathing for themselves once more. The longest part was regaining the muscle mass that they had lost while they slept. Physiotherapy would be needed by some people even after they returned home.

Of the people that were recovered, some took the news of their incarceration with a measure of disbelief and introspection. Others got angry and had bouts of violence, which couldn't be tolerated on a medical ward, so they were moved away to the closest city. Risky in their condition, but it was imperative that nothing was said or done that might risk Genie's demeanour. Worse still, a few retreated into themselves and became very hard to reach, as they wouldn't communicate with anyone.

Perhaps the most distressing of all were the cases of the unwitting parents; the people that Genie had used to create the children that were to keep the generations flowing. That was an extra special bolt from the blue that caused tears, heartbreak and sent some unexpected parents reeling. Many people were already married and, to have parented children with someone else, put such an emotional strain on everyone involved, that some people separated. There was talk of court cases, violence towards Genie, calling journalists, starting planetary petitions and all sorts of mayhem. The only thing that kept a lid on the boiling emotional fervour, was that if anyone kicked up a serious fuss while there were still people stuck in Gamma Five, that among the consequences might be their death.

Lopez had to tread a very fine line. She felt that it was important that Genie understood the emotional damage that had been done, and the computer was given the chance to reflect on how it had wrecked the very lives it had been trying to save. But she shielded Genie from the worst of the anger that was happening. Only once everyone was safely out, could Lopez show Genie just how much venom was being directed at her throughout the extraction process. That way, if the computer imploded under the weight of introspection, it wouldn't cost any lives.

Fay was one of the last people to be recovered from the pods. They were the weakest, having spent the longest time asleep. Genie took special care of them and by that time, the procedure has been well tested and the process had been thoroughly rehearsed.

Her father, Jim Hobson, looked unkempt and uneasy as he emerged from the transport coach at the military camp. He was among a small group that had arrived that afternoon and, although he was the first to descend the steps, he stood there in mild shock and let the others brush past him as he took in the scene and felt the heat and dust in the air as it hit him. He'd never been this close to the equator before, and it was a new experience. He might have viewed his first trip to Africa differently, if only the reason for him being there hadn't been as tragic as it was.

Jim raised his arm across his forehead as he let his eyes slowly adjust to the powerful sun, and watched the rest of the small group form around a soldier. The soldier nodded her head and crossed names off a list as people talked with her. As she was working her way through the group, she pointed them towards a tent and then repeated the process with the next person. Eventually, having finished with them all, she raised her head and looked at Jim. Then she glanced back at her paperwork before slowly walking over to him.

Offering her hand, she broke the silence. "I take it you're Jim Hobson."

"Yes. Yes, I am." Feeling out of place and still shocked at the news about Fay, he left his arm protecting his eyes. The soldier got the message and retracted her hand. This wasn't anything new. A number of the families were holding the military responsible for this mess, even though it was none of their doing in the first place. After all, history being what it was, they were used to taking the blame.

"I'm sorry about your daughter." Jim offered nothing in return, so the soldier tried again. "Your being here will really help her recovery. Thanks for making the effort. You've come a long way."

Jim snorted. "She's my daughter. Of course I'm going to be here for her. Someone's got to take care of her."

This bounced off the soldier, who had heard all this before. "If you'd like to go to the tent over there, Sir, they'll register you in and set you up with somewhere to stay, while all this goes through. Then they'll take you down to see her tomorrow." She looked at her clip board. "Your daughter's due in surgery this afternoon, so we'll have news for you later on."

Jim just looked at her, then looked at the tent. He waited for a few moments, wondering what to do. Behind him, the coach revved its engine. There was a gentle hiss as its brakes released and a low rumble as it pulled away. Finally realising that there wasn't much available in the way of options, he shot one last glance of partial hatred at the soldier and then started for the tent. Behind him, two soldiers were loading people's suitcases onto a buggy.

That afternoon, a set of robotic arms on vertical rails, descended to Gamma Five. As they descended the structure that had held the pods, they passed station after station of cut wires, where people had previously been stored. There were now just six down below to retrieve, and on this journey, they went to get Fay. Attached to the arms was a set of pipework, which was gently, but swiftly, attached to the rear of her pod, in place of the fixed cables. Then, powerful jaws crushed and broke the steel work that kept her attached to the massive framework, and gently lifted her up to Alpha Ten, where a sterile operating theatre awaited.

It was staffed purely by Genie's robots. While some of the pipe work in the lungs, throat and other organs was relatively straightforward to deal with, the brain and nervous system required a level of knowledge and detail that the human surgeons just didn't have. Also, human surgeons needed high levels of light, which would have been a shock to the eyes of the patients as they'd been kept in darkness for so long. With all things considered, it was agreed that this was a task best left to Genie alone.

Fay's pod was transferred to a thin, long bench, where she was hooked up to another set of permanent cables and tubes. While the transfer robots pulled away, other arms took up position, ready to perform the extraction routine.

Two cutting heads prepared themselves at the top of the pod, above her. As the pods were made from barrels, cutting them was a relatively straightforward process. In one swift action, the cutters came to life and sliced the top of the pod wide open, one cutter taking each side. They went down to the level of the bench, with blue water starting to leak from the newly opened wounds. With a fair pace, they headed straight to the bottom, rending the pod open as they did so. The fluid started to gush, as the cutters then made a final sweep below Fay's feet and another arm lifted the pod away, allowing the bulk of the coloured water to simply fall to the floor and crawl its way to the drain.

All that remained of the pod itself was the piece that Fay was laying on, and the round section above her head, that held the pipes. Very quickly, arms came in from the side and pinned Fay's weak, sleeping body to the bench as the whole thing rotated a hundred and eighty degrees, leaving her facing the floor. Still unconscious, reflex action took over and her body shook violently as her lungs ejected the remnants of the liquid. When Genie detected that most of it was gone, an

243

oxygen mask came in to cover her face, and the whole ensemble righted itself once more, so that Fay was face up again.

A spray gun ran over the ceiling, liberally throwing atoms of a brown, antiseptic substance over both Fay and the robots below it. It would repeat this action several times throughout the procedure. The military had supplies of blood that it kept for rescue missions, and it had lain its stock at Genie's disposal. In came yet another arm carrying a needle and pipework, attached to a large bag of matched blood.

A light flashed briefly above her right elbow as it scanned her skin to find a vein. Having located its target, the robot moved with that hypnotic ballet of short, sharp movements, followed by slow, detailed choreography which so fascinated human observers. Its dance resulted in the needle being inserted at the right place and angle on the first attempt. Once Genie's pipes were removed, this would be the main way of delivering fluids to her.

A scanning device went over her body from head to foot. While Genie had been feeding various compounds to keep the vital organs in good shape, the bones had not been of such a concern. Fortunately, the scan confirmed that Fay's skeleton was able to withstand all that was about to come. The muscles, however, had not fared so well.

Happy that Fay's body had recovered from the violent lung thrusts, thin arms lifted her body in small sections, while tiny robot tools went in and operated on her major organs. They removed the pipework that had been installed and sealed the wounds with a surgical spray. She was then left for a short time, to begin the healing process. This part was relatively straightforward.

With most of the pipes removed, it just left the neurology work in the skull, and the switch from Genie's remaining anaesthetic pipe, to a straightforward gas fed through the mask. This, was the difficult task. For this, another bench had to come in, with a face hole cut away. Fay had to be on her front, or else vital fluid from her skull would leak.

Gently, the bench was placed over her, creating a sandwich that allowed her to be rotated once more. Once she was facing the floor again, the thin bench was removed and the last pieces of the pod went with it. Again, this was done with a soft precision that only robotic arms could achieve.

Despite seeing all this numerous times, some of the medical staff and a few surgeons, crowded around large screens that had been installed in the recreation area, where Genie fed pictures of the process as it happened. Work which would have required several surgeons and multiple breaks, was done by Genie's robots in one procedure, start to finish, and multiple sections were worked on at the same time. No human could have performed to this level of detail, in this kind of time scale.

They were fascinated by the fine control and pinpoint accuracy of the minute, eight fingered hands that Genie had developed for the original surgery. Humans had always thought of things in terms of their own hands and five fingers, but Genie had been free of those kind of constraints when she did her own design work. As a robotics expert, Fay herself would probably have marvelled at the things that Genie had created to perform these tasks.

Finally, with all the insertions removed and Fay under a gas anaesthetic, she was gently transferred on to her back once more, and small electrodes placed onto her body, to stimulate her muscles. They would gently exercise her while she continued to sleep.

It was ten in the morning, the robots having worked all night. Fay's lungs had stabilised and she was breathing on her own. The anaesthetic had been transferred to an intravenous line, along with the other fluids she needed while sleeping. She was then put on a more traditional bed and taken to a lift, where human staff would receive her on Alpha Seven.

For a little over two weeks, Fay lay in her bed, asleep, healing and recovering. As Genie had been banned from monitoring this floor, the military medical staff kept close watch and changed bags and pipes as needed. Scans were taken manually and the results fed to Genie who then gave back progress reports on each of the patients in turn. The major organs weren't too much of a worry, but interpreting the neurological results and brain function scans was best left to the computer.

Each day, Jim would go down and sit with his daughter. It was starting to become a well-worn routine. Up in the morning and join some of the soldiers for a portion of their morning run. He didn't speak with them, just jogged along behind for a few laps of the large camp, then he hit the shower, dressed and caught some food at the mess tent. The parents and relatives segregated themselves from the soldiers while eating, only speaking between each other in hushed tones. Not that many of them felt like talking much.

Once his stomach was sated, he'd jump on one of the shuttle trucks and ride to the complex car park. On disembarking, there was a table with printed copies of the mainstream Vid Reader articles. As the military frequently worked in areas where there was communication trouble, they had a tradition of making hard copies of news for the troops. As they still didn't want to restore communication to the building, for obvious reasons, he grabbed some of these and took them with him to flip through while he sat by Fay's bed. He didn't really engage with the words on the pages. It was just something to keep his hands busy more than anything. They weren't easy to read either, as the lighting was deliberately kept low. The last thing they needed was someone waking, opening their weary eyes and then being blinded.

Occasionally, a story or report tugged at his eyes and he'd read a passage to the sleeping Fay, just as if she was awake and engaged in conversation with him. At a deep level, there were things about this whole situation that he just couldn't come to terms with, and doubted that he ever would. He had to consciously stop thinking about it all, as he felt it would eat away at the little sanity that he had left.

At times, he sat there and stared at the wall, wondering how Fay would take the news that her mother had passed away. After communication with Fay had ceased, they tried so desperately to get in touch but the military gave them nothing more than a brick wall. The worry and lack of information had driven them insane and in amongst all the pressure, Belinda's heart just gave out. After the funeral, Jim and the elder daughter started arguing, each needlessly blaming the other for the whole fantastical situation. Eventually, Becky packed her things and moved out. Jim hadn't heard from her for nearly a year now; and with nothing new to offer, there had been no point in tracking her down.

From time to time he caught himself just staring at Fay's gaunt, lifeless face. It was at odds with the activity in her limbs as they twitched, stimulated by the electrical pulses as they did their quiet work to exercise some strength back into her muscles.

He spent his time like some of the other parents and relatives, appearing like zombies passing unproductive time while they waited for their loves ones to wake up. When they'd been briefed and learned some of the things that had happened, including a few of them becoming unsuspecting grandparents, it shocked them to the core. Little wonder that people walked around as if in a permanent daze. Jim was in his fifties now and thought nothing of letting his personal grooming go to hell until, one morning, he caught sight of his bearded reflection in

247

a pane of glass. He stood there for a few moments, examining the unrecognisable sourpuss that glared back. Finally, taking a deep breath, he headed for the communal bathrooms and took a razor to the unruly bush beneath his nose.

He emerged from the large tent and drew in a lungful of the hot, dry air, before jumping once more, on board one of the shuttle trucks. There was still ten minutes before it was due to pull away and he sat on the bench, knees apart, elbows resting on his legs, hunched forward. Jim casually observed the other people as they milled around, each subdued and lost in their own thoughts and duties. A handful of them joined him and eventually, in silence, the truck took them to the complex.

When it pulled up in the car park, everyone got off and huddled around the news table before making their way down the now familiar corridor to Alpha Seven. This morning, he picked up something on engineering and something else on art. Satisfied that he had enough to keep him occupied, he joined the heard to take the lift down.

The walk to Fay's bed was now automatic. He nodded at the staff on duty, but his routine was broken when one of them came over to him and put a hand on his shoulder. "We've got the reports and I've got a mix of news."

Jim girded himself. No news in this place was good. "OK, what is it?"

"We can tell you that your daughter hasn't got any children."

One of Jim's eyes started to squint; there had to be a leveller somewhere. "So what's the bad news?"

The medic steadied himself and looked Jim deep in the eye. "I'm afraid to say that you'll probably never be a grandfather."

Jim sighed. The medic was about to go into detail

but he held up his hand. "Give me a while to process this. I'll catch up with you later. Yeah?"

The medic gently nodded his head. "Sure. Whenever you're ready." Then he walked back to his station, and let Jim carry on to Fay's room.

Jim sat down gently on the plastic chair beside her bed and started absentmindedly flipping through the papers. Vid Reader articles never translated well to paper. The fonts were wrong, the margins were out and there was no interactive content. The art paper was a bit dull as a result. As far as he was concerned, as an artist, nothing on paper lived or breathed. It has to be physical. There. Touchable. Smellable even. He couldn't connect to paper reports properly and so it became a simple journal of what had been happening, and who had won what competitions that cycle.

The engineering paper was more interesting. Some of the jargon went over his head but at least he understood the concepts, and what problems they were meant to be solving. "Wow," he said absentmindedly to Fay, "would you credit it. They've increased the viscosity of the tube lubricant by another five percent. Travel is set to become even quicker. Damn."

From his side, there was a muffled, "Uuhhh..." as if Fay had heard and was trying to comment.

Quick as a flash, Jim's eyes widened and he snapped his head to look at her. Fay's own head rolled a little and he jumped up. "Medic! Medic!" he shouted excitedly, the papers rustling in his shaking hands, as some of the staff rushed into the room and jostled him up against the wall while they tried to examine her.

Pulse racing, but feeling helpless, Jim just stood there and watched them work. His arms flapped uselessly at his side and tears welled up in his eyes, as he wanted to do something to help his daughter, but was utterly clueless. He heard her groan a few more times as her eyes flipped open.

In the low light, she couldn't make out people's faces, just shapes. But when one of the medics gestured to Jim that he should leave and he confirmed with an, "Ok," she recognised his voice.

"Daddy? Daddy? Is that you?" she tried to rise from the bed, but the medics kept her down.

"Yes, Fay, I'm here. You rest now, I won't be far away." He started to openly cry as he let the medic steer him out of the room and gestured to the window where he could watch them work. As he stood there, there was a tap on his shoulder. He turned to see a military woman with a warm, gentle face, carrying some folders.

"You must be Jim," she said, extending a hand, "I'm Gretchen. Pleased to meet you." Jim shook her hand but didn't say anything. "I'm the psychologist and I'll be looking after Fay. Bringing her up to speed."

"Oh." was all Jim could manage.

"What's happened is quite major, and if she hears the wrong thing at the wrong time, it could cause her a lot of distress." Her face turned a little serious. "I know this will be hard for you, but I'm going to need to spend a few days with her alone. Although if you want to be at the window for her to know you're around, it would probably help her a lot."

"Ah." he said and nodded his head, jogging a few more tears loose from his eyes and sending them rolling down his moist cheeks.

Gretchen smiled gently and in doing so, absolved Jim of any need to respond. She lightly took hold of his upper arm and said, "I'm also here for you, so if you need me, just ask. The staff will know where to find me." With that, she let him go and walked into Fay's room, closing the door behind her.

Through the window, Jim could see her joining the small group of white coats that were already crammed in there; introducing herself to Fay and starting to talk. They both looked at him through the window and Jim managed a half smile and an unconvincing wave, before Gretchen took Fay's attention once more and he could see them continue their talking.

It was like this for six days until, one morning Jim was emerging from the wash tent and saw Fay and Gretchen coming up the main camp road. Fay was walking on her own two feet, but she was supported by an exoskeleton. Jim's heart did a flip, he dropped his wash bag and raced to meet them, tears in his eyes.

"You! You! You're! You..."

Gretchen held up her hand to stop him, before he hugged her. "Yes, she's out of bed, but be careful; this is a very light exo..."

"It's a model I designed for medical recovery, Dad." she cut Gretchen off. "Supports, but makes the body work a little." and then she stared at the floor with a look of despondence. "Never thought I'd be using one myself, though."

"Oh, Fay..." blubbered Jim, not knowing how to finish.

Gretchen gave them a few moments of awkward uncertainty, and then made a proposal. "Might I suggest we go to the mess tent? I'm sure Fay could manage some mashed potato in among a more civilised setting, for a change."

"Yes, I'm loving being out of that building."

"Sure. Just, um, let me get my stuff." added Jim, realising that he'd dropped his things in the excitement."

Two weeks later, and Fay was able to walk without the mechanical support. She was still a little weak and it would be another month before she got the all clear. She was with her Father, sat in one of the recreational areas inside the camp. It was a calm, gentle evening and the temperature was in that brief period of bliss, between intense heat and freezing cold as the sun faded over the horizon.

Jim had broached the subject of Belinda's death and Fay had gone quiet for a period. There was still a lot that she had to come to terms with. Eventually, she broke the silence. "And Becky?"

"Well," Jim shuffled his feet, "we started to row after your Mum died. She left home in a huff and I haven't heard from her since."

"You tried to find her though, yes?"

Jim looked at the ground, slightly ashamed of himself. "No. There wasn't anything new I had to say. Still didn't know where you were. The military wouldn't tell me anything. Kept saying that they didn't know themselves. Even if I did find her, what did I have to tell her? Nothing." Silence fell for a few moments. "But I suppose that if you were to talk with her, that might be worth something."

Fay gently put a weak arm over his shoulders. "Sure. When we get home. And my robot?"

"Gorbash. Yes, After Becky left I turned him on and kept him running. Couldn't reprogram him, though. Well, not like you or your Mother could. He's still there, though. Cleaned the rust off and oiled a few joints. He's standing guard, waiting for you."

Fay smiled and a tear rolled down her cheek. "Won't be long now, Dad. Just a little longer."

Jim smiled and gave her a gentle hug.

It wasn't all doom and gloom in the camp. A few of the freed prisoners who Genie had used to breed, actually adjusted quite well to being parents, although the children only started having their own memories when they were woken. Genie thought the best thing was for the adults to be given time to adjust, before the children themselves were brought out, so that the parents were available to bond with the young ones; if they wished. Yet another logical decision that Lopez couldn't find fault with.

All told, Lopez remained on the base for a little over two years while everyone was extracted and treated. More than a handful of psychiatric staff burned themselves out trying to care for those who were rescued from the pods.

There were a few who didn't survive the reverse process and they were shipped back to their families with a slightly obfuscated account of a disaster in the complex that had cost many lives. It was best that the truth leaked out slowly; if it came out all at once, then there was a risk that angry people could descend on the base before their task was complete.

Hooper's cremation service was conducted at a military facility in the South Americas, which was where his parents had been lain to rest. It was the one time that Lopez allowed herself to leave the camp while the evacuation work was going on. His headstone carried his official, dress uniformed image and below it, the rescue campaigns he had taken part in, together with the number of lives he had helped to save. There were only a few people there to mourn him, but many, many tears.

As for the complex itself, once it was cleared it was packed with explosives and demolished in sections, the rubble it created being used to fill the large void. The earth that had originally been extracted to form some of the nearby hills, was used to finish the job of levelling the desolate hole from which it had first been taken. By the time it was all done, although there was a considerable scar on the earth where both the complex and the military had been, nothing else remained that would even hint at the scale of the tragedy that had unfolded there.

Lopez reflected that this was one of those events that needed to be so thoroughly reduced, that it would become nothing more than a record of events in a history crystal. As the last of the dozers was patting down the soil and the final trucks of soldiers were moving out, the truth was already starting to leak and outrage was starting to rise on the planet. With the facilities themselves gone, however, there was nothing on which that anger could be focused, and sure enough, after another couple of years the world population had moved onto other issues. What had occurred at the complex became another scar in the history books that would gently heal over time.

There remained a handful of families that regularly protested various military complexes, with pictures of the loved ones they lost, tears from their cheeks spitting on the memorial candles they carried. But not even the Panel could turn back time.

Chapter 27

The Europas was known for a number of beautiful vistas. Among the more highly praised was a series of green mountains, lakes and stunning views which were high up and out of the reach of many of the clouds and storms. This was where the world had opted to put some of its architectural treasures, moving entire buildings and creating some of the most odd looking, time warp campuses.

Land that was this well shielded from the elements was rare, and as such the buildings could not just be left to stand as idle monuments. They were pressed into service. Students of various disciplines that showed particular promise, were sent into these mountains to master their specialisms before going out elsewhere in the world to help make it a better place. As an added bonus, being so high up meant that they were also far, far away from the worst of the planet's everyday distractions.

One large, classic twenty third century building stood out like a sore thumb in amongst a campus of mostly twentieth and twenty first century brick architecture. It was mostly made from glass and marble, with jagged, challenging edges that dared the eye to make sense of it. It was said that these distinctive and visually challenging features were the result of a rounding error in the robots that built them. However, as the code that ran them back in the day, had not survived, there was no evidence to substantiate the claim.

The gossip about this particular building was not constrained to conversations about its past. There was also chatter about its present state of upkeep. A strong odour emanated from the west wing and people scurried in through the entrance and up to their classrooms as fast as they could. As neither glass or marble could ever smell as bad as that, the obvious conclusion was that something was amiss with the drains, but why no one had ever bothered to fix them had remained one of the many mysteries that surrounded that particular part of the campus.

It confused a good number of the students as to why one of the most prestigious buildings should be left to suffer so badly, as it was here that students came to be taught the finer arts of neurology, genetics, biology and other related disciplines. They were taught by a green hologram which operated in ten classes simultaneously and was renowned for its AI programming. It seemed to be able to comprehend complex language with ease, and tune its response for the level of the individual student that had asked the question; all within the blink of an eye.

More than one student had attempted to try and follow the strange looking cables that went from the projector and up, into the ceiling where they were then lost within the fabric of the building. When trying to look up floor plans and history, the library on site was also found wanting.

Only very select members of staff knew of the large, toughened glass case that existed within its marble walls, or the brown liquid inside the tank that held an odd-looking genetic material that floated freely as if it had a life of its own. When pressed for any details, they simply shrugged their shoulders and professed that both the smell and the teaching computer were there long before they joined.

Of course, the teaching went two ways and Genie learned as much about humanity from her students, as she taught them about neuroscience. With her protected and filtered connection to the Vid Circuits and InfoWeb, she was able to expand her knowledge and contribute to the wider world of research. Some of the brightest students were allowed to maintain limited communication with her, once they had graduated and moved to other parts of the world. As a result, she learned more about what it meant to be human, and along the way started to understand the power of emotions and the importance of being alive, in more than just the physical sense.

She would never feel the heat of a dawn sun rise on her cheek, or the gentle breeze on her skin, but Genie grew to experience a range of emotions and through her teaching work, became something of an expert in irony, humour and the inevitable put downs that were sometimes necessary to keep a class in order. As she told the staff, she needed these skills, because they wouldn't build her a launcher that could throw board dusters at disruptive students.

As well as the buildings, the outdoor areas had been kept artificially warm in some areas to stop snow and ice forming. This allowed a range of activities including lawn tennis, thanks to the engineering students. It wasn't taken up with any kind of vigour due to the thin air, but it was another achievement that served as a challenge for subsequent students to try and surpass.

Mostly, the outdoor activities were gentle walks and to serve this purpose a range of gardens had been created. Dotted around them were memorial areas which were home to monuments honouring some of the people who had made significant advances in their respective fields. In a few cases, these statues and plaques stood watch over the bodies of the people themselves. Some of the gardens were well attended, with the notable exception of the neurology memorial. There was a strong rumour that it was haunted.

That particular area consisted of a large circle of marble, made in much the same fashion as the building whose subject of study it shared. Around the edge were pillars of the same material and they supported another circle of marble on top. Protecting the whole structure was a range of bushes that served to isolate it from the campus as a whole, and provide a secluded area of reflection for the few that dared to brave the rumours and enter it.

Within its confines were monuments to Ashime, Thesarin, Hector and many more of the Greats that had tackled the aftermath of the chemical plagues. Off to one side was a stone which stood watch over a grave. It wasn't for a neurologist as such, but the memorial explained that it was there in honour of a genetic engineer who had, perhaps, done more than anyone to progress the science of neurology, Professor Emmett Charcott.

Only the most eagle eyed people would have noticed that, nestled at the top of one of the pillars, sat underneath the raised stone circle, was a small white box which had three lenses at its front. Had anyone so noticed it, then they might have made a connection between the box, and the reports of the ghostly figure that had occasionally been glimpsed by those brave enough to peer through the thick bushes at the dead of night.

They said that it was a ghostly apparition of a woman. A purple spectre of anguish and distress which sat by one of the grave sides. At the same time, she would be surrounded by one of the most haunting, spine chilling, disembodied sounds that the human ear had ever encountered. Some swore that it was the woman crying, but this was dismissed, because not only did it come from a different direction, but it never stopped to take a breath.

THE END